THE THEORY OF EVERYTHING

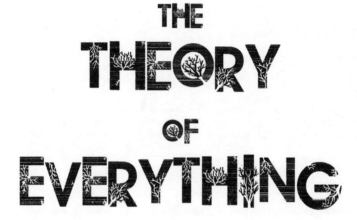

THE THEORY OF EVERYTHING

J. J. JOHNSON

PEACHTREE
ATLANTA

All the characters in THE THEORY OF EVERYTHING are fictional
with the exception of Ruby, who was very real and somewhat
feral and brought home many possums.

Ω

Published by
PEACHTREE PUBLISHERS
1700 Chattahoochee Avenue
Atlanta, Georgia 30318-2112
www.peachtree-online.com

Text © 2012 by J. J. Johnson

First trade paperback edition published in 2015.

Book design by Maureen Withee
Composition by Melanie McMahon Ives

Manufactured in July 2015 in the United States of America by Lake Book Manufacturing in
Melrose Park, Illinois
10 9 8 7 6 5 4 3 2 1 (hardcover)
10 9 8 7 6 5 4 3 2 1 (trade paperback)

Library of Congress Cataloging-in-Publication Data

Johnson, J. J., 1973-
    The theory of everything / by J.J. Johnson
        p. cm.
    Summary: Eight months after a freak accident took her best friend's life, Sarah Jones is
having trouble at home, at school, and with her boyfriend, but she gains an understanding
of interconnectedness while working for Roy, an eccentric Christmas tree-farm owner dealing
with his own tragedy.
    ISBN 978-1-56145-623-9 (hardcover) / 978-1-56145-889-9 (trade paperback)
    [1. Grief—Fiction. 2. Loss (Psychology)—Fiction. 3. Interpersonal relations—Fiction. 4.
Family life—New York (State)—Fiction. 5. Best friends—Fiction. 6. Friendship—Fiction. 7.
New York (State)—Fiction.] I. Title.
    PZ7.J63213Ran 2012
    [Fic]--dc23
                                    2011020973

For Juanita and Earl, my parentals

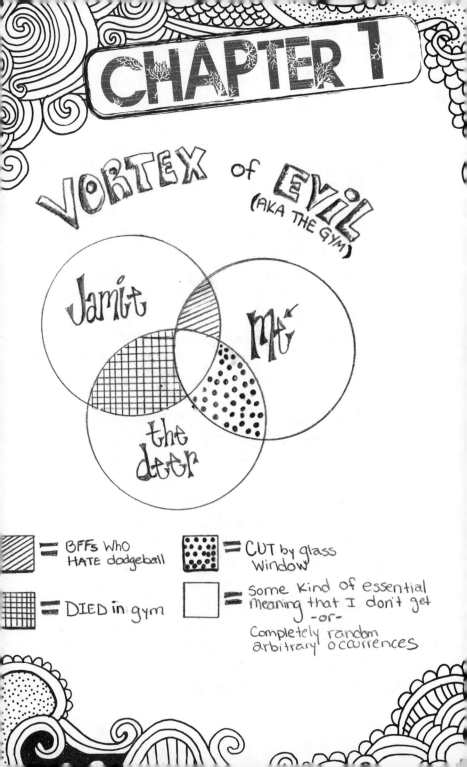

 **EIGHT** years ago, when we were seven, my best friend Jamie gave me a kaleidoscope. It sounds lame, but I loved that thing. So did Jamie. The girl kept stealing it back until I gave her one of her own. We would just lie there in my backyard, staring up at the sky through them. Prisms turning, colors changing. White cloud crystals, blue sky fractals.

Trippy, in a wholesome, Hugs Not Drugs way.

Well. My whole life is like that now—it's trippy and turny and there are no drugs involved, unless Zoloft counts.

Oh, and P.S.: Jamie's not here. She died last March.

Since then it's like I'm living inside a giant kaleidoscope: some unseen outside force shifts the world; the floor wobbles; the jagged pieces of my days get jostled into new pictures, all glassy and triangular.

The dismissal bell rings. I have to book it to the gym. The gym is the worst place on this crystalline, prismatic earth. Call it the Tenth Circle of Hell. I hate the place with the fiery passions of a million suns—not to put too fine a point on it—but I have to go there because I need my extra stash of 'pons and Advil. My period decided to bless me in the middle of chemistry, and sadly, I've failed to replenish the stockpile in my main locker.

I Handle My Business fast and sprint out through the gym. I need to get to the parking lot before my brother Jeremy takes off without me.

I run along the side wall, which is a long bank of windows, to the far exit on the parking lot side of the building. I push. The door doesn't budge. I give it a few kicks. This place is truly a vortex of evil.

Something outside the windows catches my eye.

I turn toward it. Everything unspools—a film sliding out of a movie projector, coiling on the floor.

Through the window, a blur. A train streak of momentum. The noise: a boom—thunder—then a crash—glass shattering. The sounds reverberate through the floor, through my feet, up my legs, into my spine.

Huge, shining snowflakes burst into the air, a kaleidoscope pointed at blue sky and clouds. But it isn't snowflakes or clouds. It's shards of plate glass, smashed from the windows.

Staggering in front of me is an enormous creature. A deer with massive antlers. Bellowing. Snowflakes—glass shards—jut from its body.

Holy hellmouth. My feet are stuck to the gym floor like they're magnetized.

I'm frozen: one hand raised (like I could ever stop shattering glass), the other pressing my locket as if that's the thing that needs protection.

The deer stumbles. Its head wobbles. It stares straight at me. And I swear it feels like it's telling me something. Telling me that the kaleidoscope has turned again, my life is shifting—again—and me and this deer are tumbling around inside prisms and light.

ᛦ ᛦ ᛦ

As soon as my legs start working again, I'm gone. Arms pumping, backpack jostling, boobs bouncing. My feet are on autopilot; they take me to the main office.

When I get there, I can hardly get the words out. "A deer in the gym…it's hurt…"

Ms. Franklin turns from her computer and sets down her Diet Coke. "Sarah, honey. You're bleeding."

Ms. Franklin brings her hand to her forehead. Mirroring her, my fingertips slip on slick warm blood above my eyebrow. There's something embedded in my skin. A little piece of glass. "Oh. Shit."

Dr. Folger pops out of his private office. "Is that our Ms. Jones? Indeed, there is no need for that sort of language." He doesn't really look at me. Instead, he stops to slide the nameplate on his door back to the center of its track. *James Folger, EdD, Principal.* He turns toward us. When he gets a load of my forehead, his eyes bug out. "Oh my. Are you all right?"

"Yeah. I'm awesome." (I don't mean for it to come out this way. At some point in the past eight months, my normal voice got replaced with a snark box. Somehow, approximately 92 percent of what I say comes out sarcastic, whether I intend it or not. It's beyond my control.) "There's a deer in the gym."

"There's a what?"

As I explain about the deer, Ms. Franklin whisks tissues from their box and waves them at my forehead.

I take the Kleenex and dab above my eye. Dr. Folger takes two little steps, as if he's woozy from the sight of blood. He clears his throat but doesn't say anything. Clearly he missed his calling as a paramedic.

Ms. Franklin is on the phone. "...stay a bit later. Yes, we'll come to you. Thanks." She gives Dr. Folger one of those pointed expressions that adults don't think we Youth of Today notice. "Perhaps we should take a look at the gym?"

"Yes. Yes, of course."

Ms. Franklin plucks a few more tissues and hands them over. I pocket the one I've been using and press a fresh one to my forehead. (Left pocket, garbage; right pocket, necessities like lip balm and hair ties.) She picks up her Diet Coke and we're off.

As we turn the last corner before the gym, I start hoping like crazy that the deer will have vanished. Honestly, I'd rather have hallucinated the whole thing. Sometimes being crazy seems like a better deal than dealing with reality.

But the deer is still here and now it's moaning. The sound puts Dr. Folger and Ms. Franklin into deep freeze, so I grab the door myself and pull it open. They follow. We stand there, not saying anything, for what feels like a long time. The deer is lying on its side now, facing the shattered windows—looking out toward freedom.

I set down my backpack and stare at my feet. Hear the buck struggling to stand.

Ms. Franklin drops her soda can. *Thunk. Fizz.* Brown liquid spreads over the floor, over the painted court lines. "Oh dear," she breathes.

Dr. Folger says, "Holy…" I hear him rub his neck. "Call 911."

He's thinking of Jamie. We all are.

CHAPTER 2

SNARKBOX

4 RULES OF ENGAGEMENT...

⑨ When / if person is a total masochist and comes back for more...

① Person tries to talk to me: "Hey, how's it going?"

⑧ Person runs away SCREAMING

⑦ SNARK BOX ENGAGE: HYPERDRIVE! "Oh, I'm so sorry. Did that come out bitchy? Maybe because I am surrounded by — —?"

② I open my mouth to say something normal.

③ SNARK BOX ENGAGE! (INVOLUNTARY)

④ Sarcasm pours out. "Oh, I'm awesome. I know you are awesome too."

⑥ myself pisses me off. Seriously, why can't I just be real?

⑤ Person thinks I'm a bitch. Because I sound like a bitch. "Why are you acting like a bitch?"

BEFORE

I can think too much about where she's taking me, Ms. Franklin leads me out of the gym, back down the main hall, to the nurse's office. The door swings open and I'm face to face with Jamie's mom.

Great. That's more than half a year's worth of Hypervigilant Avoidance of All Things Jamie's Family down the drain. Because Mrs. Cleary is right here, right now, and man, she does not look good.

Sadness oozes out of her like radioactive rainwater. Her face is slack and there are bags under her eyes. I guess she looks like someone whose daughter died. But then she smiles, and the smile floats up into her eyes like she's genuinely glad to see me.

I'm alive and her daughter's dead. If I were her, I wouldn't want to see me.

But she's smiling. "Sarah," she says, grabbing me into a hug, and then pushing me back so she can look at my forehead. Does she know about the deer lying on the gym floor? *No* would be better than *yes.* She doesn't need more freaky gym sadness in her life.

"She has a little cut on her forehead," Ms. Franklin says.

"It's pretty much stopped bleeding," I say. Translation: Nothing to see here. These aren't the droids you're looking for. Move along.

"Let's take a look." Mrs. Cleary pats the counter for me to sit, and snaps on some rubber gloves. She holds my chin, tilting my head to assess the situation. "It's not deep, but there's a small sliver—glass, is it?—that needs to come out. And that might make it bleed a little more."

As her tweezers come toward my eye, we hear a siren outside in the bus circle. It whoops and stops.

Ms. Franklin says, "I'll be right back."

So now I'm alone with Mrs. Cleary. She goes back to tweezing my forehead and says, "Technically, I'm not supposed to do this. Removing splinters counts as surgery. Isn't that silly? But I'm assuming your parents won't mind."

"I'm sure it's fine," I say. Since she's not suing my dad for the whole My Daughter Died In The School You're Superintendent Of thing, I'm assuming my parents won't sue Mrs. Cleary for Removing A Small Piece Of Glass From Our Daughter's Forehead. They're cool like that.

"Ow," I say at the sudden sharp pain in my forehead.

"Sorry," Mrs. Cleary says. "It's being stubborn."

Yeow, it hurts. Is she excavating my skull or what? Is there an archaeological dig in my noggin that I'm not aware of?

Ms. Franklin comes back in with the police officer. Mrs. Cleary takes a break from digging.

"Sarah, hon," Ms. Franklin says. "Officer Adams needs to ask you a few questions."

"This'll just take a moment," he says. He has a small notebook and a pen. He locks straight down into hardcore interrogation mode. Thank God, because obviously a serious felony has been committed here. "You found the animal?" he says.

I nod.

"State your name, please."

"Sarah Jones."

His pen is poised over the little notebook. "Spell that, please."

My eye roll is completely involuntary, I swear. He needs me to spell the WASPiest, most basic name ever? I start spelling, "B-A-L-T-H-A-Z-A—"

"Sarah…," Ms. Franklin cautions.

The cop glances at Ms. Franklin, then back to me. He gives me the stink eye.

I sigh. I'm not really a badass, I'm just pissed off. I hate Mrs. Cleary being sad and the deer being hurt. Not to mention that the last time a cop asked me questions like this, my best friend had just died right in front of me. "It's Sarah with an H."

"Last name J-O-N-E-S," spells Ms. Franklin.

The cop clears his throat. "Please state what happened." He looks me up and down; his eyes linger on my forehead (which is throbbing in pain, thank you very much) and—yep, there it is—he glances at my boobs, like he doesn't mean to but he can't help it. Dudes think they're completely 007 about the boob eye-flick, but I can always tell. It's a gift.

I give Officer Boob Assessment the short version of the deer story. Infuriatingly, I choke on a word or two—because Mrs. Cleary is here and it gets all mixed together with Jamie dying—and I feel blood rush into my cheeks.

Officer BA must notice my cheeks going red because he gives me a look like There Is Something You're Not Telling Me. And sure enough, he goes, "Is there anything else I should know?"

"No," I say.

"You leaving anything out?"

"No. Nope. Nothing."

Cigarette breath. "Something you're not telling?"

Wow. Power trip much? But it's working; my heart is migrating to my throat. I swallow hard. "Well, I mean, I don't really see how—"

"I need to finish taking care of her forehead," Mrs. Cleary tells the officer.

Ms. Franklin quickly adds, "You can find the gym, I'm sure, can't you, Harold?"

Ha. Go, Ms. Franklin! She's probably known Harold Boob Drooler since he was a nose-picking kindergartner; she's been working in the schools forever.

"Yes, Ms. F." He leaves.

After he's gone, Ms. Franklin pats my knee and whispers, "You told him everything he needs to know, hon." She blows out a big breath and settles onto the chair near the door.

Mrs. Cleary looks even more tired. She brandishes the tweezers and goes back to work. My skin pulls when the glass comes out. It hurts. She goes into a cabinet and comes back with a little bundle of gauze and a band-aid. "Almost done."

As she peels the wrapping off the band-aid, we hear a noise. A loud, tight, staccato pop.

Mrs. Cleary is so startled she jumps, and I'm afraid she might stab me in the eye with her finger.

"What was—"

Another pop. Like a firecracker. Which is what people say on the TV news: It sounded like a firecracker.

The realization filters through my brain slowly, like coffee dripping through a filter: *drip drip plop.*

Gunshots? Gunshots.

And it keeps filtering, until duh, I realize: Harold the policeman has shot the deer. Twice.

Probably to stop its suffering. Surely that's why.

But it still feels cruel. All of it. So much gym tragedy. Like, *enough already. Damn.*

Ms. Franklin blinks. "It's over now, hon." She pauses. "It's for the best."

I look at Mrs. Cleary, whose face has gone ashen. Her hand is at her mouth, like she can't believe any of this.

It's for the best. Sure.

What a boatload of crap.

Mrs. Cleary sticks the band-aid on my forehead. "Your parents will be wondering where you are," she says. "I'll give you a ride home."

Right. Jeremy's long gone, I'm sure. Five months and two weeks until I'm sixteen and that exact day I'm getting my driving permit and then I'm taking driver's ed and getting my license ASAP, and Jeremy'll be off to college so I'll get the car and I will never have to mooch rides ever again.

Ms. Franklin says, "I'll walk you two to your car."

CHAPTER 3

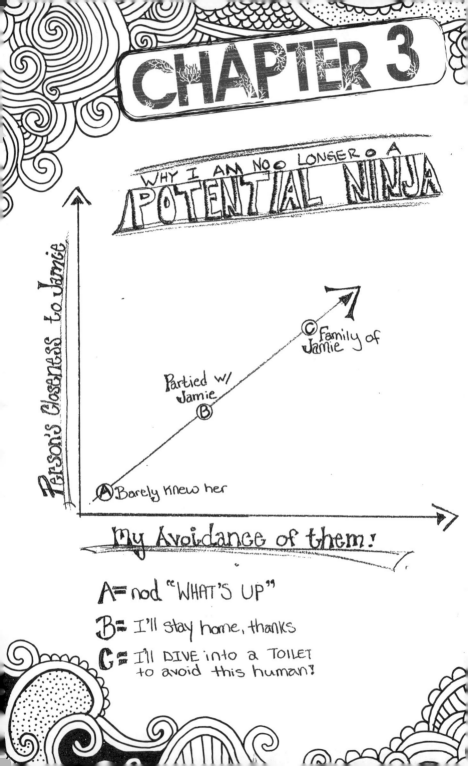

FOR the first time ever, I open the front door of the Cleary Subaru without Jamie or Emmett leapfrogging my head and screaming *Shotgun!* into my ear canal.

It's beyond weird—and that's before Mrs. Cleary adjusts the rear view mirror and says, "I need to pop by the soccer field to pick up Emmett."

Oh yay. It's not bad enough being here with Mrs. Cleary, all silent and awkward. Now I get Jamie's twin brother, too. Again, eight months of painstaking, meticulous avoidance—including two class-schedule changes—in the toilet.

Mrs. Cleary pulls into the parking lot and honks. It takes no time at all to pick Emmett out from the crowd. Same hair as Jamie's, except shorter. Same eyes. He's kicking a ball around with this kid Sam from chemistry. He flicks his head goodbye, scoops up his bag, and trots over.

Jamie's mom may look more withered since her daughter died, but Emmett is the total opposite. He's grown practically half a foot, and he's all leg muscles and lantern jaw. Damn. He looks older. And healthy, like his diabetes is doing okay.

"He's starting this year. Varsity," Mrs. Cleary says, super proud. "The coach says he could get a scholarship."

"Terrific." I actually mean it, but the snark box has a mind of its own. Mrs. Cleary frowns.

Emmett jogs over, automatically heading for the front seat. When he sees me, his eyes widen, then his face goes blank and he opens the back door, sliding in with all his gear.

What should I say? Should I nod and smile? Or give him two thumbs up—*awesome to see you, dude*! I just kind of sit there, slumped in the seat, sneaking glimpses of Emmett in the side mirror.

"Good practice, sweetheart?"

Emmett nods and looks out his window.

I guess he doesn't really feel like talking, either.

The silence in the car makes my throat ache. It hovers, presses in on us, like a fine mist dampening Emmett's hair, or a heavy blanket around Mrs. Cleary's shoulders. Or a weight around my neck, like my necklace is made of albatross.

Our necklaces. The first time Emmett saw them—it's such a clear picture in my mind. We were all in fifth grade, Jamie and I kneeling over our collages for an assignment about *Tuck Everlasting*: "Explore the theme of permanence." (Why hello there, Irony! Come on in, make yourself comfy; you've become such a permanent fixture in my life.)

Jamie's part of the locket dangled from her neck, swinging in small arcs on its chain.

Emmett had frowned. "What's up with your necklace? It looks busted."

Jamie and I had purposefully broken the locket at

its hinge. Obviously he could tell it was something important. He hated when we had secrets from him, like I was the intruder, messing with their twinsiness.

We explained it was from *Annie*: locket broken in two, symbol of a special bond, symbol of someday returning, I had the other part.

He scoffed at us. "Dang. That is so…girly."

"Oh, shut your sass trap," Jamie told him. "You know I love you, too."

That was what, five years ago? It was girly and corny then, and it is now, and I don't care. I'll never take it off. Never. Especially now.

And Jamie's locket? Buried with her. Under the ground. In a casket.

Morbid much?

Mrs. Cleary pulls the car into my driveway. "Here we are," she singsongs.

"Great." It comes out as a croak. I clear my throat. "Thanks for the ride."

"Wait a minute, I'll come in with you. Your parents will want to hear what happened."

Right. *Crap*. I'd forgotten about my forehead.

I open the car door and instantly Ruby appears, nuzzling her cold wet doggy nose into my crotch and depositing her drooly R2-D2 at my feet.

"I'll just be a minute," Mrs. Cleary tells Emmett. He nods.

I toss Artoo onto the lawn. Ruby sniffs me, sniffs in Emmett's general direction, and wags happily, running off to fetch her toy. I want to exit this vehicle, stat, but I know I should say something to Emmett. Maybe something profound. "Um. See you around."

Emmett is staring out the car window. He doesn't talk. He's holding something, like a wadded up piece of paper. Meeting my eyes for a one-tenth of a second, he half-hands, half-chucks the paper at me.

Something screams at me to launch it back at him. *Hot potato!* Or at least wait. Take it inside, read it later. But I am a glutton for punishment and I open it right here in the front seat. Smeared ink, in his messy guy handwriting.

> *Sarah,*
> *I want to know what happened. How Jamie died.*
> *Please.*
> > > *—E.*

Well. I have two responses to that.
    1. Holy.
    2. Crap.

Actually, three.
    3. No frigging way.
Sub-divided into
        A.) No way could he still not know.
        B.) No way am I going to tell him.
        C.) No way is this happening.

The *please* is what gets me. That's the knife through the heart.

I look wildly around the car, the air, Ruby, Emmett. How can he not know? Surely someone had put their hands on his shoulders and sat him down and explained it all.

But then…no. Typical. Because that's how my mom and dad, and my boyfriend Stenn, the people at school, and even the grief counselors handled it with me. They never talked about it in a specific, factual way. Oh, yes, there were ridonkulous platitudes: Have Faith; Everything Happens for a Reason. And pretty journals to write in. The advice to let it all out. The songs they'll play you: "You've Got a Friend," "Fire and Rain," "Shower the People." (Apparently James Taylor has a grief monopoly.)

But no one ever bothered explaining the nitty-gritty—the physical details of how Jamie died. Obviously I know what happened, but what actually killed her? Did her ribs break? Did she suffocate? At what moment, exactly, did she die? Inquiring minds—morbid minds—need to know.

Sure, my folks and the counselors and all, they know I saw what happened. So that's probably why they didn't bother giving me a rehash. But what if it isn't? What if that is Standard Operating Procedure in talking to the Youth? Has Emmett been fed the same shite, or lack thereof?

Unless he had asked—very specifically and probably very repeatedly—exactly, precisely how Jamie died, and unless he had asked someone who actually knew the answer—which means his parents, or mine, or Dr. Folger, the police, or…me—there's no way someone would have told him.

He's asking now.

Because no one's told him.

Well, at least he doesn't hate me for how Jamie died…not yet, anyway.

Thank God for Ruby (if there even is a God). She saves the day again, this time by depositing Artoo back into my lap, slobberier than ever, then pawing at the seat. I have no choice but to pay attention to her before she unstuffs the upholstery.

It's not my finest hour; I admit it. Because I basically ignore Emmett and split, acting all distracted by Ruby.

Mom's opening the front door of my house. Ruby's tail thumps against my leg. I shove the note in my left coat pocket and practically run into the house.

What does he think as he watches me go? *There goes the bitch who won't tell me what I want to know.*

Well that's fine. A whole lot better than *there goes the bitch who left my sister to die alone.*

Because when he finds out how it happened, that's exactly what he'll think.

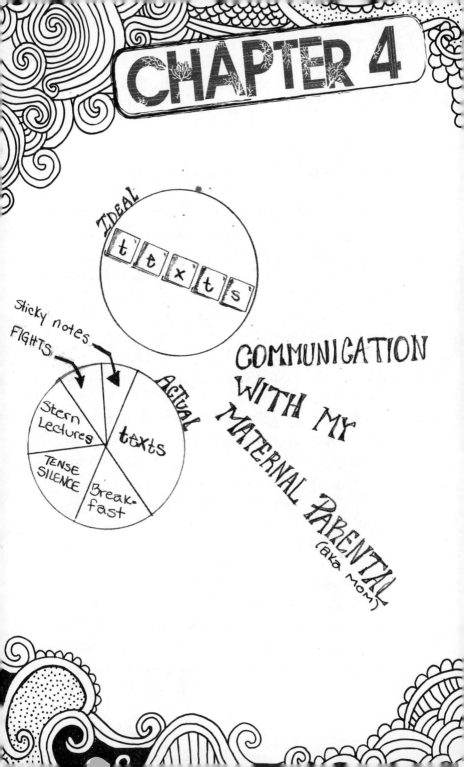

WHEN my parents open the door, Mrs. Cleary is very School Nurse about my forehead. They've probably run into each other Since Jamie Died (SJD), but I haven't seen them together since the funeral. Mom and Dad seem awkward, like Sorry We Still Have Two Kids And You Only Have One. They're sad and trying not to show it. Dad shakes Mrs. Cleary's hand and thanks her; Mom asks, "Would you like to come in for a cup of coffee?" They were never super close, but they were friendly. Kind of like extended family, in-lawsy type relationships, because me and James were so tight.

Mrs. Cleary shakes her head. "Thank you, but Emmett's waiting in the car."

Yes, Emmett's waiting in the car—and not just for his mom, but for me to rappel down from a helicopter like a Navy Seal to rescue him from confusion, help him make sense out of his sister's death. Okay, maybe that's a slight overstatement, but whatever. It seems that huge.

Dad gives me his Worried = (Sad x 2) + Disappointed look. He's used it so often lately, he probably has a trademark on it. He's sad because I've turned into such an unrelentingly sarcastic bitch. Disappointed because I don't reach out to them and let them help me. Or maybe I'm getting the causes of sad and disappointed mixed up? Anyway. He's worried because, well, apparently I'm a mess.

He turns back to Mrs. Cleary. "Another time, I hope."

"Yes," says my mom. "It would be nice to catch up."

"It would," Mrs. Cleary agrees, but without enthusiasm. She does squeeze me into a heartfelt boa constrictor hug before she leaves.

As usual SJD, the evening drags on, slow as dial-up internet. I abandoned my bag in the gym, so I don't have my homework with me. Shucks.

After dinner I watch *Star Wars* with Ruby. I toss Artoo for Rubes again and again until Mom texts me from the other room.

Mom [The Momster]: Confiscating the remote in 5 min. Go to bed. You need sleep.

Mom and I text more than we talk. When I got my first cell phone, I instantly recognized that texting is manna from heaven: a revolutionary way to avoid and/or condense communication with the maternal parental. One of my first texts was something like:

Me: Need to shop for a dress. Stenn asked me to prom.
The Momster: WTF!
Me: Mom? What do you think WTF means?
The Momster: Well That's Fantastic.

I've never set her straight because it's so much more amusing this way.

Mom peeks at me from the other room. She has her It's Not Worth Arguing With Me face, so I take Ruby out one last time and go to bed. Ruby falls asleep immediately. I wish I were a dog: get petted, get fed, never have to talk, play when you want, sleep when you're not playing or eating. Sign me up for that life.

I snuggle up with Rubes, watching her chest rise and fall. Usually that makes me sleepy, but tonight it's no use. At midnight I tug Stenn's Mercer sweatshirt over my pajamas and pad into the upstairs study. Ruby wakes up and follows me, droopy but loyal.

Jeremy's at the computer. When he sees me, he angles the monitor so I can't see what he's doing. "Go away."

"When are you going to be done?"

"Never."

"Thanks for the ride home," I say.

He shrugs. "You snooze, you lose."

"Something happened after school."

"Let me guess," he looks up at me. "More drama."

"You're so supportive. Stop it. It's overwhelming." Our whole SJD dynamic boils down to him being annoyed at me for having Irritating Emotions Like Sadness And Anger, Which Sometimes Inconvenience

Him Because They Are Unpleasant To Be Around. I sit. "You've been on the computer since dinner. Like five hours."

"Your point being?"

"How much porn can one person look at? I need to look up some stuff for school."

He rolls his eyes. "Fine. I was done anyway."

"I hope you cleaned up. Last time—"

"Oh ho ho, you are so exceedingly amusing. My sides hurt from all the laughing." He leaves.

I sign into Gmail. There's a note from Stenn saying hi, that he's in the computer lab and doesn't have time to write much; he'll try to text or call later. Mercer is strict about phones and laptops and connectivity in general. Evidently, when it comes to hoity-toity private schools, kid freedom is inversely proportionate to tuition paid.

I poke around the interwebs and can't stop myself from signing into Jamie's Facebook account. (Her password: GYSAOOMASarah. Translation: Get Your Skinny Ass Out Of My Account, Sarah. Mine? GYJRAOOMAJames. JR for Just Right. What can I say? The girl had body image issues.) When she died, her profile page exploded. Some posts were sweet, from true friends, but you would not believe the number of posers—people who were total asshats to James when she was alive—who posted crap like, "We love you, Jamie!" and "I'll miss you forever!" It was revolting. And then, because that wasn't enough, Facebook's algorithms noticed. "You haven't posted to Jamie Cleary's wall in a while. Say hello to her!" Or poke her. Poke her! That's when I bagged my own account entirely. And I didn't go back for months. But you can't delete your dead BFF's account. Though you can torture yourself by checking it.

I leave Facebook and try to distract myself by reading some blogs and stuff, but like a moth to a compact fluorescent, my mind keeps flitting back to the deer, the gym, the accident. Accidents. The deer accident and the Jamie accident. Evidently, when it comes to memories, persistence is directly proportionate to trauma (another little ratio confirmed by experience). The more traumatic and disturbing the memory, the more it sticks with you. Plagues you. Stalks you. Jumps out and says *Boo, motherfracker!*

I can't stop thinking about the way the deer looked at me, how its eyes bored straight into mine. I thought deer were supposed to be skittish. I never knew they could submarine to the bottom of your soul with their gaze.

I google *deer* and click on the Wikipedia entry. It has a link to deer in mythology. And something there flashes out at me like it's written in mercury. Ancient Scythians (cultures in Russia, China, Romania, and central Asia) were fans of deer: *The swift animal was believed to speed the spirits of the dead on their way, which perhaps explains the curious antlered headdresses found on horses buried at Pazyryk.*

Sure, Pazyryk. I just got back from there.

I read it again, and start to feel ice cubes on my spine. *The swift animal was believed to speed the spirits of the dead on their way.*

The deer died the same place as Jamie.

Is this about Jamie? Is the deer, or me, or both of us...am I supposed to be helping speed Jamie on her way? God, is James stuck in some Hell Dimension (aka high school), or some Purgatory Netherland, forever trapped until she takes care of unfinished business? Something that needs resolving, something that she needs to settle before she can be free?

I stare at the entry. Reach down to pat Ruby. Put a hand on my necklace.

The swift animal was believed to speed the spirits of the dead on their way...

I'm totally zoned out, and I jump about a foot when Chewbacca roars my text ring tone.

Stenn: Home tomorrow

Me: Great. (And I'm afraid it sounds sarcastic, even in a text) When?

Stenn: Tomorrow silly

Me: No I mean what time silly :-P

Stenn: Around 6?

Me: K. Drive safe. (Because SJD, I worry all the time about bad things happening to good people. My good people.)

Stenn: I will. Love U.

Me: Lerv U 2.

Poor Stenn. I was a decent girlfriend BJD; now I'm moody and high maintenance. But I do love the boy. Which sucks, since I can't stop pushing him away. Because, as one learns by losing one's BFF: Nothing Lasts Forever. I will lose Stenn. It is an inevitability. It might be sooner, it might be later, but the more I love him, the worse it will be.

Ironically, the long distance-ness of our relationship is probably what's saving it. I'm less annoying this far away. And sure, one might wonder if one's perfect boyfriend might accidentally fall into bed on top of a Pantene-commercial-gorgeous, rich private-school girl. But I don't think so. Call it trust, call it denial…my mental capacity maxes out before I can worry too much about it.

Sigh. Stenn and I still haven't done it. The Sex. We were about to—we had waited six looooooooooooong months. And then Jamie died, which put the kibosh on the big deflowering. Because I could not imagine de-boxer-briefing Stenn without then getting debriefed by Jamie.

About a week before she died, Jamie had gone with me to Planned Parenthood to get the patch. Stenn still doesn't know.

God, Jamie loved Stenn. He's a grade ahead of us and therefore has always had mythical, godlike, Ninja status—plus, objectively, he's freaking hot. When he asked me out our first week of freshman year (before he went off to Mercer), James was completely ecstatic, then totally jealous, and then a couple months later, dreadfully bored: "So let me get this straight: You and Stenn never fight," she said. "You are both total *Star Wars* dorks. You're basically best friends with benefits. What are you, married? Except you like each other... Hm. Does not compute."

As soon as he found out Jamie died—his parents must have called him because somehow he knew right away—Stenn came home for two weeks in the middle of the semester. I never asked how he managed that, and he never told me. All I know is he was here.

And I also know that my horniness around him is Out. Of. Control. SJD, my feelings transmogrified from normal teenage hormones into total slut lust. Because fooling around with him is the only time I feel really—I don't know—open? Connected? Loved?

But I still can't bring myself to Go All The Way with him. Not without Jamie around to talk to about it.

Ruby growls in her sleep under the computer desk. I stroke her. I know what she means.

CHAPTER 5

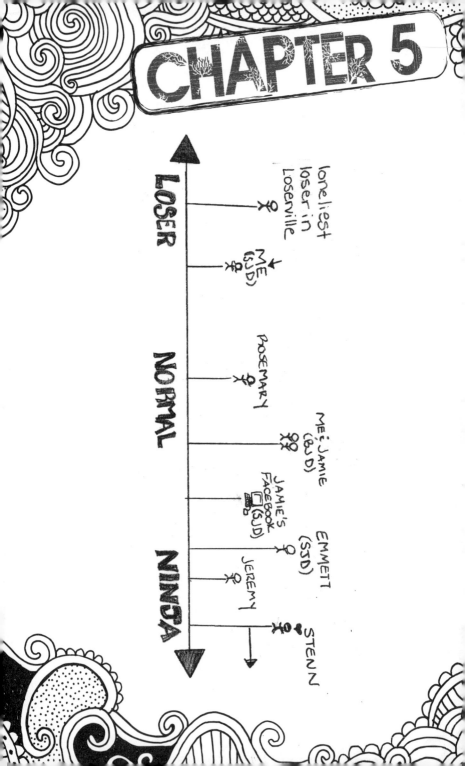

LOSER

loneliest
loser in
Loserville

ME
(SJD)

NORMAL

ROSEMARY

ME & JAMIE
(BJD)

JAMIE'S
FACEBOOK
(SJD)

EMMETT
(SSD)

NINJA

JEREMY

STENN

I wAKE up to Chewbacca roaring. I

fumble around for my phone. Chewie roars again, somewhere on the floor by my bed. I stretch over to grab it and squint my sleepy eyes so I can read the text.

The Momster: Pancakes or waffles

Mom's become a Family Breakfast Nazi. She must have read a study in a magazine: "Research Finds Families Who Don't Eat Together Spin into Different Orbits, Kids Likely to Become Serial Killers." Dinner doesn't work because Dad always has meetings, and Jeremy has…whatever it is that Jeremy does. So, unilateral declaration of family breakfast, the four of us, every weekday morning. No exceptions. (Heil, Lydia!)

Me: Don't care (I will abbreviate when called for, but I am fully committed to apostrophes in texts. Otherwise what kind of world do we live in?)
The Momster: O come on. Have an opinion.
Me: Waffles
The Momster: Yr brother wants pancakes.
Me: Then why did you ask?
The Momster: Hoped yd say p-cakes.
Me: Pancakes r fine.
The Momster: Pancakes FTW!

This, this is my life.

Shower, drag comb through hair, apply new band-aid to forehead, gird loins, etc. Jeremy and Ruby and I are in the kitchen at 6:30, good little soldiers of the Breakfast Reich.

I scoop kibbles into Ruby's dish, and even though it's hella early, my brain is on overdrive thinking about everything—the deer, the accidents, Stenn, my injured head... Everything.

Thank God for Ruby. Not much of a talker, but a good listener, and equally happy if I don't have anything to say.

Mom's as perky as a Ritalin-sniffing cheerleader. If Morning Person isn't an official diagnosis, it should be.

"Good morning, Monkey." She slides pancakes onto my plate and sets down the frying pan with a clank. She hands me my Zoloft.

Yes, Zoloft.

At first I was like, *Nokay, no frigging way, I'm not taking an antidepressant. I'm not depressed; I'm sad. There's a difference, yo. Especially when it comes to medicating people.* But they wore me down, the Grown-ups With Their Concern. So I relented. And just look at me now: Little Miss Sunshine, radiating good vibes and positive energy everywhere I go!

But truly, it does tamp down the memories of the accident—not so much hiding them as slowing down their instant replays. Except for last night. Thanks a lot, deer.

Mom gives me the official I Am Concerned About You look, frowning at the band-aid above my eyebrow. She picks lint off my sweater. "Monkey. You're wearing black again."

"Haven't you heard? Black is the new black."

She makes a face. To Mom, wearing black means you're depressed and thinking Deep, Dark Thoughts—even though I wore just as much black BJD. She bought me a bright green sweater last week. Bright. Green.

I wash my Zoloft down with gulps of juice. "You know I'm taking that sweater back. Drive me to the mall this weekend? I'm not down with the secondary colors."

Jeremy looks up from his pancakes. His eyes flick to my forehead. "Dork. Secondary disaster and malfeasance is what you're down with." He shovels more food into his mouth. How he manages to simultaneously make no sense *and* sound vaguely Shakespearean is a mystery.

"Jeremy, your sister's not a…" but Mom trails off, like maybe she can't really disagree with the assessment. She switches tack. "She's been through enough."

Wow, Mom. Your defense of me is overwhelming. Truly.

And then Dad appears, cowboy boots clunking on the linoleum. He grabs a pancake from my plate. "These boots are made for walking, Sarah."

I'm supposed to say, "And that's just what they'll

do." It's this thing of Dad's. He wants to be able to count on me saying it, no matter what else happens. Reassurance through repetition.

And I kind of want to. I want to say it and see him smile, but my snark box swallows it up.

Dad waits.

I slide my pancake through syrup. I do feel sorry for him, but I just can't get the words out. Dad looks at Mom; she shakes her head sadly.

"God, Dork, what is your problem?" Count on Jeremy to make things worse. He takes his plate to the dishwasher, stopping to check the thermometer outside the kitchen window. Ruby lifts her head off my feet to watch him. "Brr...twenty-five degrees." Jeremy reaches into his pocket and tosses the car keys at me. "You'll probably need to scrape the windshield, too."

I snatch the keys out of the air. Damn, if only Ruby was allowed to bite people. Let a girl sic her dog on her brother, already.

The car is nice and warm for the ride to school, thanks to me.

Jeremy steers with his knees while he fiddles with the music. The roads are deserted this early.

In September he started playing water polo before school with a bunch of Ninjas. Which means

I get to
1. Take the bus (hells no) or
2. Walk to school in the freezing cold or
3. Get a toasty warm ride, but arrive one whole hour before first period.

Option #3 brought to you by Mom and Dad's No Drive-y The Sister, No Borrow-y The Car rule.

Jeremy squints at the controls and turns the volume up. Loud. It's his tactic to avoid chitchat. It's amazing how we live in the same house, have the same parents, and yet barely know anything about each other. We've never been über close, but this? This is practically Stranger Danger.

Whatever. Whatever whatever. I stare out the window, try to think good thoughts: Stenn coming home today. Hanging out with him all weekend. Fooling around.

Jeremy turns down the music. "I waited for you yesterday, by the way. After school."

Wait. What happened to You Snooze, You Lose?

"Sorry. There was a...an accident..." I don't really know how much to go into it. I mean, does he care? He didn't last night.

"It must have been quite a scene. Kind of Kafka-esque?"

My brother is actually initiating a conversation? With me? And referencing Kafka?

"Um, yeah. It was definitely freaky," I venture.

How does he know what happened? "Why? What did you hear?"

"I heard Mom and Dad talking about it."

"Oh."

"You know, it would be best to keep that little incident to yourself."

"Really." Snark box, activate. "You think so?"

"Yes, really. Because everyone already thinks you're peculiar."

I stare at the road. Everyone? *Everyone* thinks I'm *peculiar*? Well That's Fantastic. "Thanks for sticking up for me."

He rolls his eyes. "Don't blame me."

"Right… Who should I blame?"

"Yourself, Dork. You're the one who acts all depressive." His voice is 2 percent sympathy, 98 percent irritation. He continues, "Mom and Dad don't know what to do with you."

"And you're telling me this because you care so much about me?"

"Actually, I'm telling you this because I'm sick of driving a total bitch around, instead of just the usual annoying kid sister. And I'm telling you because Stenn's a decent guy. And because Ruby's an awesome dog."

"What does all that have to do with…?" My stomach twists. I don't know where this conversation is headed, but I don't like Jeremy listing two of the most important things in my life like that.

"What are you talking about?"

He sighs, annoyed. "Mom and Dad were talking about how you're becoming such a deadbeat in school. You don't care about anything anymore, so they don't have any leverage."

"Leverage?" What does that mean?

"Anything to bargain with. Convince you to turn your crap around."

"You mean like, to threaten me with?"

"I guess you could call it that." He shrugs.

"But Ruby, and Stenn…" My heart freezes. "And driving. They wouldn't take them away from me? They can't."

"Calm down, Freak Show. I don't think they're planning on it tomorrow. And I bet they'd start with driver's ed before moving on to the big guns."

Driver's ed *is* a big gun. It's my freedom to visit Stenn, to drive to the mall or the movies, to stop being subject to Jeremy's lectures. But it's not as heavy artillery as Stenn himself. Or Ruby.

"If I were you," he says, "I would tread very carefully."

I groan. I can't believe this. Your daughter having a hard time? I know: take away the things that are most important to her. Awesome parenting, guys!

Jeremy doesn't turn the music back up. There's a little *clunk* when he steps on the clutch and a quiet *thud* when he shoves the gearshift into place.

"You really think they would stop me from see-ing Stenn? Or—or take Ruby away?"

The blinker clicks while he waits for the light to turn green. "I think they're getting desperate."

Cue music. End of conversation.

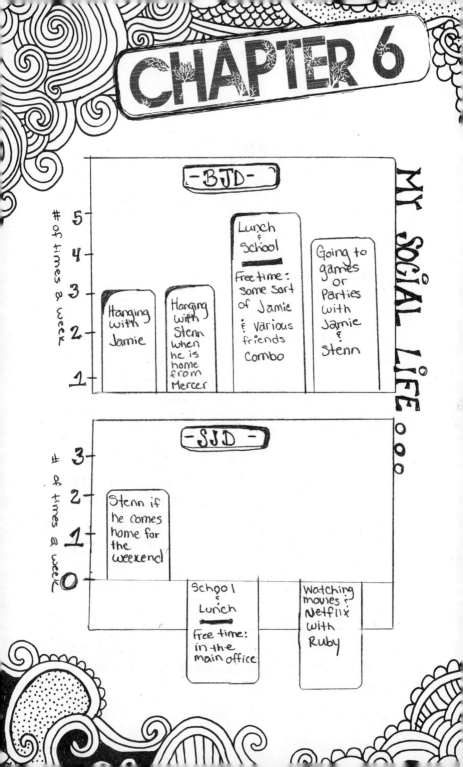

CHAPTER 6

MY SOCIAL LIFE

-BJD-

of times a week

5 4 3 2 1

- Hanging with Jamie
- Hanging with Stenn when he is home from Mercer
- Lunch & School — Free time: some sort of Jamie & various friends Combo
- Going to games or Parties with Jamie & Stenn

-SJD-

of times a week

3 2 1 0

- Stenn if he comes home for the weekend
- School & Lunch — Free time: in the main office
- Watching movies & Netflix with Ruby

SCHOOL is dark. Only the wing with the pool is lit and warm; the heat and lights in the main part of the building won't kick on for another half hour. But it's an unspoken agreement: I'm forbidden from hanging out near Jeremy, lest we actually be seen within a thousand yards of each other.

Pulling my coat tight, I head toward the office. Ms. Franklin usually comes in early with muffins and coffee. We've struck up quite the friendship based on baked goods and caffeinated beverages. The gym is on the way. I don't want to go near that hellhole, but my backpack is orphaned there, and it's better to stage a rescue than to risk Ms. Gliss confiscating it and making me do laps or scrub toilets to get it back. So I zip my jacket higher, pull up my hood, and march. Fricking Hellmouth Death Star Gym was bad before, and it's managed to get worse. I squeeze my eyes shut, trying to block out not one, but two accidents. The memories crash over me like a tsunami. Unstoppable, overpowering, unpredictable.

Good times.

All this goes on inside my head, over and over, slow motion, while outside my head things are supposed to be normal.

Bleh. Two weeks after Jamie died, when I finally came back to school, there were three Big Differences:

1. The indisputable fact of Jamie's absence. The fibers of my heart ached with loneliness. (They still do.) I kept turning around, starting to talk to her. And then. Yeah. Your BFF's dead. These feelings crowding your heart? They're called Rage. Impotence. Dread. Loneliness. Fear. Sadness. Grief. Magical Thinking. Too bad Denial didn't stick around for long.

2. Jamie's main locker was a Battlestar Galactica-esque, quasi-roadside, semi-gravestoney, dead person site. It looked like someone with Rainbow-Unicorn food poisoning puked all over it. Construction Paper and Sharpie Marker Tribute Vomitus. Seriously, the hypocrisy. It was worse than her Facebook timeline.

3. The gym's folding wall, gone. The day Jamie died—literally that very afternoon— Dad ordered all collapsible walls dismantled and removed, district-wide, overnight. Lawsuits, accountability, safety.

Request for information: Who, specifically, took

the gym's wall down? Did they know why they were called in at whatever hour of the night? They must have. Was there still blood on the carpety wall surface? Did they just leave it, or clean it off? Had they done that kind of cleaning before—the kind with blood and death?

These. These are the questions that spin through my brain. Is it any wonder I'm a mess?

I squint into the window of the gym door. A blue plastic tarp is duct-taped over the broken window. The deer is gone, but there is still a stain the color of chocolate smeared on the floor.

Somebody's slacking. Shouldn't all this have been cleaned up by now?

Sweat prickles my armpits; the hairs on my arms stand up.

There's a flicker of movement in the gym. Something gray shudders in and out of view. What the...?

I lean in to get a better look. There it is again: some sort of animal. Like a big gray rat, or a stringy-haired little dog, sniffing around the stain in odd, twitchy movements.

Great. Just what I need, another bizarre creature encounter.

But my backpack. People will start showing up before long. Ms. Gliss, especially—I've been cutting gym so much that she'd just love to have something to ransom.

I need to grab it now and get it over with. I suck in a deep breath. Whatever's in there—rat, or dog, or warthog, or other creature from the Tenth Circle of Hell—I'll just grab my bag and run.

But it isn't a dog or a rat. It's a mop. Which means I'm officially bonkers. DSM-IV Diagnosis HAG: (Hallucinating Animals in the Gym.)

Holding the mop is a man—older than Dad, younger than Grandpa—who is not one of the regular custodians. He's wearing a set of navy blue coveralls and a leather tool belt holding various spray bottles and rags. One is a particularly large, bulky rag.

Wait. It isn't a rag. It's…a possum. Which clearly means I'm having consecutive episodes of Hallucinating Animals in the Gym.

But, yes. It is a possum, hanging upside down, its tail curled around the man's belt.

Well that's normal. I mean, who isn't accessorizing with possum these days? It's almost passé at this point.

Captain Possum sets down his mop. The possum lifts its head and looks up, its tiny coal eyes glinting. The man walks toward me; the possum's whole body sways with his steps, plunking against the man's leg.

My mouth is open. I bet I look like I've just seen a man with a possum hanging from his belt.

Captain Possum says, "Just cleaning up here, didn't expect to see anyone. That yours." He says it like a statement: *That yours*, but he tips his head to one side and goes quiet, like it is a question he wants answered.

All I can do is nod.

"I'll be done cleaning up this, uh…spill…soon, if you need the gym. You need the gym." Another statement, but he waits like he expects an answer.

I shake my head and pick up my bag. Something about the way he hesitated before he said the word *spill* irks me.

"Spill?" I ask him innocently.

"Yep. Accident yesterday."

He knows something. How much, though? Does he know someone was in here when the deer crashed through? Does he know it was me?

"Accident?" I ask.

"Yep."

"Was anyone hurt?"

"No students hurt."

"No *students* were hurt?" I narrow my eyes. "Does that mean someone else was hurt? Or something else?"

The man's face changes. His good-natured expression fades. He sets his hands on his hips, just above his Possum-Holder Belt. "If there's something you're asking, wish you'd just come out with it. Still got work here." He doesn't sound mean, exactly. But it's definitely a warning that he isn't big on snotty teenagers. Which, to the untrained eye, I can sometimes resemble. A little.

I cross my arms. I don't know why, but I'm compelled to say, "I was here when it happened." *I was here when the deer burst through the window. And also when my best friend died.*

One eyebrow lifts.

"What did they do with the deer?" I ask. Suddenly I have to know. I don't even know why I have to know—I just do. With Jamie, the ambulance came and took her to the hospital. But what do they do with dead animals? What if they just threw the deer in the dumpster? It's too sad to contemplate.

And whenever there's something that's too sad to contemplate, it's all I can contemplate. I've got this slide show in my brain, see, and maybe if I have more information I can shut it down?

"They." Captain Possum rubs his chin. "They. Reckon *they* hired me to take care of it. And since your concern is personal, I'll tell you. Took it away last night. Patched up the window"—he nods toward the tarp—"until the glass gets replaced. Got late, so I came back this morning to finish up."

"Took the deer away. To where?" My hands are shaking. I'm coming unglued and I do not like it. Not one little bit.

He regards me a long time, as if I'm a puzzle he can figure out, as if he's measuring whether he will tell me. "Took it away from here."

So. It's war. He's not going to tell me. He thinks I'm just some stupid, fragile teenager.

"Need to finish up," he says. "I'll lock the door behind you. Meant to do that before. Nice meeting you, uh…"

"Sarah," I manage to say through what is now fury.

"Sarah."

He ushers me out of the gym and locks the door.

I am pissed. Seething. He can't kick me out of the gym like that! I put my bag over my shoulder and bolt down the hall. Condescend much, Captain Possum?

My cheeks burn. I'm so mad. The thing is, I know it's more than the situation warrants. It's a *Disproportionate Response.* That's what one of the counselors called it. *Disproportionate Response*, subtitled: *Being Full Of Rage All The Time, Ready To Explode For Any Reason.* She said it means that something else is going on. That there's another "issue" at play.

She loved the word "issue," loved to make air quotes around it. As in, *what's the real "issue"?*

The real "issue" is that the gym is a fracking nightmare. It was months before I could breathe in that room again, let alone get my ass kicked at dodgeball. Now I have to start all over. My best friend died there and so did this deer and there is no other soul on this earth who can understand how I feel.

I go to the office. Ms. Franklin is standing at the teachers' mail cubbies. She smiles and waves me over. But her friendliness is too much to take. I leave the office. And then I keep going.

I didn't plan it. I'm on autopilot. People are starting to come in and I just…make my way out, past kids with cold noses, puffy jackets, heavy backpacks.

Dr. Folger is in his customary spot at the main entrance. I duck my head, hoping he won't notice me.

"Hello, Ms. Jones."

Crap muffins. I turn around. "Hi, Dr. Folger."

"Having a better day than yesterday, I hope."

"Sure." Somehow I know that this is all we will ever say about the deer.

"Well. That's good," he says. With his thumbnail, he chips off graffiti, written in Wite-out on the doorjamb. "You look as if you are leaving."

Astute observation, sir. "Yeah."

He waits for me to offer an explanation: dentist appointment, stomach flu, anything.

But I don't. The thought of having to lie to him makes me tired.

I expect Dr. Folger to tell me to go back inside. But he surprises me. "Well," he says, "have a good weekend." Then he does his dorky, quasi-Japanese bow.

I take off fast, before he changes his mind. As I walk, the cold seeps into my feet and onto my face, and a thought occurs to me: maybe Dr. Folger could see that I needed to get out of there. Maybe he was being kind.

Maybe I should know better.

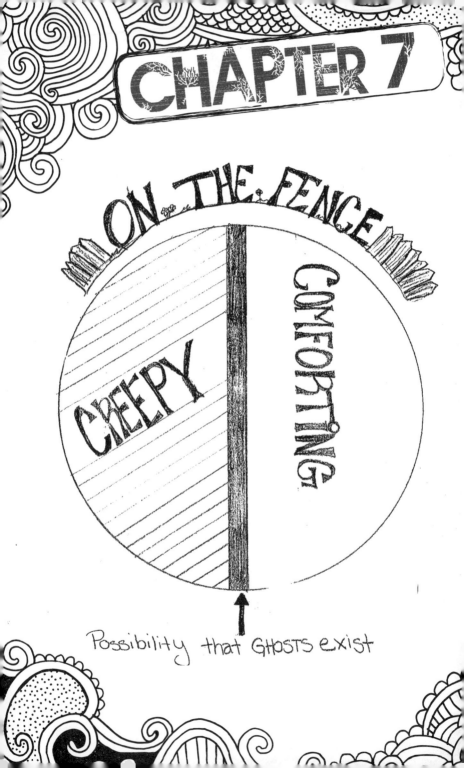

w**HEN** ditching school, there aren't many places you can go without some nosy adult threatening to call the cops. This I've learned in the past few months. I don't ditch a ton—just what I can get away with, slipping under the radar. Only when I really need to.

Anyway. There is somewhere you can always go. You can go to the cemetery. You can visit your best friend's grave.

First, I do the long, cold walk home, keeping off Broad Street and well clear of Mom's clinic. When Ruby sees me, she whips her tail at maximum revs. When I show up at home on a school day and everyone else is gone, she knows she's in for a good day. She grabs Artoo, I change into my warm hiking boots, and off we go.

When we get to the cemetery, Ruby knows where to go.

Does Jamie hover close to her grave? Can Ruby sense her presence? Or is it just habit, our trail from coming here before?

I hope Jamie's not here. I hope she doesn't have to stick around. But I do feel close to her here, and it's peaceful.

What her parents did for her gravestone, it's nice. Instead of a traditional marker, they bought a marble bench.

Even if it is pink, it's still nice.

They must have ordered it from a special supplier, because it's the only one like it in the whole place. It's a cool idea: to make a place to sit, to invite people to stay a while—to suppose they might want to. It seems like a hopeful, thoughtful thing to do. Even if it is weird to sit your ass on your best friend's epitaph. (*Jamie Anne Cleary - Beloved daughter and sister.* BFFs—no matter how beloved—aren't acceptable gravestone material.)

Jamie's mom comes here a lot. Her dad too, but they don't come together. Ruby always hears their cars, and gives a tiny *woof* to tell me they're coming. We skedaddle before they get here; there's a big tree, and then the little stone chapel, and we wait behind there. I figure it's bad enough they have to mourn their daughter; they don't need to see me hanging around in the land of the living. Seems like it would make their grief worse.

I haven't seen Emmett here. Maybe it's too weird to see your own birthday on a grave.

Today Ruby and I have the place to ourselves.

When I sit, the cold of the stone seeps right through my jeans. I pull my legs up under my coat and tie my hood around my face, leaving just enough of an opening for my nose and eyes. I pull my arms out of my sleeves and hug my knees like

I'm in a little tent. Draw my necklace out from under my sweater.

Ruby always sits on the ground next to Jamie's bench, miraculously ignoring any squirrels or birds. She waits and watches me with those big brown eyes, like she's making sure I'm okay.

Sure. I'm great.

I whisper what I always say here. *I'm so sorry, James. I miss you.*

Does she hear me? Or does the chill autumn breeze ferry my words away?

I need her to talk to. Make me feel sane again, normal. There's no one here anymore who gets me. No one who can honestly answer "Yes," when I say, "You know what I mean?"

That *Yes, I know what you mean*—that is the technical definition of Best Friend Forever.

Tears come out, making my eyes sting with cold.

Crying helps, but only so much. I bawled for hours the day Jamie died, and at her funeral, and many times since then, but it's like scooping buckets of water out of the ocean: no matter how fast you bail, it's still ocean as far as the eye can see. And when the feelings come, it's just as fresh and raw as day one.

The first weeks, I became DSM-IV Diagnosis OC-CNNW (Obsessive–Compulsive CNN Watcher). I'd sit in front of the TV, transfixed and fully freaked out. Laid out before me were the world's accidents, disasters, tragedies—all of them totally random, like

Jamie's accident—and there I sat, powerless to do a damned thing about any of it. Earthquakes, mine cave-ins, the death of your best friend… What could you do to prevent this stuff from happening in the first place?

The answer was always the same: nothing. And everything.

If Jamie and I had done just one thing—just one—differently, she would still be here.

Or the opposite: No matter what we did, Jamie would have died.

Deep thoughts. Big questions. Too deep to bridge, too big to carry.

Hypothesis—Anything can happen, to anybody, at any time.
Evidence—My best friend died, in a totally tragic, unexpected, sudden, and random (not to mention freaking horrible) way.

Hypothesis Secondo—Given that anything can happen, to anybody, at any time, you cannot trust, or put faith, in ANYTHING.
Evidence—I could be hit by a bus tomorrow. Or a zombie apocalypse virus could right now be infecting half the world.
So, what's the point? Of anything?
Answer—There is no point. It's all random. Everything. Is. Random.

It's an elegant theory, if I do say so myself. Simple, concise, all-encompassing. Yet it's not so popular with the grown-ups. Especially counselors.

Everyone—the array of counselors, and my parents, and some of my teachers, and even Stenn—told me the same thing, in one form or other.

Everything happens for a reason.
God has a plan.
You must have faith.

Riiight. I attempted to take that approach. But it didn't stick for more than a day. I mean, my best friend, fourteen years old and totally healthy and happy (except for the occasional mood swing or whatever), dies for no good reason, and I'm supposed to *Have Faith* and believe *God Has a Plan* and *Everything Happens for a Reason*?

It's horseshit. And eventually, I told them so. All of them: grief counselors, parents, guidance counselors, teachers, boyfriend.

Until I learned *not* to tell them so. Because if you do start speaking the truth, guess what? People freak. They get scared you're going to commit suicide or go on a shooting rampage based upon your theory that everything is random. It's hard enough to control your own reactions when someone dies. But when you pile on other people's reactions to your reactions? It all becomes an enormous, unmanageable, intolerable heap of Sucktacular Suckiness.

Eventually, I turned off CNN. I wandered around aimlessly. My parents' foreheads wrinkled with worry. (This was before they added frustrated and annoyed to the range of emotions revealed in their expressions.) They gripped the tops of my arms and looked into my eyes. They said things like, "We're concerned about you. You're not yourself. We think you should see a counselor."

First stop: my guidance counselor. I didn't get past the first "crisis" meeting with that moron. The man can barely figure out how to transfer me to a different gym class or find the correct honors English schedule, and I'm supposed to *relate* to him? Moving on.

Next stop was a social worker. She was nice—frazzled, but nice. She had mugs of hot tea and a big smile; I almost started to trust her. Until! During our third meeting, I kind of broke down and before I could stop myself, I blurted, "If everything that happens is random, doesn't that make everything meaningless?"

Well. That did it. She stopped listening to what I was actually saying and started listening for what she was afraid of hearing. But I wasn't going to hurt myself or anyone else, and I'm still not stockpiling guns or ammo. I just want some honesty.

So. After the social worker, my parents ratcheted up the stakes, climbed the hourly fee scale, and sent me to a bearded, loafer-wearing psychologist in

Binghamton. I got to do a Rorschach test and the MMPI. It was super fun. And it turns out I'm gifted! And slightly depressed! But normal! And not psychopathic! With no evident personality disorders!

Still, our therapeutic relationship ended up not being, as he put it, *simpatico*. Mostly because I called him on his pretentious bullshit, and told him I didn't appreciate him conflating grief, sadness, and honesty with depression. Thank Christ, Mom and Dad kind of petered out on finding me another therapist after that.

I did try to talk to Stenn. More than once. *Use your resources, call on your support network*, as the counselors say. Example:

"Do you think there's meaning in the way things happen?" I asked him. We were cuddled on the couch in his parents' basement, post almost-intercourse.

He got super earnest. "Yes. I believe God has a plan. Jesus guides everything."

Holy cats. He sounded like a Cylon. In my head, I was all, *Say what, now? God has a plan? And Jesus is in on it, too?* Since when was my boyfriend Mr. Religion?

He must have noticed the not-so-slightly horrified look on my face, because he dialed it back. Hard. "Like in *Star Wars*," he said. "Everyone has their destiny—Luke has his, Han and Leia have theirs. Obi Wan, he knew his. Even if it's sad or scary. Even if you don't understand it until way later."

Points for speaking my language, but still. I gave him an I'm Not Buying It face.

"Seriously, Sare. Whenever you want to talk, I'm here for you. You know that."

It made me feel better. Until it dawned on me that he hadn't bothered to ask me what I thought, what I believed. Just a slight oversight.

Truth is, it's lonely as hell. Because the thing about knowing what I know? It is Not Helpful. It's not conducive to normal, happy teenager relationships. Observe.

1. Knowing that life is random makes it damned hard to motivate. All of a sudden, for some strange reason, cute jeans and a tight little ass and perfect hair and looking good and being cool and Facebooking and homework and SAT prep don't seem terribly important.

2. You can't really let yourself be close to your boyfriend, or your dad, or your old friends if you know they could die at any moment.

3. It's a case of "all dressed up and no place to go." Because I know this Big True Thing and nobody wants to hear it. Nobody.

Message received from everyone, loud and clear.

Talk to us enough to think you're okay, but don't say what you really think. It makes us uncomfortable. And God forbid we should be uncomfortable.

I can live with it, though. I do live with it. It's not the worst part.

The worst part is not being able to talk about it with Jamie. Because she would understand how I feel, and what I think. She would get the theory.

The second worst part? Not being able to talk *about* Jamie. Look, if I can't be with James, at least let me rip on her and laugh about stuff.

The first few times I waxed Jamie-sophical, and started in on how the girl used to add sugar *and* Splenda to her lattes, people were fairly sympathetic. But after a month or so, it was like *Time's up! You should be over this by now*. When I'd say her name, shoulders started to stiffen, mouths turned down. In Stenn's case, fingernails were bitten. Apparently people preferred posting to a dead girl's Facebook timeline, or abandoning her memory entirely, to feeling a modicum of...anything.

And the longer it goes on, the more it feels like I'm in some parallel dimension where my BFF never existed. Like in the movie *Back to the Future*. Michael J. Fox goes back in time and keeps checking a photo from his past to make sure the people he knows are still there. To be sure they still *exist*. But they start fading from the photo, a little at a time.

Could that happen with Jamie? Could she dissolve from my memories, leaving just a swath of background scenery, with no one standing in front of it?

The thought makes me sick. So for a couple of hours here in the cemetery, I concentrate on making Jamie's picture come back. I let myself be comforted by Ruby, and I hold my necklace, and get cold, and miss Jamie.

And then my dad shows up.

CHAPTER 8

"And Now, Young Skywalker, You Will Die"

HORRIBLE!

- Slowly digested over 1,000 years by the sarlacc in the Pit of Carkoon.
- Smushed in folding wall @ age 14
- Anaconda
- Crocodile
- Plane crash on LOST
- Ejected from Battlestar into vacuum of space
- Parachute doesn't open while skydiving
- Flash-frozen à la *The Day After Tomorrow*
- In your sleep when you're 95
- licked to death by puppies (PUPPIES!)

NOT too BAD
(if you have to go)

DAD rips into the cemetery, driving so fast that Ruby doesn't have time to warn me. *Et tu*, Dr. Folger?

So. Dr. Folger hadn't been showing me kindness earlier when he let me leave school. He was just waiting for me to leave so he could turn around and call my dad.

Dad pulls up so the Jeep's passenger side is next to us. He puts the window down; his face is hard and angry. There's none of the usual softness of worry in his eyes. He looks one thing only: pissed off. Times infinity. He pushes the passenger door open.

"Sarah. Get in the car. Now."

I'm dead. Most of my teachers have overlooked the occasional skipped class—either out of pity, laziness, or not wanting to upset the superintendent. Sure, Dad has had to sign a few detention slips for skipping gym. (Ms. Gliss never lets anything slide.) But this—this is multiple classes; this is being caught off school grounds. This is a big one. I'm in for it.

What is he going to do? Nix my driving permit? Forbid me from seeing Stenn? Take Ruby away? He wouldn't really do that, would he?

"Get in the car," he repeats.

"No." It just comes out.

"Now, Sarah."

"Come on, Rubes," I say. With pounding heart, I start walking. Where am I going? What the hell is wrong with me?!

Dad drives beside me, the passenger door still open. To be honest, I'm scared out of my intestines. Not getting in the car is making it worse. My dad looks like he's going to burst into rage flames. I've never, ever seen him this mad.

Ruby, panting happily, looks from me to Dad's car and back at me. Then she hops through the open door into the Jeep. It's her way of saving me from my own stupidity. I'm not about to let her go anywhere without me, so I open the back door (because I'm a stubborn jackass) and slide in. Ruby jumps over the front seat onto my lap.

Dad reaches over and pulls the door closed. You'd think he'd peel out, lay tracks, the way he's fuming. But he just continues to drive slow. Really slow. Way too slow. In the kind of silence that can suffocate. I can't survive it for long. So I say, "Where are you taking me?"

"Back to school."

"I'll just leave again."

He eyes me in the rearview mirror. He stops the car. "Get out."

"You just told me to get in!"

"Now I'm telling you to get out."

This time I do what he says. I open the door and gently nudge Ruby out, then get out myself.

Dad gets out, too. He stands there staring at me and Ruby. "Just what...just what in the *hell* do you think you're doing?"

"Well, I heard there was the big party here in the cemetery," replies my snark box. "It was supposedly a three kegger, and I just—"

"*Enough!* Enough with the sarcasm, Sarah. I have had it up to here with you." He puts his hand to his forehead like some sort of salute. "Jesus. What am I supposed to do?"

I have no idea. I don't know what I'm doing, and I just need you to be... I don't even know what I need you to be! Patient? Understanding? Persistent? But none of those words come out, because that's never what comes out SJD. Instead, the snark box strikes again: "You're just upset because it looks bad. The super-intendent's daughter cutting school—"

"Oh, cut the crap! You have got to be kidding me. You think I give a... You honestly think that's why I'm upset?"

No. "Isn't it?"

He starts laughing. It's a crazy, bitter laugh. He sits down on the ground. And then, somehow, he's weeping. "Where have you gone? Where is the Sarah I knew?" He puts his head in his hands. "I just want her back."

To see your dad cry like that. Because of you.

Not just because of something you've done, but because of Who You Are, because the person you've become is so profoundly messed up and unreachable... It's beyond sad. And it's an entire marathon past guilt.

Shame. That's what I feel. Ashamed. Not ashamed of him—although it is embarrassing to see him this destroyed. But no, I'm ashamed of myself. This strong, smart, capable man—my *dad*, for God's sake—is blubbering on the ground because of me. Because I don't know how to get rid of my snark box. I literally do not know how.

And so I stand there like a stupid idiot. And after a while, Ruby and I get back in the car.

Eventually, Dad stands up, gets back in the car, and starts driving, even more slowly this time. "I'm taking you back to school. And don't think this is over. Not by a long shot. You understand me?"

Pretty sure it's a rhetorical question, so I don't bother answering. I just stare out the window at the rows of graves. Dad turns, following the twisty cemetery lane, and we pass a white van parked on the grass. Dad's going so slow that it seems like I could be pulling the van toward me on a rope.

Past the van, a man is kneeling at one of those double graves, the kind with one headstone for two people. His head is bowed like he's praying or deep in thought. As Dad curves the Jeep around the path, the man looks up. Dead on, straight at me, like he knew I was looking at him. He has gray hair, he's wearing coveralls, and there is a small gray thing—a possum—curled up nearby.

It's the man from the gym.

My stomach flips, my scalp prickles like birds are pecking at it. Captain Possum from the gym is here. Sure. Makes perfect sense. I live in a small town and I've seen him exactly never before in my life, so why wouldn't I see him two times, back to back, first where Jamie died and then near where she's buried?

He watches me pass, and there is no doubt that he recognizes me. He remembers me from this morning just as surely as I remember him.

The whooshing sound comes, like seashells clamped over my ears, and then the tidal wave. It's happened before and I. Do. Not. Like. It. The sound is the Harbinger of Doom, along with the aluminum foil saliva taste in my mouth. And then the rush of memory—and the panic, the fear, the anxiety. No. I don't want this. But inexorably, the light goes funny and the worn seat smell of Dad's Jeep turns rancid. I try to fight it, squeezing my eyes shut and hugging Ruby close to my face. The seashell noise, this feeling, it means remembering. *I will not think about it. Don't think about it.*

But it comes anyway.

That day.

Jamie and I had ducked into the gym after school. It was empty—away games, teams had left early—and she was panicked. She'd lost her locket. Maybe the necklace had broken during gym class?

First, we searched the locker room.

"It's not here," she'd said. "Let's check the gym."

It was crazy to think we'd find it. Needle, meet haystack. I would have given up after the first ten minutes, but Jamie had started to cry, and her drippy, bear-cub eyes were un-ignorable. So I kept looking.

Something caught my eye. "James! Come here!"

She ran over. I pointed to a thin gold chain pooling out from under the folded gym partition. The collapsible wall was pushed to one side of the gym, its large sections folded tight. I knelt down and tugged the necklace, but it wouldn't budge. "It's stuck."

"Crap." She sat down next to me. "Mr. D and Ms. Gliss had the wall open—wait, closed? Whatever. You know what I mean. To separate us from the boys. Because they're so dangerous to our virtue." She rolled her eyes. "My necklace must have caught while I was sitting against the wall."

I thought a minute. "We could break the chain. Maybe the locket will slide off."

"Nokay!"

"James. How else are we going to get it?"

She looked at me, pained, but she knew I was right.

I jerked the chain. It broke and more of it came out from under the wall, but it was still stuck. The locket didn't appear. "Shoot. What is this made of? Titanium?"

Next to me, Jamie hugged her knees. "What if we open the door? The wall, I mean?"

"The controls are locked."

She got a wide grin and pointed to the other side of the gym. Mr. D's keys were hanging from the control box, next to the red power button.

"No," I said.

"Yes," she said. "It's important. We'll just get my locket and fold it back up. Mr. D won't mind."

I wasn't so sure about that.

James jogged across the gym.

"Wait," I called, catching up. "I'll do it." Perks of being the superintendent's daughter: I always got in less trouble than other kids.

She was grateful. We bumped hips. "Ninja bitches!"

She went back to the folded wall. "I'll tell you when I've got it, and you close it back up quick."

"10–4." I studied the control box. It looked simple enough: there was a slot with the key in it, and one big red button. "Ready?"

"Affirmative!"

I pressed the button.

Nothing happened. "It's like the hyperdrive on the Millenium Falcon," I said.

James threw me one of her looks. "Don't nerd out on me. Try it again."

I fiddled with the key and pressed the button.

The motor whirred and the wall started spreading

out along its track, opening like an accordion. As the wall sections pulled away from each other, Jamie stepped in and disappeared between two of them.

"Got it! Back her up!" She sounded happy.

I turned the key and pressed the button again. The motor made a grinding, ratchety sound, and the wall shuddered and reversed direction.

"That didn't sound good!" I laughed, walking toward Jamie. She was still hidden between sections.

"Oh shit!" She was laughing, too. "I'm stuck!"

"You are high-larious."

She was quiet a moment. The motor kept humming. "Not funny! My sweater's caught in the hinge." She sounded a little nervous. But not terrified. Yet. "Abort! Abort!"

I jogged back to the control box. "There!" I shouted as I twisted the key and pressed the button again. "I think I got it."

But the sound of the motor didn't change. The wall kept folding.

"Sarah!" Jamie shouted.

She sounded really scared now.

I pounded the red button and worked the key back and forth furiously. "It won't stop!" I screamed. "Jamie! Get out of there!"

"I can't!"

"Take your sweater off!"

"I'm stuck! Sarah! Help!"

I slammed the button again.

The wall kept collapsing.

This wasn't happening. It couldn't be happening.

I ran toward Jamie. There must be a safety override.
The wall would sense that it was blocked—

The motor made a sick, groaning sound.

Jamie screamed. Screamed. And then fell silent.

I stopped running.

I didn't know what to do. What should I do?

I sleepwalked.

A rivulet of blood appeared under the folded wall.

I threw up.

You'd think I would have sprinted, run for help, but I couldn't. I could barely balance.

I walked to the office.

It was all I could think to do.

But at what cost?

Jamie. My best friend.

♀ ♀ ♂

Was she dead when I left? Or did she hear me walk away from her?

Did she die alone?

Jesus Christ. I still don't know how it happened. I don't know why I couldn't make the door stop. I don't know how it could be heavy enough to crush a person.

I'm so sorry, Jamie.

Please tell me you don't blame me. Please tell me you know I tried to help you.

Please tell me you didn't hear me walk away from you.

Please tell me you're happy now. That you're not lonely. That you are one with the universe, part of the Force or something.

Please tell me you're not hanging around, hovering over your grave, waiting for some sort of resolution.

Maybe she is. What if she is?

Maybe I wish Jamie was haunting her grave. Because at least that would mean she's still herself, and she's still nearby. But I know I'm a selfish creep for wanting that. Maybe that's why I can't overcome the snark box. Because it's too much. It's too selfish and it's too sad and it's too much. All of this. I don't want it anymore.

CHAPTER 9

GEOMETRY

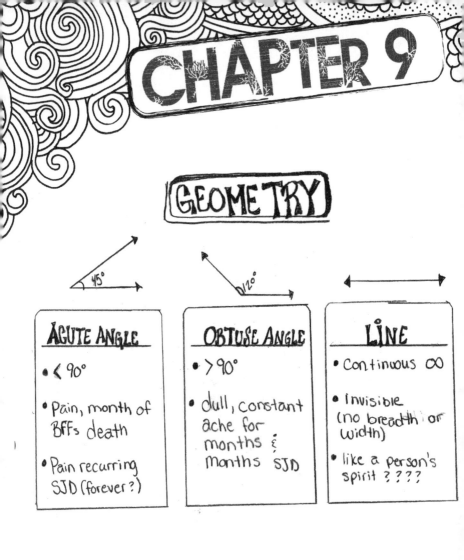

ACUTE ANGLE

- < 90°

- Pain, month of BFFs death

- Pain recurring SJD (forever?)

OBTUSE ANGLE

- > 90°

- dull, constant ache for months & months SJD

LINE

- Continuous ∞

- Invisible (no breadth or width)

- like a person's spirit ????

DAD parks in the bus circle and walks me into school. He escorts me to my locker and then to class. He seems cold and distant. Which is fair enough, I guess, because that's how I seem to act around him SJD. Plus there's the Superintendent Effect, which comes into play whenever he steps into a school building. He's the Darth Vader. He's the Admiral Adama of the battlestar. It's all forced smiles and/or averted gazes.

Trigonometry has already started. Dad nods at Mr. Haas and Mr. Haas nods back, gesturing for me to take my seat.

Dad squeezes my shoulder and tells me, "Come straight home after school." I feel his eyes on me—his, along with everyone else's—as I walk to my desk. I sit. Dad leaves. Good thing I don't care about being cool anymore, because this would have been complete social ruination.

Mr. Haas drones on and on. "You'll remember from geometry that a locus is a collection of points that share a property. Sarah Jones, are you listening?"

Focus. Locus.

Locus. The word gets me thinking. The frazzled social worker talked about something called a locus of control. She said it meant that when the world seems completely bonkers and totally overwhelming, you should concentrate on what you can actually do about it. That is your locus of control: the stuff that is within your power to change. She said to stop for a moment. Breathe. List everything that's going on, and then go through the list and analyze what you can and can't control.

So I turn to a fresh page in my notebook.

WHAT UP, BEE-YOTCHES! THIS IS MUH LOCUS O' CONTROL.

1. **Jamie.** My best friend died and I miss the hell out of her and there is nothing I can do to control that, so moving on.

2. **Parental units.** They are pissed, and they are kind of justified. What would I do if I had myself for a kid? But what are they going to do? What are they going to yank away from me? Driving? Stenn? Ruby? Damn. What can I control about that?

   (A) Not let my grades keep plummeting. That would make them happy. I used to get mostly A's, for crying out loud. It can't be that hard to get back up to snuff. So—

   (i) Do some homework once in a while.
   (ii) Study.
   (iii) See about maybe extra credit.

(B) Stop ditching classes. Actually...dunno if I can do that. Sometimes I just have to get the hell out of Dodge. So—

    (i) Be smarter about when I ditch.

    (ii) Chose classes whose teachers won't rat.

    (iii) Avoid blithely walking by Dr. Folger when leaving.

(C) Try to be a little nicer. At least throw the parentals a bone now and then.

3. **Getting my license.** Driving = freedom from being under Jeremy's thumb. Freedom to go where I want, and visit Stenn. Must. Get. License. (Sadly this is mostly in Parentals' Locus of Control. Therefore refer to point 2, sections A and B.)

4. **Ruby.** Best dog in the universe. Light of my life. Cannot risk losing her. Again in parentals' hands. So, appease parents. (Refer again to point 2, sections A and B.)

5. **Stenn.** Fire of my loins.

(A) Would my parents seriously forbid me from seeing him, taking away pretty much the last human interaction and kindness from my life right now? Good idea, guys! (OK, once again, back to point 2, sections A and B. Tread carefully.)

(B) How long is Stenn going to deal with me being moody and sarcastic? How long would I deal with myself? Good question. Family is obligated to put up with you, but boyfriends have a choice. So. What can I do about it?

> (i) Have sex with him? For most guys that would work. But Stenn's not most guys. He actually cares about me.
>
> (ii) Maybe try to talk to him more?
>
> (iii) Be less hostile and sarcastic. But the snark box seems to have a mind of its own.

So—

6. **<u>Snark Box.</u>** Work on it. Rip it out. How?

(A) At least I'm not in denial about it! Hey! Step one, complete.

(B) Recognition = the next step. I do seem to be noticing it more often, even though it's been installed for six months + . Therefore—

(C) When noticed, try to say something non-snarktastic instead. Or in addition, as the case may be.

(D) Failing that, just shut up.

7. **<u>Jeremy.</u>** $\longrightarrow$ "Everyone thinks you're peculiar."

(A) Out of my control = what everyone thinks

(B) In my control = not acting like a snarktastic (see point 6) weirdo bereaved peculiar kid. (Also it would be a refreshing change to not be hated by my own brother.) Make an effort to go back to normal. Sure, easy! Which probably means—

8. **Effort to go back to normal.** It's like the social worker said: "Fake it 'til you make it."

(A) Stop hanging out in the main office before school and during lunch and free periods. Question: BJD, what would I have thought of someone who made the office their HQ? Answer: fingers in the shape of an L on the forehead. Capital L, Loser.

(B) Stop using long-distance boyfriend as excuse to be antisocial. Go out again.

> (i) Baby steps. Set goals. Goal: start by going out to at least one party/shindig/movie/game/whatever a week.

> (ii) With Stenn is okay when he's home. Figure out another plan for weekends he stays at Mercer.

(C) Reconnect (did I really just write that word? Reconnect?) with some actual friends. Ones who are alive. Breaking apart into more do-able chunks—

> (i) Maybe some of my old Star Wars-centric nerdy guy friends who do not require lots of talking or effort? See if Banks, Mike, and/or TJ have third period free. Hang with them instead of in the office. This will not advance any Ninja agenda, but at least they are

>> (a) easy to be around and
>> (b) alive.

(ii) Emmett? Or is that too weird? He wants to know how J died. This might need a whole new section.

(iii) Quasi-close girlfriends who were supportive for a month and then moved on from my sorry butt. Gah! Girls feel too complicated. Plus the betrayal factor—them of me SJD, me of Jamie's memory. WWJT (What Would Jamie Think)?

(iv) Make new friends? Table this thought. Too overwhelming for now. All of this is

(v) Easier said than done.

9. **Emmett.** Back to Point 8, Section C ii.

(A) Worth repeating—he wants to know how Jamie died.

(i) In my control = telling him.

(ii) Out of my control = freaking out about the memories of it, and all the feelings I'd have when telling him. Can you say Panic Attack?!

(B) Also out of my control = he will hate me when/if I tell him, because he'll think

(i) It's my fault, and

(ii) I left his sister to die alone.

Bah! My head is swimming. Table decision/action re: Emmett until later date. Possibly forever.

Hmm. What else.

10. **The deer.** Holy crap. Is "speeding souls on their way" my otherworldly spiritual job? To tell Emmett the details of the accident? Is that the unfinished business that needs to happen for Jamie to be at peace? Whoa. I so can't deal with that anytime soon. Again with the moving on. Table this also indefinitely.

11. **Living in Coincidence City.** Hello, Captain Possum! Hello, two freaky deaths in one gym! Take me down to Coincidence City where the grass is green and…oh hell. Next.

12. **Adults around here** (I'm talking to you, Dr. Folger) telling on me, being condescending and sneaky. Out. Of. My. Control.

Now, to go back and count up the within-my-locus-of-control stuff. Great. Out of all those points and sections, looks like…a tiny fraction of the list is things that I can actually do something about. And honestly, most of the changes feel impossible anyway. Case in point: if I knew how to shut off my snark box, I would have done it at the cemetery, when it would have mattered.

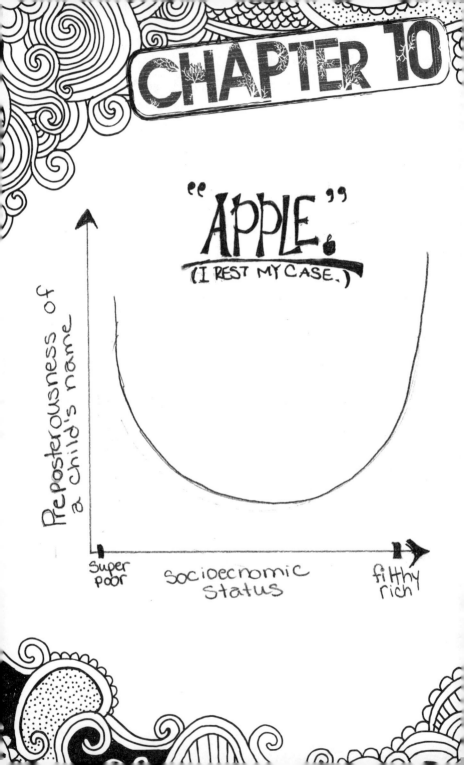

CHAPTER 10

"APPLE."

(I REST MY CASE.)

Preposterousness of a child's name

super poor

socioeconomic status

filthy rich

THE day wears on, until the final bell rings at last. I get my stuff from my locker and drag my ass out to the parking lot to get a ride home.

Jeremy's by his car, talking with a bunch of guys. I slouch down, trying to make myself inconspicuous so I don't annoy my driver. But one of the guys looks over and right at me. Blond hair, great smile.

Stenn! What a sight for sore eyes.

We wrap our arms around each other. He's into big, squeezy hugs, and I let him hold on to me for a while. It's a combo of smothering and comforting and semi-tingly. A small peck on the lips—kissing in front of my bro seems too icky. "Hi, silly," he says.

"You're early! I thought you weren't getting home until later."

He laughs. "I finished my midterm early."

"Yay!"

"I got home around noon," he says. "Which reminds me, where were you today? I thought I saw you in your dad's car? When I was rolling into town—" He stops abruptly, his eyes locking on the band-aid above my eyebrow. "What happened?" He holds my elbows and maneuvers me to face the sun, to get a better look. He cups my chin in his hand.

It is such a classic Stenn move, straight from a movie. It both melts me and, somehow, pisses me off.

SJD, my knee-jerk reaction when I start to feel something that makes me feel cared about, and therefore vulnerable, is anger. It's like the snark box is connected to something deep and ugly, a tempest of anger that wasn't there BJD.

"Let me see, Sare. What happened?"

"Gym accident." *I don't want to talk about it.*

Stenn raises his eyebrows. He's no dummy. The word "gym" raises particular concern.

Which makes me angrier. Which makes so much sense.

"I'll tell you the whole story later," I say.

"Why not now?"

Because the deer thing was sad, and the speeding-their-souls thing is freaking me out, and it all makes me think of Jamie, and I'll probably start screaming right here in the parking lot. "It's just a long story. Boring." Change of subject, please. "Does my mom know you're here? Or my dad?"

He shakes his head. "Why?"

"I'm kind of in trouble."

He sighs. "What did you do this time?"

I was at the cemetery because I don't know how to be anywhere else. "Long story again." Quick! Another change of subject. "I'm supposed to go straight home... But they won't be home until five." I smile up at him.

He nods over at Jeremy. "I'll take her home."

"Sure, man." My brother shrugs. Stenn is doing him a favor; now Jeremy doesn't have to drive me or deal with me. It's so nice to feel like a useless sack of potatoes. Jeremy says, "Tell Mom and Dad I'll be home after dinner."

"Okay," I say.

Stenn takes my hand and we weave through the parking lot. Lots of people say hi to him. They are glad to see him, and when I'm with him, their smiles extend to me. My boyfriend, my last tether to social normalcy. Stenn's a guy's guy, for sure: dudes give him the handshake/hand smack/half-hug thing. Upperclass Ninja girls say hi. Freshman and sophomore girls, most of them Normals, not yet eligible for Ninjadom, are more demure. Only one fellow sophomore has the nerve to say hello to us directly: Rosemary Sturt. Solid mid-to-high Normal. She seemed cool enough when we suffered through a semester of health class last year. Still, she's maybe a little too eager to say hi to my hot boyfriend. Me no likey.

Stenn clicks his key; his Audi beeps and unlocks. The Wagners are richer than God—not the ascetic skinny Mother Teresa kind of God, but the plump Republican prosperity gospel God. They're the wealthiest family in Norwich, that's for sure. I slide onto the leather seat and roll the dial to fire up the seat's tush toaster. Another thing about Stenn is that you know he's got money, because he's all polite and well dressed—and he has his own Audi—but he is not a snot. He doesn't have a diamond-encrusted stick up his ass like, oh I don't know…say…his mom?

Stenn waves to more people as he drives away from school. Then he gets quiet. Not companionable-silence quiet, but tense quiet, like riding-with-Jeremy quiet.

"Is something wrong?" I finally ask. I manage to get it out without too much snark.

Stenn looks at me for a moment, then back at the road. The music changes. Stenn flips the blinker.

"What?" *Just spit it out already.*

"I'm just wondering why you're in trouble, Sare. Maybe we shouldn't—maybe I should just drop you off at home."

"You don't want to come in? For Business Time?"

"Of course I do! I was just thinking… I don't want to get you in more trouble. What did you do, anyway?"

"I skipped a couple classes. My dad found out."

"Why!"

"Because Dr. Folger is a narc."

"No, I mean, why did you skip? Wait, does it have something to do with your forehead?"

I shrug. "No. I just…I wanted to get out of there."

"You can't just cut school, Sare."

"Yes, I can."

"No, you can't."

I look at him. "I cut school, okay? It's done. Can we move on? I'm not as perfect as you are."

He slumps in his seat. "I'm not perfect, that's not the point."

"I needed to get out of there. I was freaking out; I needed some fresh air."

"Freaking out about what?"

"What do you think?"

He sighs, part worried, part annoyed.

I nod. "Yeah. You don't want to hear it. So let's just go inside."

"I *do* want to hear it! It's just you're frustrating as hell—"

"Oh, I'm *so* sorry I'm *so* frustrating. Sorry it's getting old that your girlfriend is damaged."

"Sare." His tone is going cold. He looks over at me and grinds his teeth on a cuticle.

I'm pushing him too far, and I know it, but I just cannot get out in front of this anger and snarkiness. Despite the deal I just made with myself in trigonometry. Try, Sarah. Try, try, try not to be a total bitch.

No. Do, or do not. There is no try.

Right you are, Yoda. I take a deep breath. "Yes. I was freaking out and I left school. I went to the cemetery. I was having a hard day and I needed to get away and I got fully busted by my dad and I'm probably going to be grounded. And I'm trying really hard, I am. But that's all I'm going to say about it right now, okay?"

He looks surprised. "Okay." He nods. "All right."

I stare straight ahead. My head feels like it will explode with all this effort. "So." I try to sound casual. "How were your exams? How's school?"

He squints at me like he's trying to decide whether to let me off that easy. But he's über generous—or he can see this is killing me—because he says, "School's okay. Midge helped me study for—"

"Stop right there. *Midge*?"

"Short for Mildred?" He frowns. "Or Millicent, maybe?"

"Oh my God. Why do the rich curse their children with such names?"

"Midge is better than Apple."

"There's an *Apple* at your school?"

"You don't like Apple?"

"Apollonia, maybe, if she purifies herself in the Lake Minnetonka. But Apple? Like Gwyneth's Apple? That's just wrong."

He laughs. "Apple claims she's going to change her name when she turns eighteen."

"Ooh, rebellious!" I say. "Won't Dadsy and Mumsy cut her out of the will? Or trade in her trust fund?"

We're here. Stenn pulls up my driveway. "Probably. She'd never do it. It's all talk."

"How can you stand it there at Mercer with all those trustafarians?" Stenn is rich, but Norwich rich is not the same as Manhattan aristocracy rich.

Stenn shrugs and turns the car off. "It's not so bad. Mom had a cow when Stiv didn't go, you know that."

"Yeah." His brother had bucked family expectation by staying at Norwich High School for his junior and senior years. His mom was so upset they practically had to book her a room in a psych ward.

"Midge is nice. You'd like her."

I narrow my eyes at him. "How nice is nice?"

Whiplash-fast, Stenn grins like the Cheshire Cat. "You're jealous!"

"Why would I be jealous of a rich girl who you actually see every day?" Who is probably gorgeous and undamaged by grief and rancid sarcasm? "Should I be?"

"No. It's just kind of adorable." He tucks my hair behind my ear. "I didn't know you still cared."

"Der."

Thump. Something thwacks the car door. *Thump thump thump.* I swing the door open. There is Ruby, a mouse dangling from her mouth. Terribly pleased with herself, she's wagging her tail so hard it's about to dent the Audi.

Another reason to be glad my folks aren't home yet. They blow gaskets every time she chucks a carcass onto the porch. Or worse, sneaks one into the house.

Ruby is so proud of herself. It's sweet, in a revolting way. She never offers her kills to anyone but me. Still, I'm sorry for the animals she's killed: umpteen mice, enough garter snakes to fill a bucket, lots of moles, even a small woodchuck. Part lioness, my dog.

I fake enthusiasm: "For me, Rubes? Thank you! Drop it, girl." Ruby sets the mouse at my feet. I rub her velvet ears. "Thank you so much!"

Stenn is already out of the car. "Nice one, Rubes," he tells her. To me, he asks, "Want me to deal with it?"

I smile in a way I hope looks 50 percent cute, 50 percent sexy—although probably I just look like the Joker. "Yes, please?"

"You're gonna owe me."

"What? I'm just giving you a chance to be chivalrous. You know you love it."

"I do, I really do. Anything for you."

Sigh. When we first got together, he used to say that all the time, all moony-eyed. Lately it sounds annoyed and a little sarcastic.

"Come on, Rubes," I say, and she follows me into the house. She laps from her water bowl while I watch Stenn through the kitchen window. Midge. I've never really worried too much about Stenn cheating on me; he's so honest and...*good*. But maybe I should be worried? Everyone says long-distance relationships are doomed. Even Jamie worried about it. Seeing each other a couple of weekends a month...and me being a bitch approximately 45 to 90 percent of that time...

Stenn's got a shovel from the garage. He uses it to scoop up the mouse, carries it to the little animal graveyard under our big maple tree. He peels back the chicken wire covering the ground, an addition I made after Rubes exhumed several moles, thank you very much (I felt quite brilliant coming up with that solution), and digs a little hole. He tips the mouse in and covers it with dirt, then rolls the chicken wire back over it, setting rocks on the edges to hold it down.

Stenn lays the shovel down, bows his head, and folds his hands in prayer. I freeze. Stenn, my boyfriend, believer in God with a capital *G*. And a Divine Plan. Mister Everything-Happens-for-a-Reason. It plucks my nerves, but it's also strangely sweet. It reminds me of the way he prayed, silently, eyebrows furrowed, tears on his cheeks, at Jamie's funeral.

It's easy to overlook that he's such a believer: he's not one of those Abstinence Club kids; he doesn't wear a *WWJD?* bracelet; he doesn't go door-to-door trying to convert people (that would be a deal breaker). Honestly, his religion never really came up until Jamie died.

Which is funny. Not funny *ha ha*, but funny strange. Why does death bring out religion? Isn't faith supposed to be about affirming life? Joy? Love? That kind of thing? Am I missing something?

Stenn comes into the kitchen, takes off his muddy shoes, and then wraps his arms around me. He's such a good kisser. Good. Good kisser. Extremely good kisser.

"Thanks," I say about the mouse, not mentioning the prayer.

Whatever his religious beliefs, they don't include chastity.

"You're welcome." He nuzzles my neck so that

my legs begin to weaken. It feels so good. Why not try to forget everything for a while?

"Let's go to my room," I say. I start taking my sweater off as I lead the way.

We're halfway up the stairs when the back door slams.

"Shit!" It's my mom. Or my dad. And they'll be so pleased to see me stripping down for Stenn.

Stenn groans.

I throw my sweater back on. "You're probably not supposed to be here."

"Should I try to sneak out?"

"No, they must have already seen your car." We scuttle downstairs.

It's Mom.

"Hi, Mom," I say, trying to look as uncrumpled and non-flushed as possible.

"Hi, Ms. Jones," Stenn says, pulling a hand through his hair.

Mom shoots me a look. A bad, scary, Kiss Your Teenage Liberty Goodbye look. Like she knows what we've just been up to (or were about to be up to), *and* she's talked to Dad about me ditching classes, *and* she just Does. Not. Know. What. To. Do. With. Me. Anymore.

"Hi, Stenn," she says, managing an amiable tone. It's good that Mom and Dad love Stenn, because maybe they won't kill me for having him over right now. Unless that puts Ruby on the chopping block? Or driving? Argh! Cannot deal.

Mom asks Stenn, "How is school?"

He nods. "Good. I just took my midterms..." And off he goes, speaking fluent Parent-ese. Stenn is bilingual in English—he speaks Normal Kid and Educated Young Man. Also Spanish. Mom smiles and nods, asks questions, has an actual conversation. Her eyes look grateful. Grateful that he is a normal person, that he is still my boyfriend, and therefore perhaps there's hope for her daughter to be normal again, too.

Mom hangs her work bag up and sits at the kitchen table. "I think I parked so you can get out, Stenn."

"Lucky she didn't crash into you," I say.

"Hilarious, Monkey," Mom says to me. She appeals to Stenn. "I'm a good driver. I don't know why my entire family gives me such a hard time."

Stenn takes my mom's hint while deftly deflecting the subject. "Thanks, Ms. Jones. I'm sure I can manage to get out of the driveway. Good to see you."

"You, too."

We put on our shoes and Ruby and I walk Stenn to his car. "So," he says, kissing me. "I'll come by to pick you up later?"

"Are we going somewhere?"

"Soccer party?"

I nod. This means I can cross something off my Things To Do To Regain Normalcy list. Yay me. "Sure. But I might be grounded. I'll have to sneak out."

Stenn cringes, like he doesn't want me to get in

more trouble, but he also wants to see me later. "I'll text you."

We kiss again until I realize my mom is watching from the window. Then it's all prim.

"Well, good day, sir," I say.

"Lovely to see you, miss." We shake hands. And Stenn leaves.

Back in the kitchen, Mom's looking into the fridge. She moans a heavy, Martyr Mom sigh, "What should we have for dinner?"

"Pizza. And cookies for dessert."

"Done." She grabs a bottle of wine before shutting the fridge door. "And just so we're clear. When your father gets home, we are going to have a chat." She pours herself a whopping big glass of wine.

Pass me the bottle, lady. I need to brace myself.

DAD gets home the same time the pizza arrives. My weekly batch of chocolate chip cookies is baking in the oven. Jeremy's still out. Clearly Dad and Mom already conferred about their Problem Daughter, because after dinner they sit me down on the couch and tell me the deal straightaway.

"You're grounded," Dad says.

"For how long?" I ask. *Months? Until I'm sixteen? Forever?*

"The weekend," Mom says.

Only the weekend? Unbelievable! I hide my elation, lest they realize they're letting me off way too easy.

"And we're taking away your phone for the weekend, too. And no internet or computer."

I try to look totally forlorn and appalled by this additional punishment. But come on. It's only two days!

"And you're also writing letters of apology," Dad says. "To Dr. Folger and all your morning teachers."

"Um, why exactly would I do that?" Revenge of the snark.

Mom says, "For showing such total disrespect the way you did. Skipping their classes."

"Sure, I'll get started on those right away," I say

with no disguise of the sarcasm in my voice. But I manage not to add, *as soon as I'm back from ice skating through the flames of hell.* So, really, this is progress.

Before I can feel too proud of myself, Dad says, "We're more worried about you than we are angry." He looks as sad as he did in the cemetery.

"I wouldn't say that," Mom disagrees. She hates it when Dad uses the Royal We. "I'm angry *and* worried. And frustrated, and annoyed, and concerned—"

"I get it, Mom."

"I don't think you do," she says, crossing her arms. "You're going to a counselor."

"I already did that. Multiple times."

"We'll find someone new."

I do not like the way they keep eyeing Ruby—who is lying on my lap, fifty pounds of alert dog weight—and then looking at each other. Do not like it one little bit.

Dad says, "Your behavior needs to turn around, young lady."

Mom says, "We know you've had a hard time since...since..."

"It won't kill you to say it," I offer helpfully. "Her name was Jamie."

Mom presses her lips together. "We know how much *Jamie*"—she emphasizes the name—"meant to you, how traumatic the accident was. We want to help you with that. But we need to separate that issue—your grief—from this behavior you're trending toward—"

Dad interjects, "It is absolutely unacceptable. Truancy, poor grades, abysmal attitude. Unacceptable. You are a smart girl, Sarah. You are ruining your future."

Mom is nodding. "It's got to stop. All of it. You can be sad and bereaved all you want, but if you don't turn this ship around, and soon, there are things we are prepared to do."

"Like what? You already grounded me." *Danger! Skating on thin ice!* But I have to know how far they'll go.

"We wouldn't want to prevent you from seeing Stenn, because he's a social support for you, but we will if we have to. And we can take away your computer privileges. Indefinitely," Mom says.

Youch. That came out of nowhere. Still, no mention of—

"And your phone. And the possibility of driving when you turn sixteen, if we decide—if you keep showing us—that you are just not capable of responsible behavior. And people who are not able to be responsible don't get to have dogs. Ruby might go live with Aunt Mara—"

"You can't do that!" I squeeze Ruby so hard she yelps. I've been so worried; hearing the words is like a stab to my chest. Tears fly out of my eyes. "You love her, too! She's part of our family!"

They look at each other. I detect a hint of pity in my dad's eyes, like maybe he's not fully on board with this plan. Then again, maybe not, because he says, "When you found her, and we agreed to let you keep Ruby, you signed a contract."

"Yeah, that she wouldn't bite anyone or act wild. And she hasn't! I trained her and she's the best dog ever!"

Mom says, "You also agreed to be responsible for—"

"I do everything! I feed her and pick up her poop and walk her—"

"Your behavior at school is making us doubt your ability to be responsible."

"That's bullcrap!" I say. "School has nothing to do with Ruby!"

Dad sighs. "You're right."

Mom gives him a murderous look. "Dear, we talked about this…"

Dad looks at Mom, "I know." He looks back to me. "I'm saying, I see that school and Ruby are not the same thing. But what you have to see, Sarah Elizabeth, is that we are this desperate. We are grasping at straws here. What else can we do?"

So, it's war. It's leverage. No holds barred. All guns loaded.

And it's working; the bejeezus is being scared right out of me. There is a lump the size of an apple—or maybe an Apollonia—in my throat. "Can I go to bed now?"

"Do we understand each other?"

Holding Ruby tight, I nod.

"This discussion isn't over," my mom says.

I scoot Ruby off my lap and we go up to my room. On the way I mutter something along the lines of, "According to you, it's never over," sprinkled with a lot of F-bombs.

"We heard that!" Mom yells.

They are asleep by ten. Clockwork.

My parents want me to be normal and responsible. Normal teenagers are supposed to rebel, right? And be responsible for looking after their dogs?

I shrug on my coat and red mittens, and Ruby and I are out the back door without a sound. Whenever I sneak out, I have to take her with me. Otherwise, she'll give me away by scratching at the door until I come back. Besides, the soccer party is outdoors; how could I force my sweet doggy to stay inside when I'll be out in nature with lots of good smells and leaves to snuffle around in?

Yes, it would be smarter to stay home, but I can't. I can't stay in the House of Evil Parents, not when there's an alternative. A hot, great-kissing alternative named Stenn.

He's waiting in his Audi at the corner of Locust Street and West Main, as aforetexted before Mom remembered to actually confiscate my phone. I open the back door for Ruby and she hops in, dropping Artoo on the seat. Stenn's gotten used to me taking Ruby everywhere. I get in the front.

"Where to, milady?" He seems in a good mood. "Soccer party still sound good?"

"Hm…let's see. Will it be freezing? Will there be a keg of Pabst Blue Ribbon?"

"Or something equally revolting. Milwaukee's Beast, maybe."

"And red Solo cups?"

"But of course."

"Then what are we waiting for?"

He gets serious. "You sure you're up for it?"

"What, you don't think I can be social?" I say, and it's only halfway snarky.

He shrugs. "Pig Farm Party Shack can get pretty rowdy."

"Please. After everything I've been through? Bring it on."

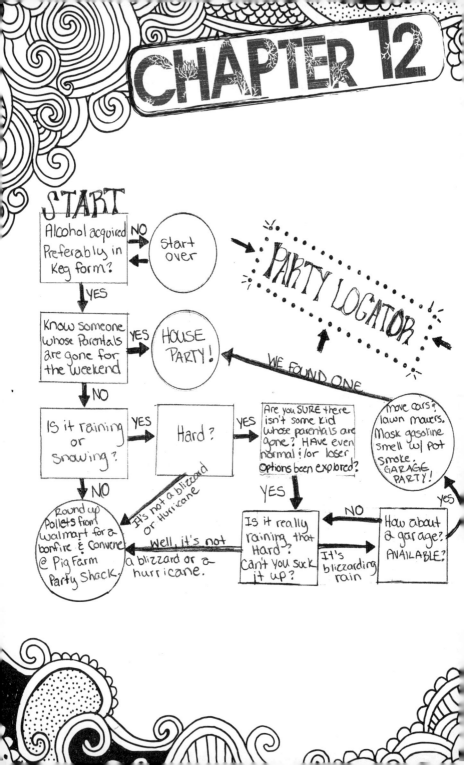

CHAPTER 12

PARTY LOCATOR

START

Alcohol acquired Preferably in Keg form? → **NO** → Start over → (back)

↓ **YES**

Know someone whose Parentals are gone for the weekend → **YES** → HOUSE PARTY!

↓ **NO**

Is it raining or snowing? → **YES** → Hard? → **YES** → Are you SURE there isn't some kid whose parentals are gone? HAve even normal &/or loser Options been explored?

↓ **NO**

Round up Pallets from walmart for a bonfire & Convene @ Pig Farm Party Shack.

It's not a blizzard or hurricane

Well, it's not a blizzard or a hurricane.

↓ **YES** (from "Are you SURE...")

Is it really raining that Hard? Can't you suck it up? → It's blizzarding rain → How about a garage? AVAILABLE? → **NO** → (back to "Is it really raining that Hard?")

YES (How about a garage) → Move cars, lawn mowers. Mask gasoline smell w/ pot smoke. GARAGE PARTY!

WE FOUND ONE → HOUSE PARTY!

THE rumor is that the Pig Farm Party Shack used to be on a pig farm, in, like, 1970. It's a shack, if the definition of shack means three flimsy particle board walls and a plywood floor. That it's the place to be on a Friday night is just part of the Norwich charm.

It's less than ten minutes from my house, but it feels like the middle of nowhere. Stenn drives all the way up West Hill and partway down the other side. He turns left at a tiny church I've never really given any thought to before. It looks white and dainty in the Audi's headlights. Above us, the clouds look haunted, lit by an almost-full moon. It's freezing cold, way too cold for November: Hoth Rebel Base cold. I turn the heat full blast while waiting for the seat to toast my buns.

Stenn knows the way better than I do. A mile or so down the church road, he slows down and leans closer to the windshield.

"You see it?" I ask.

"Not yet." Ruby pokes her head between us. Backseat driver. Stenn jabs a finger at the window. "There it is."

A wooden sign, weathered and gray, announces Loblolly Road. Two parallel tracks of mud, gravel, and huge potholes disappear up into the darkness.

"Looks really steep," I observe.

"We can make it."

"Your mom will kill you if you break the car."

Stenn's face is glowing from the dashboard lights. He turns onto Loblolly Roadercoaster. "Hold on to something."

He guns it. We surge ahead, Mach 10. The car slams through ruts and potholes, shooting mud everywhere. I claw the dashboard. Ruby yelps.

"Slow down!" I yell.

"Can't," says Stenn. "We'll get stuck."

The road goes up, steep as a cliff. I look over at Stenn; his jaw is clenched so hard that his cheeks are puffed out. With a whimper, Ruby slinks down to the floor of the backseat. More stability there.

The car shoots up the hill like a bat out of hell.

"We're going to tip over backward." I am strangely calm.

"You said you wanted to be around when I made a mistake…"

I love a man who can quote *The Empire Strikes Back* at a time like this.

"I take it back!" I say.

We make it up Loblolly, almost to the top of the hill. Stenn wrestles the steering wheel to keep us on the road. When the incline decreases, he slows down a lot. "Fun, huh?" He smiles.

"Yeah. I just need to change my undies and I'm all set."

"Sarah," Stenn says.

"Stenn," I say.

"Was that a joke? Were you…did you just say something funny?"

"I thought it was pretty freaking hilarious. Why?" Pretty sure I know why he's asking, but…

"It's just…a joke and going to a party in the same night?"

"I know. It's a whole new me."

"It's the whole *old* you."

"Come on, I haven't been that bad."

"If you say so." The guy is smart; he knows when he needs to let things drop. He reaches into the backseat to give Ruby a pat. "You know, we're basically behind your house, on the other side of the hill."

"Thank you, Captain Obvious."

"I'm a helper," he says, grinning. He is coated in Good Mood Teflon tonight. My sarcasm slides right off.

Something glints red in front of us: reflectors. Taillights of parked cars, lined up on each side, half in ditch, half on road.

"Soccer team," I say.

"Thank you, Captain Obvious."

I manage to swallow my snark, instead doing my best to match his Good Mood Teflon. "You…are welcome."

Yay, me! Look at me go. A whole new (old?) Sarah.

Stenn pulls forward and shifts into park. He leans toward me and moves his head back and forth, swaying like a cobra, until he catches sight of something. "There," he says, pointing past my window toward a small structure. "They revamped the party shack."

Squinting, I can make out some silhouettes, backlit by a big fire, sparks drifting up.

"It's supposed to be big tonight. They were talking about getting two kegs." He looks at me, gives me a kiss on the cheek. "Ready to say hi to everyone?"

No, definitely not ready. Not used to parties without Jamie. Can't I just stay antisocial? Awesome. Thanks.

He must notice my pronounced lack of any kind of movement toward the party, because he squeezes my mittened hand. "You know, I think this is really good. A good step. You've been so not into the party scene."

"Thanks a lot," I say. But it manages to come out soft.

"You…" He kisses me on the cheek. "Are welcome."

I take a deep breath. "All right. Do I look okay?"

He makes a face at me. "What kind of question is that? You always look gorgeous."

Which is way too sweet a thing for him to say. I peel my lips back. "Anything in my teeth?"

"Can we go?"

I stick up my nose. "Any bats in the cave?"

"You are booger-free. And you're beating around the bush."

"You know full well there isn't any bush."

"Come on, we're going." He pulls the latch on his door and starts to open it.

Immediately, so fast it's a blur, Ruby slips out of the car and tears off into the woods.

"Was that Ruby?" Stenn says. He's as shocked as I am.

"She must have smelled something," I say, trying to keep the desperation out of my voice. I stumble out of the car and slam the door. "Ruby! Come back here! Rubes!"

Nothing.

"Ruby!" I cry. "Get back here!"

Nothing nothing.

"Did you see where she went?"

Stenn points across the road, "That way somewhere. I'm so sorry, Sare. She always sticks with you. I didn't expect..."

My heart is in my throat. "What if she gets lost? We should—"

"You stay here. I'll find her."

"Nokay!" Has the boy not met me? He has to know I'd never just sit here and wait. Ruby is my heart—if your heart can have black fur and carry an Artoo and run around outside your body. Plus this wouldn't have happened if I hadn't brought her. If she gets lost, it's my fault. "I'll go this way," I say, meaning the dark woods. Since Jeremy's lecture, I've been petrified of losing her—but not this way. Irony is such an utter bitch. "You go that way." I point down the road.

"Sare—"

"No time to discuss this with the committee," I snap. But I don't know if he hears; I'm already halfway into the woods.

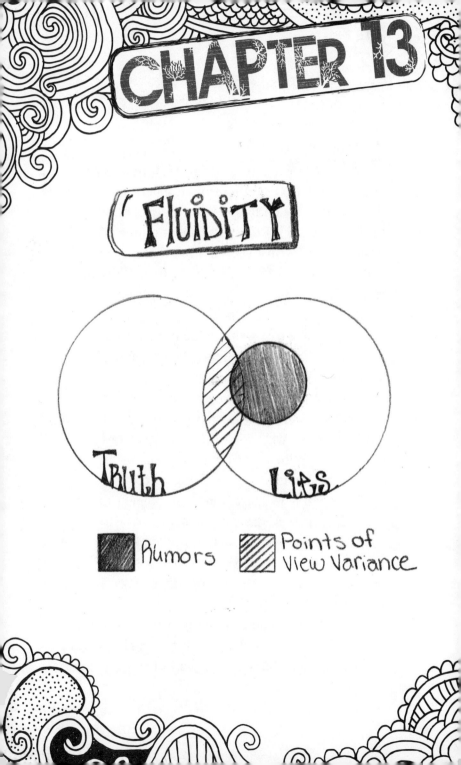

I RUN, stop to listen for Rubes, run some more. Oh my God. Hunters and trappers are out this time of year. Leaving out those horrible foot traps for foxes. What if Ruby gets caught in one? What if it snaps her leg in two? Or it catches her and she can't escape and she's just lying there hurt and I can't find her and she starves or freezes or bleeds to death, or all three? All alone?

I trip over a tree root and belly flop onto frozen moss. Standing, I try to wipe the cold mud off my jeans and coat. Outstanding.

Pine needles, crumbling leaves, icy patches of dirt crunch and slide under my boots. As my eyes adjust to the dark, trees begin to glow gray in the moonlight. A jingle, distant, like bells. Ruby's collar! Thank Christ. I jog, listening hard.

The trees slide apart from each other; I turn my ankle in a rut. A tire rut. A driveway? I follow it uphill. The trees get shorter and fuller, forming neat rows as I pass. It's a tree farm. Christmas trees?

There it is again: quiet jangling of tags. Just up the hill.

I run. A small house comes into view, outlined in moonlight, so dilapidated that it tilts slightly, into a rhombus. Blue television light spills from a window.

Next to the house is a one-story garage, casting its light onto a white van and a pickup truck parked outside. The big garage door is closed, its horizontal row of windows glowing, but there's a regular door on the side that's ajar.

"Ruby!" I call in a loud whisper. Her tags jangle louder. Near the garage. My heart is pounding. Please let me find her. Before she gets hurt. Before we get in trouble.

"Rubes!" I hiss. Is she inside the garage? I creep to the big door, the kind that slides up to let a car in, and set my mittened hands on it. I peer in. My eyes are foggy from the shock of bright light and it takes a moment for things to come into focus. Blood in a washtub. Mops clattering onto the floor. Buckets clunking as they roll. Ladders. Workbenches. Pegboards covering the walls.

And Ruby, a blur of motion, attacking…

And I realize what I'm seeing. Hanging on a chain, swinging from Ruby's attack.

Oh my word. It's here.

The deer from the gym.

No mistake, it's the same deer. Dead deer. Skinned deer. Glass-shards-still-sticking-out-of-its-muscles deer.

How did it get here? Here, of all places?

Is this Captain Possum's place? No fracking way.

The white van. And the deer. Which is swinging from a hook, hanging upside down from its hind legs. Near it, hunkered on the concrete floor, is

Ruby. She's gnashing a gob of meat torn from the carcass.

I hope there's not any glass in that meat.

I lurch through the door on the side of the garage. The smell of raw meat and blood hangs in the air, sick and metallic, and sweet like rotten plums.

I watch in horror. The dog in front of me can't be Ruby. This one is feral. Violent. Like the dog my parents used to worry she was, back when I found her, hurt, on the side of the road. This is the Ruby they said should be put down.

I'm terrified to go near her, but we have to get out. She's making such a racket that anyone within a mile must have heard.

"Ruby!" I plead, "Let's go!"

Her eyes roll, savage as a shark. Bloody animal, raw meat. She's turned into a wolf.

"Ruby! Please!"

A door slams. From the house. Oh, no. No no no!

I duck, scamper to the windows, and look. The front porch light is now shining like a beacon, illuminating a figure walking toward the garage.

I run back to Ruby. "Come on, Rubes," I hiss. "Someone's coming!"

Ruby keeps gnashing. I reach out to her. She raises her hackles and growls.

Feet crunch over gravel in the driveway.

"Ruby, please! We're not supposed to be here!" I grab her collar. She snarls and curls back at my arm.

A flash of teeth.

A stab above my wrist. Oh God, she bit me!

"Please, Rubes!" I beg. My arm kills. The cold air stings my fingers. My mitten hangs, stuck in Ruby's collar.

Crying hard now, I grab her with the other hand. She doesn't bite me this time.

I drag her across the cement floor. The garage looks like it's been hit by a tornado. There is no way I can cover our tracks, even if I could let go of Ruby. She has tipped over a washtub of blood and there is a chunk of meat missing from the carcass. The best I can do is get us out of here, fast.

Gravel crunches louder. I pull Ruby out the side door. I run, dragging her, towards the trees.

I can feel his eyes on me. Captain Possum, who lives in this weird dilapidated house, a man who will skin and butcher a deer that was already dead when he found it.

And I'm about to get caught. Sneaking out while grounded. Trespassing. With blood on Ruby's lips and a dog bite in my arm.

Well That's Fantastic.

CHAPTER 14

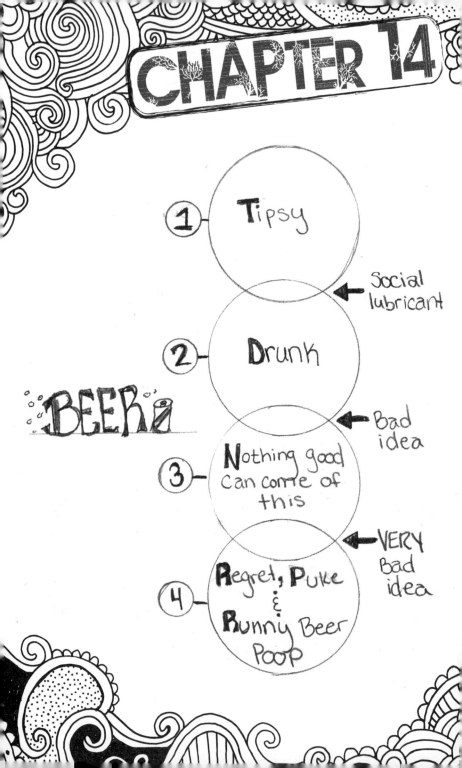

1. Tipsy
← Social lubricant

2. Drunk

BEER

← Bad idea

3. Nothing good can come of this
← VERY Bad idea

4. Regret, Puke & Runny Beer Poop

HEY!"

The voice is gruff, gritty as driveway gravel. I drag Ruby into the trees. We make it one, two, three trees into a cultivated row before Ruby skids to a halt, stopping stock-still, like a boulder. It throws me off and I fall, my hand tangled in her collar. My arm already smolders where Ruby bit me; now it burns like someone stubbed a cigarette out on it.

"Know you're out there!" It's him. Same voice. Same man.

Ruby turns and cocks her head to listen. My hand and wrist are so twisted in her collar that I can barely move. I get to my knees. Unless I want my arm to break, I have to let go of her for a second. One second. She bolts. I dive at her, grab the end of her tail. There's a distinct *crick*. Ruby yelps, but stays put.

"Come on out!" He's louder, closer. I press into the ground, clutching Ruby. Captain Possum steps toward us, his boots visible between tree trunks.

Snap. What was that? A twig or a stick breaking—somewhere in the trees behind us.

Well, that's awesome, because I'm not freaked out enough.

Captain Possum's footsteps stop. A gray lump scuttles down his leg and across the ground: it's that possum. Of course it is. And of course Ruby wants it—the perfect after-deer dessert. She digs her paws into the earth and pulls hard, barking and growling.

The man's hand shoots down to scoop up his pet.

Hand over hand, I inch up Ruby's tail, to her body, to her collar, and hold it tight, my fingernails digging into my palm. *Please do not bite me again. Please do not bite me again. For your sake and mine.* I stand, then stagger-run, dragging Ruby with me, stumbling, twisting my ankle. We run like crazy.

We run until the trees get taller, more uneven, no longer in neat rows. Then I stop to listen. Is Captain Possum following? My heart thumps, banging blood around in my ears, making my arm throb and burn. But the woods are silent except for the creaking of trees from the cold air.

After a while, I get brave enough to let go of Ruby. She trots beside me like nothing's happened. The little monster.

I flinch when she turns to sniff me.

But I can't be scared of her. She didn't mean to hurt me. She was just being a dog, and I got in her way—like when I first found her, stray and hurt. No one has to know she fell off the wild-dog wagon. Especially certain parental units. It would lead to all sorts of questions—including the fact that I snuck out—and end with them taking her away from me.

I clench my teeth and swallow hard. Okay, time for predicament prioritization.

1. Where the hell am I? Lost in the woods super late at night, that's where.
2. Where's Stenn? He'll be thrilled that I decided to take off without him.

My hair is falling in my face. I pull my ponytail tighter to help me think, and pain lances through my arm. My eyes threaten to start leaking tears again. Seriously, I just want to stand here and partake in some primal scream therapy. But that would be the opposite of stealth.

Ruby by my side, I walk/jog/stumble in what I hope is the general direction of Stenn's car and/or Loblolly Road, picking my way through the dark woods. And suddenly there is a beacon in the darkness: a spot of glowing orange.

Hallelujah! Praise you, sweet lords of drunken high-schoolers!

I run, watching the orange spot grow into a fire, a shack/shed structure, people in the woods. In my whole life, I will never be happier to see a tottering mass of inebriated doodles.

Faces turn toward us as Ruby and I make our way toward the bonfire. Normals stand around the outer rim of the party, clutching their red plastic cups with both hands. Ninjas—cool seniors, varsity soccer players, football jocks—stand closer to the fire, clustered in circles, beer cups dangling from fingertips. There are a lot more guys here than girls.

Maybe because of the cold. Hard to look hot when you're trying not to freeze.

Conversations seem to stop as I approach. Huddle by huddle, people fall silent. The fire pops. Ruby's collar jingles as she sniffs the air. A cup here, one there, rises to silent lips.

Right. Think of something clever to say. *Thanks for saving a cup for me*? Or something simple like *hey, how's it going*? All casual and chill. But really I must look the exact opposite of casual chill: I'm a red-eyed, grimy thing with muddy ice on my jeans, a dorky band-aid on my forehead, and a mud-caked dog at my side.

I lift my hand in an awkward, arthritic wave. Lightning shoots through my arm. Oh yeah, that. "Hi."

Resounding silence. Crickets-chirping silence. A collective, actual *WTF*?

Trump card: "Stenn—my boyfriend?—he's home for the weekend," I follow this with a *heh heh* that can only be described as spasmodic. The very definition of quiet dignity, that is me. "Um, Stenn's on his way. So it'll just be, er, a little while and he'll be here."

Some of the dudes exchange glances.

"I just need to call him and he'll be…like I said, he'll be right here," I practically wheeze. Jesus, put me out of my misery, here. "Um. Does anyone have a phone I can borrow?" *Because I'm technically grounded and indisputably phoneless.*

Glances are exchanged again. Apart from turning their heads to look at each other, no one moves. It's slightly brutal.

Maybe Rubes could dig me a hole to crawl into and die.

Just when I'm going to keel over from mortification, I hear feet crunching over pine needles. Someone's coming over. I can't tell who; he's backlit by the fire. Mystery guy reaches into his pocket. Extends his arm. In his hand, a phone.

His last step brings him out of the shadows. Yowza. He looks so much older, and so calm—no, *dignified*. And he's saving my ass. I give him a ginormously grateful smile. "Thanks, Emmett."

He hands me the phone, nods a silent *you're welcome*, and goes back to the shed. Then another miracle: conversations resume, the party goes back to normal. It's like Emmett unweirded my weirdo emergence from the woods.

I dial Stenn's number, hoping he'll pick up, even if he probably doesn't recognize the phone number.

He answers on the third ring.

"Hello!" His voice spits out of the phone.

"It's me."

"Where the hell are you? Are you okay?"

"I'm at the soccer party. I borrowed someone's phone." I look over at Emmett. Why didn't I say whose phone I'm using? He's sitting on the edge of the raised plywood floor of the shack, warming his hands by the fire. He's not holding a cup. Yay for that. What would beer do to his blood sugar? It doesn't seem like a good idea for a diabetic kid to get hammered. Then, a more important question dribbles through my brain filter: What the hell is he doing here? The Clearys would sooner shove him into traffic than let him go to a party. Strict isn't even the word for how they are with Jamie. *Were.*

Either his parents have been body snatched, or Emmett is one sneaky sneaker-outer. Nice. Takes one to know one.

Stenn curses, snapping my attention back.

"I found Ruby," I say. "Can you get to the party?"

"Oh sure, no problem." Damn, he sounds really pissed off. "I'll be right there. *If* I can find my way back."

"Where are you?"

"Where do you think? You really think I'm going to let my girlfriend go out alone at night in the woods? I followed you. I'm at some tree farm or something."

Stenn's protective streak—equal ratio sweet to annoying.

"I told you to go the other way," I say, because everyone loves to hear *I told you so.*

"Sare. I—*OW!*" A *thwunk*, and another curse, sounding far away.

Cringing, I wait for him to pick up the phone, then say, "Stenn, listen to me: you have to get back here."

"No kidding."

"I'm serious. Someone's outside, looking around. The guy who lives at that tree farm. He...kind of...might have...heard me and Rubes. We had to hotfoot it out of there."

Silence.

"Stenn?"

"Damn it." He sounds even angrier. "I'll be there as soon as I can."

"Don't be mad," I say. "I mean, I'm fine and safe, so that's good, right?"

"Just do me a favor and stay there." He swears again. Then Emmett's phone beeps and goes dead. *Call ended.*

I palm the phone and make my way to Emmett. Ruby trots next to me, sniffing at the hem of some guy's jeans.

"Stop bothering people," I tell her. I try to sound commanding, but the bite on my arm still burns.

"S'okay," the guy slurs. He pats Ruby, then puts his hand out to me. I stare at it like a moron while he says, "I'm Rich. Stenn's friend."

"Oh, right. Hi, Rich."

"Uh, your brother's in my...physics class?" he says, sort of like a question, until it dawns on me that he's still holding his hand out. I shake it—a solid ten seconds worth of dweeb awkwardness later than a normal person would—and it makes my arm hurt more. Then he pulls me into a hug.

Question: When did hugging become the normal greeting for high-schoolians? I did not get that memo. My vote was not counted on that particular referendum. Seriously people: stick to the handshake or the fist-bump. Fist-bump explosion if you must. But save the hugs for your significant other, your BFF, and your parents.

"Pull up a beer," Rich drawls. "Keg's that way."

"Thanks."

Rich bobs his head and starts playing air guitar. Man, he can really shred. Okay, then.

Ruby and I slalom through little groups of upperclassmen. I know most of them by name, but they're not strike-up-a-conversation friends, even BJD. As I walk, a few people say hi, some nod, but two guys grab me into a group hug and everything suddenly feels very *off*. They are beyond wasted. They are zombie undead wasted. They are Making Poor Decisions, That Moment When Everything Starts Going Terribly Wrong wasted. More girls here would be nice, balance out the testosterone.

I head over to Emmett. Safety.

"Thanks again." I hand him his phone. "Mind if I sit?"

Emmett looks at me. Really looks at me, for a few excruciating seconds. Then he scoots over to make room.

I sit. But how do I even begin cutting through all the stuff in the air between us? Um, yeah. Not my skill set. So I just try to shut down my brain for a while. I push my feet and hands toward the fire to soak up its warmth. The heat makes my skin feel thick and chapped. As I turn my wrists to warm the backs of my hands, my dog bite flares again.

Ruby is curled on the ground between us, resting her chin on Emmett's foot. He reaches down to pet her. For a post-traumatic second I picture her taking a great white bite out of him, but she just eases closer. Ferocious.

"Looks like she misses you," I say.

Emmett smiles. He rubs her ears. I wonder if the Clearys would ever relent and let him have a dog, now that he's an only child by default.

Now there's a word for you: de-fault.

Emmett runs his hands down Ruby's back, fluffing her fur. He tugs her tail amicably. She jumps and howls like a sick turkey.

"D'oh! I forgot!" I say. "I think her tail might be broken."

Ruby starts whimpering. So much for the bloodthirsty wild dog.

I rub her and, with only the slightest hesitation, press my forehead to hers. "I'm sorry if I hurt your tail earlier, Rubes." In a whisper, I add, "I guess that makes us even."

Emmett leans down and whispers something into Ruby's ear, too. He keeps his eyes on me the whole time. There's a glint of mischief in his eyes, those eyes just like Jamie's. Stab me in the heart.

"Aren't you the lucky one," I tell Rubes. "He seems pretty picky about who he talks to." *Especially SJD.*

Emmett's smile—which had seemed tense, aloof, maybe slightly annoyed—deepens. It transforms into the smile from years ago, from up high in the trees of his and Jamie's backyard. That Just Try And Catch Me grin flashing between tree branches when we played hide-and-seek. Emmett tips his head back and laughs. And God, it's good to hear.

"Sarah," he says, his tone flashing from laughter to super serious. *Uh oh.* I do not like this change of direction, not one little bit.

"Emmett." He's going to ask me about the accident. Demand that I tell him right now.

"I believe Jamie used to say it best: Just shut your sass trap."

A laugh comes out of my mouth; it's such a surprise I practically choke. "Jamie didn't used to say that. *You* used to say that."

"Never." His big brown eyes twinkle and he sticks the tip of his tongue out. The old Emmett. I keep laughing, and so does he.

And that's it. So much of what's been weighing me down dissolves into laughter. For a few seconds, at least.

Turns out Emmett's full of surprises. Because while I'm still laughing my arse off, he reaches inside his coat and pulls something out. A joint. Which he sets between his lips.

It's not the first time I've been face-to-face with the herb.

But Emmett smoking pot? This is news.

He pats his pockets, looking for a lighter, and smiles at me.

I gape at him. He winks.

My mouth is now hanging open. I manage to close it, but then open it again to ask, "What are you, Easy Rider now? Smoking the marijuana and winking at the ladies?"

The cheeky wanker responds by sparking the joint. And clearly it ain't the first time, because he looks like a pro. He puts the flame to the tip, pulls a huge toke, and waits a long, long time before exhaling.

"Haven't you heard?" I frown. "Pot is a gateway drug."

Emmett smiles and takes another drag.

"Jamie wouldn't approve." I try to sound as sister-y as possible. But I have to say, most of me, the non-sister-y part, is like *whatever*. Not even whatever; more like *right on*. Because I've just realized that Emmett and I share a secret: when someone close to you dies, the entire world changes. Once the kaleidoscope has shifted that drastically, the usual rules—well, they no longer apply. Like me, Emmett's had to figure out what's real and important in life, and what's not. Fear That Marijuana Is A Gateway Drug, or Abiding By Parentals' Outmoded Lifestyle Regulations, or Making Small Talk With Ninjas To Ascend The Social Continuum—Emmett's figured out these aren't the Big Things In Life. Maybe that's why he seems so quiet and aloof? It's not that he doesn't care about anything, it's that he's trying to only care about the things he thinks are worth caring about.

Noted.

And there are the physical changes, too. His shaggier hair suits this whole pot-smoking wisdom dude vibe. And his eyes have changed. Still brown, of course, but they look kind of molten. They remind me of that saying, "Still waters run deep." These days, SJD, he's Emmett "Still Waters" Cleary. And I'm not the only one who's noticed. After all, here he is, one of the few sophomores in the center of the party. That makes him full Ninja.

Nice. Leave it to Emmett to slog through the sewer of grief and emerge wiser, cooler, and better looking. Leave it to me to come out covered with crap and wadded toilet paper. Metaphorically speaking.

Emmett holds out the joint to me, his fingers opening like petals of a flower.

"Jamie wouldn't approve," I repeat.

Emmett looks at his feet, pats Ruby's head with his other hand. He says, very matter of fact, "Jamie's not here."

"Well. Duh." But I know he means more than those small words. "Maybe some other time."

Emmett nods. Ruby sits up suddenly.

"Hey, now. What do we have here?" It's Stenn. And his voice is laced with irritation.

"Stenn!" I jump up and hug him. On tiptoe, I whisper in his ear, "I'm so sorry. I didn't mean to make you worry," and I realize maybe I'm talking about more than just that I took off after Ruby. Maybe. Before he responds, I say, "So you're okay? You found your way back?" Which is a total tactic, taught by my dad, for how to get people onto your side: ask questions that make them answer yes. Or, at least, not no.

"Eventually. Obviously."

I cross my arms. "So you followed me, huh? Instead of spreading out and covering more ground to look for Rubes?"

Stenn narrows his eyes. "You're not mad. You're just trying to distract me from being annoyed."

Damn, he's tough to manipulate. Got to respect that.

"How about we just call it a tie?" I arch an eyebrow. "Your friends are stoked to see you."

"Smooth change of subject. Well played, Sare. Well played." Stenn looks around as if he'd forgotten we're at the soccer party.

Next to me, Emmett stands, joint in one hand, extending the other to Stenn. They do the Hand Smack/One-Armed/Hit Each Other's Back Boy Hug.

Stenn says, "Hey, good to see you." Polite as ever, very smooth, but he looks over at me with eyes that say he's surprised I'm hanging out with my dead best friend's twin brother.

"Emmett was keeping me company while I waited for you."

"Awesome. Thanks for looking after Sarah, man." Simultaneously, he and Emmett reach down to pet Ruby, who is standing between them. *Clonk*. They knock heads.

Awk. Ward.

Ruby looks from one boy to the other and then lies down over my feet, like *y'all are cool, but Sarah's my girl.*

I break the silence. "So…do you want to say hi to your friends and then get going?"

Stenn makes a face. "Yes to saying hi, no to going. I just got here."

"I know, but I'm freezing. And it's all weird, it's not as…social as I thought it would be." I don't even know what I mean.

Emmett heads over to the fire to finish his joint, leaving me and Stenn alone.

Stenn says, "You wanted to come. We thought it would be good for you."

"And now I want to leave." I contemplate telling him Ruby bit me. Surely then he'd take me home. But I'm not really ready to talk about that.

Stenn gives an annoyed sigh. "Can you just keep hanging out with Emmett?"

"Fine. At least he's being nice to me," I mumble.

A dagger in his weak spot. To Stenn, being called unkind or impolite is worse than a kick in the nads. He's tough to manipulate—but not impossible.

"Probably because he didn't drag his ass through the woods for an hour just to find a dog."

A Dog? She's not *A Dog*. She's Ruby. "You forgot to mention dealing with your bitchy girlfriend."

"That is not possible for me to forget," Stenn says.

"I bet you've tried."

"What's that supposed to mean?"

It means I don't know how to be nice to you. I want to, but it just doesn't happen. It means I'm scared you'll get sick of my shit, and you'll decide to be with a perfect Mercer girl instead of me. It means I'm hanging on by a thread. I don't know what I'd do if we broke up.

"Nothing."

He eases up a little. Because he's a saint or something. "Just give me ten minutes. Fifteen, maybe."

But I'm not done pouting.

He reaches for my hair, strokes my cheek, which of course turns me to Jell-O.

"Okay, Sare?"

I make a sound like *hmf*.

He pinches my chin gently. "Okay?"

"All right."

A quick peck, and Stenn jumps the short distance from the floor of the shack to the ground. I sidle up to Emmett. He raises his eyebrows.

I shrug. "I've become high maintenance in my old age. Bitter and shrill."

He offers me the dregs of the joint. It looks more appealing after that little spat. What, precisely, is my problem? Why do I insist on making a good thing rotten? What happened to my resolve to be good and normal again? Seems like any time anyone makes an effort to be nice to me, I bite their head off and flash my teeth and dare them to come back for more.

The only person I haven't been a total bitch to recently is Emmett—probably because I haven't had much of a chance. Not in my favor is the fact that he wants to know about the accident, and I haven't exactly been forthcoming with that information.

Which leaves Ruby as the only person—animal— I haven't been a bitch to (except for breaking her tail). I sigh and stroke her ears. Sit quietly on a log with Emmett and watch Stenn make the rounds.

When Stenn's ready to go, I get up to leave. Emmett surprises me again. He says, quietly, "You should come to a game."

"Oh, like soccer, you mean? To watch you play?"

He nods.

Happiness! *Why am I this happy?* "Okay. Yeah, I will. This week?"

He rewards me with a smile. Then he does that hand-smacky thing with Stenn, who says, "Oh yeah. Heard you made varsity, bro. Congrats."

"Thanks." Emmett gives Ruby an ear rub goodbye.

We walk to Stenn's car in not-uncomfortable silence.

In the car, careening down Loblolly road, Stenn goes, "You know that guy?"

"What guy?"

"At the tree farm." He thumps the Audi onto the road by the little church.

"You saw him too?"

"Wish I hadn't. That whole place was eerie as hell." Stenn shudders. "How do you know him?"

"Wait. What?" I thought he'd asked, *You know that guy?* As in a rhetorical beginning to a story. Not as in, *Do you KNOW that guy?*

"Well, he obviously knows you."

My spine prickles. "Say what, now?"

"He was looking for you."

"Well, obviously he knew *someone* was skulking about."

"No. By name, Sare. He was shouting your name."

"No way." I blink. This does not compute. "No way. How could he know it was me?"

"He must have seen you."

I shake my head. There's no way he could have gotten that good a look at me. Right?

"Does he know your dad, maybe?"

"Everyone knows my dad."

"Then I hope he doesn't know him very well. Because if he tells your dad you were out tonight—"

"I'm screwed."

This is bad. Bad bad bad. Bad for me, bad for me and Stenn, bad for Ruby.

It's so scary it's nauseating. Throw-Up-In-My-Mouth-A-Little nauseating. Maybe…maybe it's time to spill some of my guts to Stenn, just so I can get this stuff out there, outside of me, so I don't feel so sick about it.

The words stick in my throat when I try to get them out.

But I do. I tell him about the deer, and how I met Captain Possum in the gym.

And I tell him that Ruby bit me.

It feels weird to put it all out where Stenn can see the words, I feel like they are visibly hanging in front of us, here in the Audi. But also it feels good. To get it out.

Stenn is…he is *kind.* He stops the car and hugs me and kisses me and tells me it'll be okay.

It's nice. But it doesn't resolve anything.

Maybe I should have smoked that joint with Emmett, like a prisoner's last cigarette before the firing squad. Because if Captain Possum knows it was me, and knows who my dad is, and tells my parents, I'm dead. Sneaking out while grounded, plus Ruby busting up the place. I can kiss Stenn goodbye, and so much for getting my license. And Ruby? She is doomed.

CHAPTER 15

JONES FAMILY MEALS

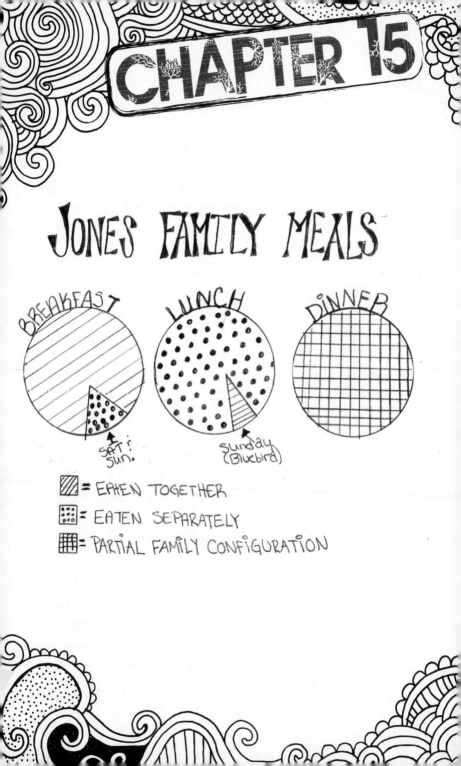

BREAKFAST · LUNCH · DINNER

↑ SAT & SUN.

Sunday (Bluebird)

⬜ = EATEN TOGETHER

⬜ = EATEN SEPARATELY

⬜ = PARTIAL FAMILY CONFIGURATION

THE next day is all vigilance and agitation. I keep Ruby close and wait for the end of the world as I know it. And I do not feel fine.

Waiting: super fun!

Everyone loves waiting!

It's better than menstrual cramps!

It sucks so much because waiting does not fall within my locus of control. Nope. Not at all. And I'm so scared about my fate, and Ruby's future, that my stomach hurts and I can barely see straight. There's nothing to do but try to distract myself and...wait.

Friday night, when Stenn dropped me off, we stayed in the car a good while, steaming up the windows. His kindness after I told him the stuff about Captain Possum, and the deer, and Ruby, totally softened me for a while. And, oh, the epic goodness that is kissing Stenn: the bite on my arm, the drama with my parentals, everything that happened earlier, it all dissolved into sparkly tingles when Stenn and I got going, doing what we do best. Doing everything but *it*. Finally, all rumpled and sweaty, I snuck back in the house—my parents, God bless them, were snoring like bears on roofies—and I slipped onto the forbidden computer. In privacy mode, I searched for *dog bite treatment*.

1. *Wash out with soap and water.* Which turns out to be a little procedure that hurts so bad I see stars.
2. *Apply antibiotic cream and dry bandage.* Check.
3. *Watch for signs of infection, including weeping pus.* Yummy, weeping pus! Om nom.
4. *Be sure your tetanus shot is up to date.* Um. Does "pretty sure" count?
5. *For the love of all things good and holy, keep it hidden from your parents.* That one's mine. Actually number 5 was really, *Report the incident to the proper authorities, as the dog may need to be reported and/or quarantined.* Sure thing. Report this, mofo.

Saturday morning, Mom and I took Ruby to the vet to see about her tail. I wanted Rubes to be as healthy and strong as possible for whatever grim future awaited us. (When Mom asked how Ruby got hurt, I told her I'd grabbed her tail and heard a crack. End of story. Details = the kiss of death when lying to parents. Be safe, people: keep it vague.) The vet said Ruby's sprained tail would heal on its own.

And, back home, Ruby does seem fine except for her pitiful absence of tail wags. No more feral Ruby, just fifty pounds of furry sweetness. But all weekend, her limp tail—and my throbbing arm—are like flashing neon arrows pointing to West Hill and Loblolly Road, lighting it up like the Vegas strip.

I try to read *Crime and Punishment*—oh irony, you naughty vixen!—for English, but my thoughts keep following the imaginary neon signs up the hill to the deer and Captain Possum. Is it normal to butcher a deer that died in an accident? Aren't you supposed to go hunting, wait in a tree stand while drinking beers, kill a deer, and *then* butcher it?

But perhaps I'm not the most qualified judge of human normalcy.

And Ruby. How could I be so stupid? Why did I have to sneak out? I probably could have figured out a less risky way to hang with Stenn and get my social on. The soccer party was so not worth the trouble. And it is trouble. Certainly enough for my parents to feel justified in—

No. I refuse to think about it. Well, I refuse to not try to not think about it. Because there's nothing I can do about it now. Captain P knows my first name. He knows I was there when the deer crashed into the gym. He's worked at the school so he might know my father. It's within the realm of possibility that Dr. Jones or some other rat fink would say something about the superintendent's daughter witnessing the deer accident. So it all comes down to whether Captain Possum decides to raise a ruckus about what happened at his place. Which I have zilch control over.

Locus of control? More like locus of disaster.

Argh! So much for concentrating on homework.

Outside, the day is Unseasonably Warm: temperature in the low 60s, sunny, with those puffy white *Simpsons*-theme-song clouds in the sky. Boyfriend-sweater weather. Might as well go outside and help Dad, who's raking the backyard.

My parents don't believe in allowance or any kind of wages-for-chores. Their stance is old school Russian communist: Jeremy and I will do our chores—and be happy about it, damn it!—because we are a part of this family. We shall work for *ze common good, comrade*. Not for monetary compensation.

Which is so lame, especially when I have to beg them for money every time I want something.

But the yard needs raking, and I need the butt-kissing points, Grounded Troubled Daughter that I am. Plus I must admit that the fresh air feels good. I grab a rake from the garage while Ruby sits wanly on the back porch, poor thing. West Hill seems to loom over us, the yard, the entire house.

"Hey, kiddo," Dad says, a little too happy that I've volunteered for this drudgery.

"Hi." I turn my back to West Hill and rake, watching grass appear beneath the leaves as I work. After a long time, I say, "Hey, Dad. Can I ask you something?"

"Anything except to get rid of these ass-kicking boots, kiddo." Dad lifts his jeans to flash his boots.

"By the way, I meant to tell you. *Midnight Cowboy* called from the year 1969. He wants his boots back."

"Blasphemy!" Dad says. "Don't listen, boots. Now, what do you want to ask me?"

"Just making sure—you think Rubes' tail will be fine?"

"Sure, kiddo. She's a scrapper. Sprained tail's nothing compared to the broken leg and ribs we found her with, and she recovered from all those injuries very quickly."

Fair point. Poor, hurt, snapping-at-everything stray—before we got her fixed up and re-trusting and she morphed into my awesome Ruby.

"You worried about her?" He pats Ruby's head. She's now lying on the leaves.

I nod. *Her, and a whole lot of other stuff.*

We work a while. I have to move Ruby as we rake.

"Hey, Dad?"

"Yup."

"I was just wondering. How come you don't go hunting with your buddies? Or take Jeremy hunting?"

Dad stops raking, starts again. "What do you mean?"

"I don't know. I mean, you're sort of outdoorsy—"

"*Sort of* outdoorsy? I was an Eagle Scout, kiddo! I've been taking Jeremy through the ranks—"

"Dad. Chill."

"You're freaking me out here. That's it. We're going on more family camping trips. We'll canoe down the Mississippi—"

"Stop! You're incredibly outdoorsy, all right? You're Super Outdoorsy Man."

"That's better," he says. "That's true."

"But my point is that you're the only *incredibly outdoorsy* grown-up I know of, in this town at least, who doesn't hunt every weekend."

"You trying to get rid of me?"

"Dad."

He nods toward a pile of leaves. "Let's make one really big pile."

I'm about to say, "What a novel idea," but instead I say, "Okay." Look at me, not being snarky. "But I'm serious. Why don't you hunt?"

Dad flips his rake to pull off the leaves stabbed by its tines. "Well, Jeremy has zero interest in it, for starters. So, that's one. Two, I don't feel good about guns, whether it's rifles or handguns. There are too many guns in the world." He flicks the leaves onto the pile. "Also, it's pretty boring, waiting all day, doing nothing. And cold." He shrugs. "Now that I think about it, one of the best things about being an adult as opposed to being a kid, is that you get a lot more say about who you spend your time with, and how you spend it. I'd rather be with your mom and your brother and you, my darling daughter."

I push a leaf into the pile with the tip of my shoe. "Did you ever hunt, when you were a kid?"

Dad nods. "I went with your grandpa a few times."

"Did you ever kill a deer? Have to, like, skin it and gut it and stuff?"

Dad's eyebrows go up, like he's finally figured out why I'm asking. "Are you thinking about the deer you saw at school?"

I nod and study my hands. Blisters are beginning to swell on my palms. Stupid chores.

"Well. Then you know how strange it is to be up really close to a big animal."

I nod. "Yeah."

He sighs. "I shot an elk once. Pop—your grandpa—made me field dress it. And made me eat some of the raw meat."

"Was that a hunter initiation thing?"

"Yeah." He rests both hands on the hilt of his rake. "Once was enough. After that, I always missed on purpose. And I swore if I ever had kids, I'd never force them into hunting."

"Ugh. Thank you."

The wind moves a few leaves from the top of the pile back onto the lawn. Dad says, "Thank *you*, for actually talking—I worry about you when you don't. You sure you're okay?"

"Except for being grounded and having my phone taken away? Yeah, I'm great."

"You reap what you sow, kiddo," Dad says. "No more cutting classes or it'll be worse. Now I have a question for you. How are you doing, really? What's new? What's happening? How's life?"

"That's one, two, three, four questions."

Dad smiles. "Well, we've got lots more leaves. Lots of time for conversation."

"It's a trap!" I say, but my Ackbar reference is lost on him.

By three o'clock, my hands are bubbling with blisters and an enormous pile of leaves rises up in the middle of the backyard. Ruby and I collapse onto the pile, deflating it, to nap in the sun.

Dad gives our nap his almighty blessing. Apparently I've worked hard enough to earn the Sleep Of The Righteous. But he is a sneaky bastard: his giggles wake me up. I blink, shading my eyes with my hand to block out the late afternoon sun.

Dad is sticking his phone in my face, clicking the camera button for an extreme close-up. "Gotcha!" He does the twist in his cowboy boots and shouts, "Like lightning!" He runs back into the house.

Later, I grab his phone to look at the picture. In it, I am asleep, soaking in sunlight, surrounded in leaves, resting my head on Ruby. You can't see that my arm is bandaged underneath Stenn's sweater. And even though I'm relaxed, dozing with Rubes, it's like something in my face has changed: you can see that my soul is overfilled with the knowledge that things have changed, irrevocably, SJD.

Things happen with no warning.

Bam! And your life is different.

Five minutes, and your best friend is dead.

The day Jamie died, after my parents picked me up from school, I went upstairs and stripped naked and stepped under the hot shower and stayed in there for a long time. I scrubbed until my skin was angry red, and then wrapped myself in a towel to walk, slow as a snail, back to my room, where I stood and stared at the clothes I'd taken off.

The weave of cloth in that shirt, the buttons, the jeans, the shoelaces...when I'd gotten dressed that morning, it had been a normal day.

I stood there looking at the jeans and shirt and sweater rumpled on the floor, and something rose up in me. My stomach filled with acid, my face burned, my hands turned cold. I threw myself on the floor and attacked my shirt, sweater, jeans, bra, underwear, socks. I grabbed scissors from my desk and cut and ripped and screamed and tore until I was panting, sweating.

My mom came to check on me, but I snapped and snarled and chased her away.

And then, like nothing happened, I gathered everything up and stuffed it all into the back of my closet.

The shredded pile is still there, in my closet, and it will stay there. I can't throw it out. It is too significant. The fibers are filled with meaning. Not as much as my necklace, but still—some things you can never get rid of.

🌷 🌷 🌷

At eleven o'clock on Sunday morning, I drag myself out of bed, let Ruby out, and go back upstairs to shower, re-dress the bite on my arm, and get ready for lunch at the Bluebird Diner. I don't need my forehead band-aid anymore, so at least there's that.

My mom relaxes her breakfast rule on the weekends. Church is optional—Jeremy won that fight for the sibling coalition long ago, God/gods/The Force bless him—but lunch is mandatory. Every Sunday, noon, Bluebird Diner. Usually, we arrive from the four directions: mom from the church kingdom, Dad from the trail-jog kingdom, Jeremy from the Ninja netherlands, and me and Ruby on foot from the land of the lame. The waitress holds the big round corner booth for us. Someone even made a sign: *Reserved— Jones family*. Yes, we're rock stars.

The cool thing is they let Ruby stay in the manager's office, where they feed her table scraps while we eat. I'm sure it violates all sorts of health codes, but it can't be any worse than the rumored mouse poop and kitchen roaches.

Our waitress brings our drinks—always the same, she never bothers to ask—and I search my pockets for quarters. (Playing the antique Pac-Man game with Jeremy is the sole remnant of voluntary sibling bonding. Better to play Pac-Man with your peculiar little sister than sit at the table with your even less cool parentals.) I'm a pocket pack-rat; my jean pockets are bad enough, but my coat pockets are worse. I pull out a couple of lip balms, hair elastics, candy wrappers, nickels and quarters, crusty tissues, and a lone red mitten. Um…only one mitten. I set it on the table and stare. Where is the other one? I search my other pockets, and then all around the booth, and then the restaurant, and then the sidewalk. Later I'll have to sneak a call to Stenn to ask if it's in his car. But I'm almost positive it isn't.

Cold dread marches up my back, over my shoulders, into my scalp. Because I know. I know where it is.

Captain Possum's place.

I ripped it off in the garage, when I was grabbing Ruby's collar to drag her away.

Think. *Think.* Have I worn my mittens since the tree farm? At the party, I'd held my bare hands out to the fire, and then to the heating vents in the car. And then I'd put them on Stenn. By the time I'd snuck in the back door—horny and flustered—my parents were in bed and Jeremy wasn't around. I'd gone straight to the bathroom, to clean and cover the bite on my arm.

No, my mitten isn't at home, isn't at the party, almost certainly isn't in Stenn's car. It's on Captain Possum's garage floor.

I get this picture of him stepping into his garage, inspecting the mess we left, the chunk of flesh missing from the deer, the upset bucket of blood. And my little red mitten.

Maybe it's in the rows of trees. Maybe he won't find it.

Please let it be somewhere in the trees. Please let a snowstorm come and bury that sucker under five feet of ice!

I try to concentrate on Pac-Man with Jeremy. Distract myself. He beats me by five screens, because my brain isn't working.

Think. Think!

What about sneaking back into Captain Possum's garage to retrieve my mitten? No—I would have to go at night, and Stenn has to go back to Mercer, so he can't drive me.

The mitten doesn't have my name on it, so that's good. But what if Captain Possum did see me and figures out it's mine? He'll bust me for trespassing. There's evidence. My parents would have concrete proof that I snuck out.

Goodbye, driving. Goodbye, Stenn. And Ruby?

I follow Jeremy back to the booth, and slide in after him. My whole body is stiff. I pick at the edges of my paper napkin.

"Earth to Sarah, come in, Sarah!" Jeremy waves his hand in front of my face. "She's waiting for your order, dork."

The waitress's pencil is poised over her order pad. My parents are looking at me like You're Acting Strange, Even For You.

"Unh. Veggie burger and fries, please," I manage to squeak. *And someone to help me out of the mess I've gotten into.*

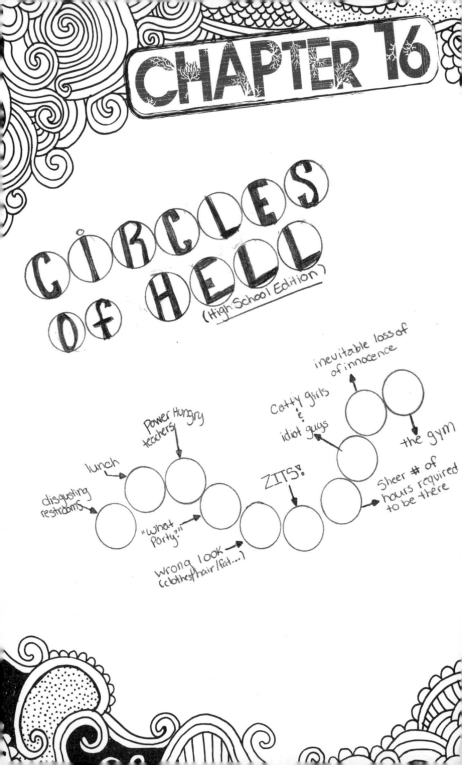

BACK to the unending joy that is Norwich High School. Monday morning, groggy and sleepy, I wander into the main office in search of coffee and company. I know I'm supposed to be hanging in Dweebsville less, being social more, but it's 7:30. No one's here. And I need coffee.

Besides, Ms. Franklin's nice.

A rational person probably would not go straight to the main office after having ditched school Friday. But honestly, I'm over it. Plus: free coffee.

It's the first time since The Great Tree Farm Deer Carcass Debacle that Ruby hasn't been within a limp tail-length of me, or at least in the same building. I'm shaky. I'm terrified I'll go home and she'll be gone. Disappeared, removed, stolen, missing from my life forever. I never should have gone to that party, and I definitely never should have taken Ruby along.

Ms. Franklin smiles as I arrive. She waves me in like nothing's amiss, no trouble is brewing. The only thing brewing is coffee. Har har.

"Well, good morning, sleepyhead," she says. I probably have bed head—and not the good kind. "I brought bagels. Go ahead and fix yourself one and then go in and say hi to Dr. Folger. There's someone here to see you."

Excuse me? Say what now?

Ms. Franklin sees my surprise. "Mm-hm. Came in a few minutes ago. Nice man."

Man?

Sure enough, I can hear low voices in Dr. Folger's office.

Okay, calm down, Sarah. No way is it Captain Possum. Get a grip. Life isn't a movie. Things don't happen that way.

Ms. Franklin is business-as-usual. She hands me the mug I like, the one with a fading cartoon of a kid under a "School for the Gifted" sign. He's pushing on a door that says *Pull*. It's a metaphor. Or actually, in my case, sometimes literal.

Ms. Franklin's still talking. "I believe his name is Roy Showalter. Owns a Christmas tree farm. And a"—she hesitates, frowning—"a small business."

Oh no. No no no no no. No way.

Breathe!

Can't.

He tracked me down. Which can only mean he wants to nail me for trespassing and vandalism. And bust Ruby. Oh God.

The empty mug lands on the carpet with a *thunk*. I reach down to pick it up. My hands are trembling.

Maybe I can pretend I didn't hear Ms. Franklin and just slink away. I'll look like an idiot, but what else is new?

Feet shuffle on the carpet; Dr. Folger's head pops out of his office.

"Ms. Jones! Come in here for a minute, would you?

Someone would like to say hello."

My heart is galloping, kicking up mud on a race-track—so loud I bet Ms. Franklin can hear it.

Dr. Folger ducks back into his office, says something I don't catch, then pops his head back out the door again, like Whack-A-Mole.

"Well? Come, Ms. Jones," he says. I'd like to whack that mole.

Turning to Ms. Franklin, I try to make a silent plea for help, but she's completely preoccupied with putting cream cheese on her bagel, spreading it so the grooves in her plastic knife leave wavy ridges. Zen sand-garden bagel.

I accidentally let out a whimper when I set my mug on her desk; Ms. Franklin finally lifts her head. "You okay, hon?"

"Uh…" I shake my head. "Uh-unh."

She chuckles like this is priceless, and returns to Zen cream-cheesing.

I move toward Dr. Folger's office; it's like he has me in a tractor beam, sucking me into the Death Star.

Dr. Folger is sitting at his desk, fiddling with a Slinky from his collection. And across from Dr. Folger, there he is. Him. Captain Possum, Christmas tree farmer and deer skinner and small business owner, sitting in one of the two chairs facing the desk. He is wearing a heavy, and heavily worn, dirt-smeared Carhartt jacket and thick boots. His possum doesn't seem to be here. He turns to look at me.

"Sarah," he says slowly, and then he throws his head back, laughing maniacally in a classic villain laugh.

Okay, maybe that last part is only in my mind.

Dr. Folger sets down the Slinky and clears his throat. "Mr. Showalter asked to see you." He smiles at Captain Possum—Mr. Showalter. My judge, jury, and executioner. And Ruby's.

I swallow. My throat is dry. How did he find me?

"Mr. Showalter came in this morning to settle some business. He asked about you."

I shift weight, ready to bolt.

"I told him you usually arrive early," Dr. Folger says. "And that if he stuck around, you'd probably come visit." He stretches a rainbow Slinky between his hands, moving them up and down like a pan balance. Tomorrow's headline: *School Principal Found Strangled with Colorful Slinky. Young Female Suspect at Large.*

"Well," Dr. Folger says.

I study my shoes and don't say a word.

Eventually, the man speaks in that gravelly voice. "Dr. Folger. Could me and Sarah have a minute." Not a question; a statement.

Looking sort of surprised, Dr. Folger collapses the Slinky and sets it on his desk. "Of course. I'll just help myself to another bagel. You two take your time." He leaves the door open when he goes, probably because of state regulations. *To Catch a Predator* or something. Fine by me.

My scalp is burning: fear, nerves.

"Won't you sit."

I don't move. I kind of can't.

He shrugs as if to say, *suit yourself.* Leaning back, he digs into his jacket pocket.

A flash of red yarn.

"I believe this belongs to you." He tosses my mitten onto the desk. Oh, crap. Yeah, I've been looking for that. But how does he know it's mine? I'm still in the realm of plausible deniability.

He reaches back into his pocket. He pulls out a crumpled piece of paper, smooths it onto the desk.

I stare at Emmett's handwriting: *Sarah, I want to know what happened. How Jamie died. Please. —E.*

Oh my God. The note was in my jacket pocket. I'd shoved it in there and left it to rot—never wanted to look at it again. He must have shown it to Dr. Folger, who would have confirmed exactly which Sarah it referred to. We are way out of the land of deniability now.

"I'm going to ask you again: won't you sit. We've got some things to discuss."

Sitting is starting to sound like a good idea. Keeping my distance, I walk around Dr. Folger's desk and sink into his swivel chair, flatten my palms on his desk blotter. Here I am in The Seat Of Power. Except I don't have any.

Captain Possum sets his face into an expression I can't read. He says, "Well then. Why don't you start by telling me what you were doing in my garage

Friday night. You and your dog."

At the mention of Ruby, I go from terrified to furious, zero to sixty. Snark box engaged and going into overdrive, subsuming my whole body. Anger pulses into my arms and legs, setting fire to the bite on my arm. *I won't give Ruby up. Just try it. You can all go straight to hell.*

"Well," he prompts. "I'm waiting."

My vision tapers into lasers. How can this man be holding Ruby's fate in his hands? Not possible.

"What does it matter why we were at your place?"

"It's trespassing, for one. And the deer, the meat that was ruined…"

"The deer meat! That poor creature was dead in the gym before you even showed up. What are you, a buzzard? Circling for carrion?"

Well. That shocks him. He presses back in his chair like he's fighting g-forces. "Excuse me," he says after he recovers. It's a question.

"You heard me." I'm on a roll. Panic has swept away all good sense and fear and I'm past angry. Just gone.

Captain Possum blinks rapidly, like he's trying to process my attack. His gaze turns downward; he rubs the arms of the chair.

When he looks up, he seems sad. *Whoa.* That throws me off. Why is he sad? And then I remember him kneeling at the cemetery. And I realize what a completely irrational bitch I am. I've torn into the man without even knowing for sure what he's up to.

This is more than snarky. This is cruel.

Captain Possum, I mean Captain Showalter—what the hell is wrong with me?—*Mr.* Showalter, sucks in a breath, starts to talk, and then stops. Sucks in another breath, lets it out slowly. "Got off to a bad start. Might be my fault, I don't know. Sure don't know why you're so mad, when I'm the one wronged." He pauses; it feels like he's trying to put aside his frustration. "Reckon one of us needs to back up, give in a little, or we'll get nowhere. And from the look of things, it's going to have to be me."

His voice is smoke in the air—if I inhale, his words will singe my nose, char my lungs. They're too unselfish.

"All right," he says. "I'm going to give you my point of view." He leans forward and slides his hands onto his knees. Dirt darkens the tips of his fingernails.

Doubt starts to creep into me. Remorse. And my old frenemy, guilt.

Clearing his throat, Mr. Showalter shifts in his chair. "I heard some trouble in my garage Friday night. And who did I see come running out but you. And your dog."

Ruby. I swallow.

"And I thought, *huh, that's strange.* Tried to see where you were going, but off you'd run and, from the sound of your dog, it wasn't a good idea to get Buddy close to him. You disappeared. And then I saw my garage. Do I have to tell you what a mess you left."

I don't answer.

"You and your dog." He lifts a hand and rubs his chin. "Your dog ruined a fair amount of meat. Any rate, I found your mitten. And then the note." He turns a plain silver band on his finger, then shakes his head like he's pulling himself out of his thoughts. "Now I don't know you, although I know some about your family, and you don't know me. Seems we think about some things different. You seem upset about me having the animal for venison. Not sure why. To me, well...I set out to see that it didn't die pointless. Seems more kind." He sighs. "Besides which, it was good meat. Would have got me through the winter."

I study my cuticles. I've shrunk to about an inch tall.

"Now maybe you don't agree with me. Way I see it, that isn't neither here or there."

Nor. Neither here NOR there. Sweet. How cool of me to be correcting his grammar right now.

"Fact is," he says, "you were sneaking around my property and you cost me meat. Fair thing is for you to pay it back." He sits back and takes a deep breath.

I do, too. I breathe. Open my mouth to speak, but nothing seems right. I'm a deflating balloon; Mr. Showalter has been sticking pins in me with each statement: *Seems we think about some things different.*

I set out to see it didn't die pointless. Seems more kind. Fair thing is for you to pay it back. Out of me hisses confusion and anger and fear, dissipating into the air. Plus, I'm a grade-A snob. Correcting the dude's grammar? That's awesome. Judging him for using an animal's meat? Not like my own grandfather isn't a farmer and a hunter. Not like I'm not an utter hypocrite.

My cheeks prickle with shame. I stare at my mitten and the note on the desk. "I'm sorry," I whisper. Clearing my throat, I say, louder, "I'm sorry. And I don't know how much the meat was worth, but I don't have any money to pay you back."

I wait for him to make some crack about Mom and Dad floating me a loan. Instead he seems to soften: his shoulders come away from his neck. "Don't you," he says.

I shake my head no. How much money do I owe him? I have no clue. But I'm pretty sure the piddly $12.50 in my Darth Vader piggy bank won't cover it.

"I would think your parents have the money."

And there it is. My chin presses in on itself and starts quivering. Mr. Showalter undoubtedly knows that my dad is the superintendent. If he didn't already, Dr. Folger would have told him. Maybe he even knows that Mom's a physician assistant at the clinic on East Main. In our town of 7,000 people, we're not a low-profile family.

So this whole conversation has been a total mind job. He's just going to go to them anyway.

Forget the trouble I'll be in for sneaking out. Forget Stenn aiding and abetting. Forget driving. They're going to take Ruby away. And it's my fault. I hate myself for starting to cry in front of Mr. Showalter, but I can't hold it back.

His eyes widen, but the rest of his expression doesn't change. "You can pay it off by working for me."

"What?"

"Could use some help."

I wipe my nose and ask, "You mean being a janitor with you? I…I guess I could do that…"

He chuckles. "No, no. With the Christmas trees. Harvesting the trees."

Oh. Duh.

Yet again, I'm not sure what to say. Without the snark box, the script doesn't write itself.

"Way I see it, this is our business. Between you and me. What you tell your folks is your business. Don't intend to make it mine. Made Jim—Dr. Folger—clear on that point, too. Took some convincing, but we go back a long way. He agreed to go along with me on this one."

Oh sweet deliverance! Ruby is saved! Ruby is safe. I'm light-headed with relief. I could almost pass out. I swipe at some rogue tears.

I can't meet Mr. Showalter's gaze, but now it's

because I'm so grateful that I feel defenseless and vulnerable, which is the worst. "Thank you."

"Expect you on Saturday. I'd tell you my address, but I have a feeling you already know where the farm is. Eight o'clock sharp." He waits like I'm supposed to say something.

"Okay," I say. Then, because I'm both a masochist *and* a moron, I blurt out, "Friday is a teacher workday. I don't have school. I could start, you know, on Friday. If you want."

He cocks his head to the side, looking surprised and amused. "That so."

I nod. Now that I'm thinking about it, it will be easier to help Mr. Showalter on Friday, when both parentals are distracted with their work, than on Saturday.

"Friday then. Now I'll let you be." He pushes his chair and stands, walks to the door. "I'll ask Jim to give you a minute."

The door sweeps across the carpet and clicks shut.

I drop my head onto the desk. What just happened here?

Eventually, the bell rings. I wipe my nose on my sleeve. Five minutes to homeroom. The fun never stops. I take my mitten and Emmett's note off Dr. Folger's desk and stuff them in my backpack. Head down, I walk out of the office and try to clear a path through the rest of the day.

✿✿✿

There's just one tiny hiccup. I have to convince my parents to let me work for Mr. Showalter.

Like, "Oh, by the way, I heard about this cool job and it will look so good on my college applications…"

No problem! Every parent of a fifteen-year-old girl is just waiting, nay, *hoping* their child's first foray into the world of employment will be on a Christmas tree farm. With some random dude. In East Next-to-Nowhere Bumblefart.

I spend the entire school day mulling over strategies, tactics, alibis.

But in the end, I decide to slap my instincts in the face, since they seem to keep leading me in crap-all directions lately. My instincts tell me to lie like a cheap carpet—so I'm going to be as honest as possible.

Honest, yes. Forthcoming, no. Big distinction.

So, after school, when Mom makes me go grocery shopping with her, I, delicately and with great finesse—because those are my middle names—broach the subject of working for Mr. Showalter. As we load groceries into the trunk, I just come right out and say, "I've been thinking about getting a job."

"Perfect timing," Mom says, and my heart leaps. Can it be that easy?

"Really?" I set a gallon of milk into the trunk.

"Sure. We've been thinking about charging you and your brother rent."

And I wonder where I get my sarcasm.

Mom pulls the last bag of groceries out of the cart. "But I don't think you should drop out of school just yet."

I take the cart to the corral, telling myself to go forth and prosper. You can totally do this. I join Mom in the car. "Seriously," I say, "A job. Just a weekend kind of thing."

Mom barrels out of the parking lot. "Hm. Where are you thinking of applying for said job?"

"I was talking to this guy at school. Dr. Folger knows him. And he knows Dad. He has a business."

"This is a student?"

"No, a grown-up. His name is Mr. Showalter."

Mom crinkles her forehead as she hits the brakes at a stop sign. Worst. Driver. Ever.

"He has a Christmas tree farm," I explain. "He thinks I could help with the trees."

"You already talked to him about it?" She's annoyed.

Backpedal! Backpedal! "Well, I told him I would have to ask you first."

Mom is quiet, so I talk to fill the space. "He was talking about it—Mr. Showalter was—and he grows the trees himself and then he sells them. You know, for Christmas?"

"Christmas? Christmas. I think I may have heard

of that holiday. Sounds vaguely familiar." She drills her eyes into me, "Do you really think you can handle a job on top of school and…how you've been feeling?"

"Watch the road, Mom? You nearly sideswiped an ambulance."

"Don't change the subject."

"It's hard to stay on topic when there's a maniac at the wheel."

"The job, Monkey."

"Okay, okay." It's strange, having a normal-ish conversation with Mom. In person. Not texting, not harping too much on what has become of me SJD. "Um…I think it would be good. I know I need to bring my grades up, and I'm trying, but it's like inertia."

"Inertia? How so?"

"Objects in motion tend to stay in motion. I think it will be good to stay busy. And learn the value of a dollar and all that."

"Understanding personal finance is not my main concern for you right now," Mom says as she plows through an intersection.

"Red means stop, Mom."

"It was yellow. Yellow means go faster."

"Seriously, how can you heal people for a living but be such a menace behind the wheel?"

"Don't exaggerate." She stomps on the gas. "You know, there's plenty of time for you to learn life lessons about work and money when you're older. Your grades need to be your main priority."

"I know. But I honestly, seriously, think this will help."

"Hm. Maybe. I'll discuss it with your father."

"Thanks!" Skippidy doo dah! *I'll discuss it with your father* means she'll inform him of her decision. In theory, Dad has veto power, but he almost never uses it. Mom is the Decider.

"I'm not done," she says, screeching up the driveway and slamming the car into park. She takes the keys out of the ignition but doesn't get out. "As I was saying. I'll discuss it with your father, but I think…yes, my answer is no."

Frost forms on my neck. "Yes, your answer is no?"

"Yes, my answer is no. You do not have my permission."

"I don't have your *permission*?" Like I'm in second grade and a need a signed note to take a field trip?

"You need to bring your grades up first. You need to attend all your classes. You need to earn back our trust."

"What I *need* is for you to get off my back! Let me have a life! What I *need* is for you to be fair!"

She sighs. "Life isn't fair, Monkey."

"Oh my God! This is perfect." I'm starting to see red, literally see red. "*You're* telling *me* life isn't fair. Um, news flash! Jamie died right in front of my eyes so don't even tell me about how life isn't fair!"

"You've been through a lot. No one denies that.

157

But you're just a kid, Monkey. We want you to be a kid."

"Make up your mind! Am I supposed to be super responsible, or am I supposed to be a kid?"

"This discussion is over. You're just proving my point that you're not ready for a job. You can't even sit here and have a rational—"

"GO TO HELL!"

Mom takes a deep, angry breath. "Get inside and go to your room. Now."

"You're such a hypocrite. I hate you."

"Go."

I slam the car door as hard as I can.

Gee, that went well. Just when I thought things could be getting a little bit better, they come crashing back down. Plus, thanks a lot, honesty.

Well screw her, and Dad, and every other person on the planet. If I wasn't determined to work off my debt before, I sure as Hades am now. No way am I not paying back Mr. Showalter; no way am I giving him a reason to rat me and Ruby out to my parents. You can bet your sweet hoo-ha I'm going to work at that tree farm. I just have to figure out how.

AS the week trudges on, my bite and Ruby's tail both get better, my forehead cut barely even shows, and it's good to have my phone and internet "privileges" back. Too bad I can't say the same for my employment prospects. All day, and during the windows of wakefulness at night, I knock my head against the wall, trying to jar some ideas loose for:

1. An excuse for being out of the house all day Friday (how long will I have to work to pay Mr. Showalter back? Saturday, too? Sunday? Longer?)
2. Transportation to and from the tree farm

I'm so desperate that I even risk activating Stenn's overprotective streak by telling him about working for Mr. Showalter. Of course he hates the idea of me working in the middle of nowhere, with a strange man, all alone. *But* he likes the idea of my parents forbidding us from seeing each other, revoking potential driving privileges, and/or taking Ruby away even less, so…he deals. But no, he can't come home this weekend and doesn't have any brainwaves for an alibi.

Wednesday after school, for only the cost of a

large fries and a Coke, Jeremy agrees to take me home to get Rubes and then over to Emmett's soccer game. (Money left in Darth Vader piggy bank: $8.50.)

The game has just started when we arrive. Ruby is the perfect excuse for avoiding the dreaded Who Do I Sit With moment—moments I never had BJD. I should be inured to them by now, but honestly, they still kick me in the guts every time. It's just another of the millions of reminders that my BFF is now my DFF.

But Rubes gives me heart. Strength. Fortitude. We truck up the bleachers to the end of the top row; Ruby lies down on the bench next to me, resting her head in my lap. Our perch gives us a good view of the crowd: parents sitting in clusters, students sitting in bigger groups.

Mrs. Cleary is here. And Mr. Cleary, too. But they aren't sitting together. Does it mean something? It seems bad. Maybe they're just making the social rounds?

They each see me; they each wave hello. Mr. Cleary looks older than he did seven months ago and he's packed some fat around the belly and chin. Both Cleary parental faces seem friendly enough, but I have to wonder: Do they realize I'm here specifically at Emmett's request? Would that freak them out? Like, would they tell him to stay away from me for his own safety? Protect the remaining child, in case I carry some sort of curse?

I try to look cheerful and return their waves. Both of them press their lips together in what must pass for smiles these days. Then they turn back to the game.

Emmett is the starting (I assume, since it's only two minutes into the game) halfback. He plays amazingly well. The kid is on fire. He just tears up the field. Jamie would be so, so proud. Whatever else has changed about him, his soccer mojo remains. And damn, I have to admit, he looks good. Then again, ew. Incesty.

At halftime I hide behind the pages of *Crime and Punishment*. Which, by the way, should be called *The Novel That Would Not End. Ever. Really. Seriously, This Novel Never Ends.* Because that would be both honest and descriptive.

My invisibility plan fizzles, though, when Ruby sits up and gives a friendly *huff*. My bleacher bobbles; someone has plunked down next to me and is petting my dog, who is thumping her tail happily. The canine traitor.

"Is this your dog? She is gorgeous! What a gorgeous girl you are—she is a girl right?—yes you are, yes you are gorgeous." It's Rosemary from health class and from saying hi to Stenn in the parking lot. The girl is über-extroverted. Or else someone put her up to this—double-dog dared her to come talk to the outcast.

"I didn't know you were such a dog hater."

She smiles. "I can't stand the things. Ugh."

"Her name's Ruby. Careful, she bites."

Rosemary laughs and smushes Ruby's ears. "I can tell. She looks positively scary."

Okay. You know there's that saying, "The way to a man's heart is through his stomach." It's super outdated, but whatever. Point is: the way to Sarah Jones's heart? Ruby. And right now Rosemary is totally copping a feel of my atrium.

Still stroking Rubes, Rosemary nods at my book. "Is that what the brains are reading?"

"I guess." The Brains. Egad. This brain isn't getting very brain-worthy grades. Just ask my folks.

"Is it any good?"

"If you like your books confusing as crap and boring as hell, it's awesome."

Rosemary laughs. "It's got to be better than *The Old Man and the Sea*. I mean, what a *guy* book. So the man caught a fish—who frigging cares?"

"So true. It is as if our teachers do not realize there are actually books published after 1952."

"I know!"

"Or by women. Shocker."

Rosemary laughs—a raucous, horsey laugh. She's so loud that some groups of kids look at us, and some parents give us Girls, Settle Down looks.

Oh wow. When was the last time I've been at the business end of one of those looks?

With Jamie, of course. At Victoria's Secret, probably. We went to the mall in Binghamton the weekend before she died. To pick out sexy undies and bra for my deflowering. When I'd decided on the perfect ensemble (off-white lace, black ribbons) and was getting my clothes back on, Jamie decided it would be high-larious to make people think we were the prototypical horny old couple getting it on in the dressing room. She was all deep-man-voice moaning, thumping the partitions. She was so preoccupied with her performance that I finished dressing, snuck out, and left the door wide open while she kept moaning and gyrating. Ha. Served.

A sharp twinge, like a bad cramp, pinches my stomach. It's guilt. Painful and strong. To be laughing, watching Emmett's game, getting looks from parents, and it's not with Jamie...

Rosemary covers her mouth in deference to the grown-ups, but their disapproval has given her the giggles; she is practically falling off the bleachers.

It's contagious. I get giggly, too, and try to tighten my stomach against the feeling that I'm betraying my best friend.

Happily oblivious to my inner turmoil, Rosemary launches into a new subject: "Ron and I have been going out for two weeks, so I started coming to his games. You know Ron Halverstead?"

I shrug. "Not very well, but I know who he is."

"Well, I don't know much about soccer," Rosemary says. "I've always been more of a football girl myself, but I figure if I watch his games, he'll owe me. I'll bring him to the mall and make him hold my purse while I try stuff on. *Mwahaha*." She curls her fingers and drums them together. "That's my evil laugh, in case you didn't realize."

"Got it."

"So how come you're here?"

She's got the attention span of a fly.

Rosemary continues, "I mean, Stenn's away at school, so why are you watching boys' soccer?" Her smile dissolves and her face fills with horror. "Oh my God. You guys didn't break up did you? I have such a big mouth! I'm sorry—"

"Don't worry." Speaking without thinking first? I may have done that. Once or twice. *May* have. "Stenn and I are still together."

"Well, thank God. You guys are like, the power couple."

"The power couple?" Really? People think that?

"Yeah, you've been together so long, and even long-distance and everything."

"Oh." I don't know what to say. All of a sudden my snark box is malfunctioning. "Uh, well. I just...I told a friend I'd come to the game."

"Oh, that's cool. Who?"

Holy Nosey Parker, Batman. But putting that aside, it's nice to be sitting with a human, someone my own age, of the female gender, talking about normal things. Girl things.

A fresh pang shoots through me. Girl stuff is Jamie's territory. Me and Jamie's territory, together.

"Um, Emmett. Cleary," I say. Waiting for Rosemary to connect the dots (Sarah —> Emmett —> Emmett's dead sister Jamie), I picture her playing roulette. She spins the wheel. *Click click click* goes the little ball, but instead of numbers, this wheel has words: *pity, discomfort, panic, platitudes, awkward silence. Pity, discomfort, panic, platitudes, awkward silence.* Around and around it goes. Where it stops, nobody knows!

"Oh…," Rosemary says. "Jamie's brother."

"Yeah." The wheel is slowing down. Where will it stop? My money's on awkward silence. With a side bet on pity.

"That's cool you and Emmett are friends. I didn't realize." She squints like she's thinking. "Makes sense, though. You two probably miss Jamie the most out of everyone. I don't know who was closer to her—I mean, twin or best friend? It's practically the same thing, in some ways."

Hold up. The ball just landed on *Say one of the truest things Sarah's heard, ever.* My throat contracts; I can't speak. So I nod.

Rosemary looks stricken again. "I'm sorry! I always say too much." Then, without hesitation, she adds, "Does it make you sad, talking about Jamie? Should I not? My friends told me not to, but I—"

"No!" I snap. Rosemary looks confused. The girl is trying really, really hard. I start again, more quietly, "No. I don't mind talking about her." *Actually, sometimes it's all I want to do.*

Rosemary slouches, maybe from relief, but she still looks worried.

I say, "Here's the thing. Of course it's sad." I kind of laugh at myself, "Duh, right? But it's nice, too."

Rosemary nods like I should keep talking. Ruby has settled her weight onto me again, but we're taking turns petting her.

"Hearing you talk about her is just"—what's the right way to describe it?—"surprising? Because no one ever does. Want to talk about Jamie, I mean. Or even say her name. Like people will burst into flames if they do. It's pretty impressive you didn't spontaneously combust right then." *That alone elevates you from high Normal to low Ninja.*

She nods more vigorously. "Probably because everyone's worried they'll say the wrong thing. Like me! But if I kept my mouth shut in order to not say the wrong thing, I'd never be able to talk at all, you know?"

Yeah, that sounds about right. Hey, look at me! Another snarky comment I managed to not say.

Rosemary continues, "It's like, when my cat died, my parents wouldn't mention him in front of me because they didn't want to make me sad, but that just made it worse, you know? I kept thinking, didn't they think Picky Picky was important enough to remember?"

"Picky Picky?"

"Yeah, it's from—"

"*Ramona*. I loved those books."

"Me, too! I was six when I named her."

"I approve." Although I can't say I approve of the

comparison of cat death to BFF death. Then again, I am slightly attached to the dog lying on me right now.

On the field, the soccer players take their positions for the second half. Emmett kind of jogs in place, waiting.

"I know it's not the same," Rosemary says after a while.

"What's not?"

"A cat and a person. Picky Picky and Jamie."

"Yeah."

"But, then again," she says. "Picky Picky was a good cat. More like a dog, really."

Hm. Girl sitting next to me: funny, with an edge? Or clueless and airheaded? I'm on the fence, but hoping for the former. And when I notice she's looking at me sideways, struggling not to grin, I take it as a good sign.

The referee blows his whistle and the field is swept into motion.

"He looks older," Rosemary says. "Emmett. He got hotter." She bumps my arm. "But don't tell Ron I said that!"

"It's in the vault."

"The what?"

"The vault."

"Oh, like a safe? In a bank?"

"Yes."

"Oh. Thanks."

We watch the game, and I try to pay attention.

But I'm wondering why Rosemary hasn't gone back to sit with her crew. And I can't stop thinking about Jamie. She would know what *in the vault* meant, even if I'd never said it before. No explanations necessary. And the joking thing. Even when she had everyone else fooled, I always knew when James was kidding. She was a diabolical genius. So. There's that.

And then there's the teensy matter of betrayal. Is sitting here with Rosemary, is it like cheating on Jamie, trying to replace her? Because I would never. If James were still here, I would never. Even if Rosemary turns out to be awesome, I will never split a locket in half with her and put it on a necklace and wear it forever.

Or…therapy session time: Am I projecting? Because if I really think about it, there's no way James would want me to mope around like a social pariah. She'd smack me and tell me to get a life.

A little later, Rosemary says, "It's nice to get a chance to hang out."

I nod.

"I've been wanting to, but…I don't know. You've kind of gone off the radar. And my friends are like 'Give her some space.'"

"Who said that?"

She shrugs. "Everyone. It's not that people don't like you, Sarah. It's just that you make people kind of…uncomfortable."

I snort. "Uncomfortable." Wow. I don't want to

care, but this stings. Like onion in my eyes, stings.

"That came out wrong! I just mean, it's a hard situation. No one knows how to handle it. I'm sorry. I'm really sorry. That came out totally wrong."

"It's okay." I will not cry. I will not cry.

"Anyway," she gives Ruby a pat and then smacks her knees, stands up. "I should probably get back down there. Do you want to come?"

I shake my head. At least I'm managing not to cry. "It's best if I stay up here. Because of Ruby. You know." Plus, God forbid I should make anyone uncomfortable.

"Um, okay." She takes a few steps down the bleachers before she turns back around. "Hey, you used to take dance lessons, right?"

I nod.

"Well, this might sound stupid, but I signed up for this Salsa-Thon? It's one of Ms. Gliss's stupid fundraisers. But it's for Breast Cancer Awareness, which you can't really argue with. It starts Friday morning and goes all day Friday and Saturday. She's giving extra credit for it, which I need, and no one else will go with me, and I was just wondering if maybe you want to do it?"

Oh, nice. So none of her other friends want to go, so I'm the last-ditch effort? Or the pity invite.

Then again, she didn't have to ask at all.

Then again...it's all day Friday and Saturday. The perfect alibi.

"Hey, Rosemary?"

"Hey, Sarah?"

"This might seem weird, but do you think you could help me out with something?"

She crosses her arms. "Depends. Are you going to do the Salsa-Thon?"

"Possibly. Eventually."

She gives me a confused look. "Are you going to help me raise money for it?"

"Possibly. Eventually."

"Wait. Is this something I'm going to get in trouble for?"

"Possibly," I admit, "but not…"

"Ooh!" She claps her hands excitedly. "Is it shocking and outrageous?"

"No, it's more…sneaky and rebellious."

"Then yes. I could use some excitement in my life."

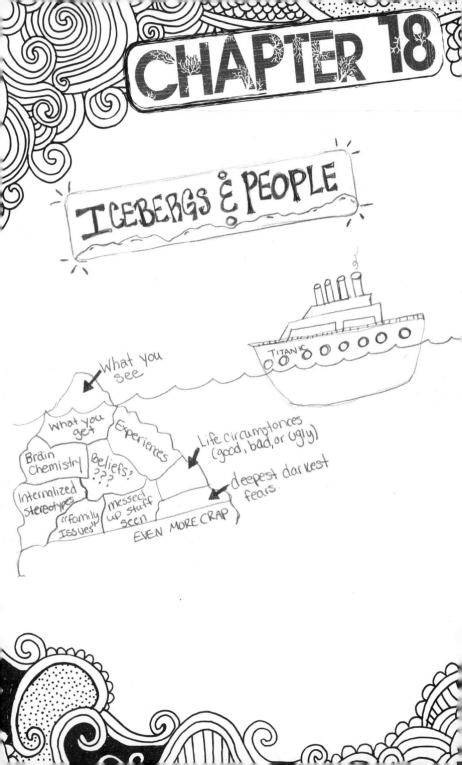

CHAPTER 18

ICEBERGS & PEOPLE

TITANIC

What you see

What you get

Experiences

Brain Chemistry

Beliefs?

Life circumstances (good, bad, or ugly)

Internalized Stereotypes

"family Issues"

messed up stuff seen

deepest darkest fears

EVEN MORE CRAP

AFTER school the next day, Rubes and I walk over to the cemetery. To spend some time on Jamie's bench, yes, but also for a bit of recon. I want to check out the area where Mr. Showalter was on the day Dad so rudely interrupted my truancy. I want to know more about him, this strange man who—*bam!*—appeared out of nowhere, and now keeps turning up. And holds my fate in his hands.

Google won't help me much; all I can figure out is

1. There are a whole lot of Showalters, none listed in my town, and
2. That I can't for the life of me remember what Dr. Folger had said his first name was. If he said it at all.

So, recon. Going back to where he was, I find two Showalter graves, right next to each other. One of them is a double grave, the kind with two overlapping hearts.

It says

Roy Showalter
November 11, 1961–

Donna Showalter
December 30, 1964–
October 13, 2005

You were born together, and together
you shall be forevermore.
You shall be together when the white wings
of death scatter your days.
Aye, you shall be together even in the
silent memory of God.

Holy crap. Is this possible? Was Donna Showalter his wife? And he has this grave reserved for himself? Talk about commitment. If he is Roy Showalter, he's completely given up on ever remarrying, or even having a girlfriend again. I mean, who's going to date a guy whose cemetery space is already waiting, right next to his dead wife?

And. If this *is* his wife, Mr. Showalter must have chosen the epitaph. Gruff Captain Possum picked out this crazy tender love poem. I imagine him reciting it to the engraver. Standing there with his possum and his dirty fingernails, having known this poem, having chosen it. It just doesn't go with my image of him.

The grave next to the double heart is also a Showalter.

David Leonard Showalter
June 28, 1990 – October 13, 2005

Oh, man. Fifteen years old. His son? With the same date of death as his wife. So his wife and son died on the same day? Must have been an accident. Something sudden. But what?

One thing's for sure, it didn't happen in Norwich. A tragedy like this, even if it was just a crazy fluke— actually, *especially* if it was a crazy fluke—everyone would know about it. Everyone. And these names are new to me.

Now that I have first names, and dates, I go home and Google it again. Ruby curls up on my feet while I tap out the search and scan the results. First hit is a news story from the Binghamton *Press & Sun Bulletin*. It's kind of a long one, with a byline, instead of just a snippet-type accident report.

Reading it, I go numb and cold.

MOTHER AND SON DEAD IN APPARENT MURDER-SUICIDE
OCTOBER 14, 2005

BRISBEN, NEW YORK—Local painter Donna Showalter, 40, and son Leon Showalter, 15, were found dead yesterday in their home on Route 12.

Police report that Leon Showalter shot his mother to death, using a handgun registered to his father, Roy Showalter. Roy Showalter reported hearing "four or five" gunshots as he returned from his job at Spence Green Architects in Johnson City. Mr. Showalter claims he found his wife dead and his son in a "manic state," allegedly threatening to shoot his father. The elder Mr. Showalter tried to calm his son, but Leon Showalter turned the gun on himself. His cause of death is listed as a fatal self-inflicted gunshot wound to the head.

Police report that the gun was kept in a lock-box in the basement of the Showalter's residence, and that the lock showed signs of tampering. A neighbor, who declined to be identified, said that Leon Showalter was known to have suffered from bipolar disorder. "He was a great kid, real smart, but you could tell he was always either really up or very depressed," the neighbor said.

The county district attorney says no criminal charges have been filed.

Suddenly chilled, I hug myself.

"Are you done yet? Get off the computer." Jeremy in the doorway. Impeccable timing, as usual.

"Go away."

"You get five more minutes."

"Says who?"

"Says me."

"Or what?"

"Or...there will be dire consequences."

"Ha. You got nothing. No leverage."

"I mean it. Get off the computer. I need it."

I close the door and prop the chair under the doorknob.

Mr. Showalter had found his wife dead. Had seen the gun in his son's hands. Knew his son had killed his wife. Then watched his son shoot himself.

It's beyond awful. How can a person survive something like that?

Is there a comparison chart of horrible experiences? Losing your son and your wife—and knowing that your son murdered your wife and then committed suicide—isn't that even worse than watching your best friend die?

It's totally morbid to compare. But that's what people do, isn't it? Life is a constant comparison—yourself to others. You figure out who you are, how good or bad you have it, in relation to other people's situations and experiences.

Like Stenn: he has it great. Never been through anything majorly bad, has a family who loves him, gobs of money, friends, private school. My brother's got a pretty sweet deal, too: no major traumas, decent parents, friends, that stuff. To be honest, I had it pretty good, too, BJD. But the JD changed everything.

Did Roy have it good before his wife and son died? Or does he come from the school of hard knocks? Does that make it easier? If you had a crappy childhood that made you tough, maybe it's easier to deal with a tragedy.

So what's my theory here? Abused kids have it easier? Sure, that's not problematic at all.

The newspaper said Mr. Showalter had worked in an architect's office. As a janitor? Or something else? Did he used to be Captain Successful Architect until one day he went home and found his life completely shattered?

One thing's for sure: Captain Possum has been through hell and back.

CHAPTER 19

CHILDHOOD, TIME SPENT DOING STUFF
(IN THE U. S.)

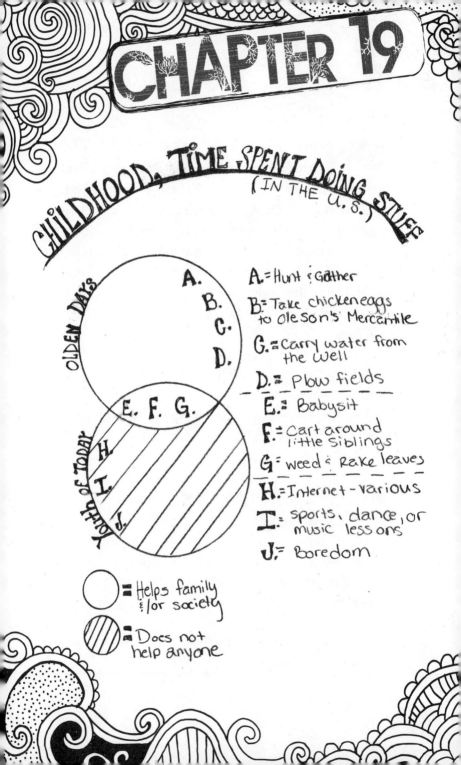

OLDEN DAYS

A.
B.
C.
D.

E. F. G.

Youth of Today

H.
I.
J.

A. = Hunt & Gather

B. = Take chicken eggs to Oleson's Mercantile

C. = Carry water from the well

D. = Plow fields

E. = Babysit

F. = Cart around little siblings

G. = Weed & rake leaves

H. = Internet - various

I. = Sports, dance, or music lessons

J. = Boredom

◯ = Helps family &/or society

▨ = Does not help anyone

ON Friday morning, seven o'clock plows into me even harder than usual. Brutal. It should be a sleep-in day. What else is a teacher workday good for? You can't tell me teachers actually *do* anything on teacher workdays except stand around drinking bad decaf and complaining about the internet and Kids Today. It's a day off for everyone except me. For me, it's Don't Get Caught Going To Your New Job day.

Even Ruby groans when my alarm goes off. Her tail is pretty much healed, but she's too sleepy to wag it. I slump out of bed to take a shower; Ruby brings Artoo and falls back asleep on the bathmat.

I dress in multiple layers and stuff more warm clothes in my backpack.

On my way downstairs, I knock on Jeremy's door. "Wake up," I whisper. "You have to pick me up in half an hour."

Muffled groan.

"If you're late, the deal's off," I tell him.

In the kitchen, Mom sets my Zoloft next to my breakfast plate. "I still don't know about this, Monkey."

"Dad said it's okay." Ha! Take that, lady! Turned the tables and went to Dad first.

"Two whole days, though. It's too much." She hands me a bag lunch. "Can't you just collect pledges and not do the entire Dance-A-Ma-Tron?"

"Salsa-Thon, Mom. You should be happy I'm being social. And philanthropic. It's for a good cause."

She makes a face. "This wasn't exactly our agreement."

"If you will recall, I got an A on my trig test this week. And all homework in on time, thank you very much."

"And that's the *only* reason I'm agreeing to this. If your grades slip at all after this…this Dancy-A-Jiggama, you are in back in the dog house."

"Noted, Mom. Jeez. Most parents would be stoked their kid was going to get exercise and raise money for a good cause," I take my Zoloft with orange juice and bite into whole wheat toast. "Plus, I made a new friend. Aren't you proud? Dad is."

"I'm going to ignore the manipulative attempt at triangulation of me and your father, and say that, yes, I am pleased you've reached out to someone."

Rosemary did all the reaching, but let Mom think what she wants. A car horn beeps outside. "That's her. I'll be home around 4:30 or 5:00."

"Love you, Monkey. I am pleased that you're—"

"Bye."

Ruby sits at the back door and wags her tail. She always wants to come with me, but this time it's like she knows I'm going somewhere more exciting than usual. "Sorry, Rubes." I nuzzle her. "No dogs allowed at dance-a-thons." She looks at me with those big dark eyes. Ouch.

In the car, Rosemary's mom is super chatty. Apparently the apple didn't fall far from the tree. When she drops us off at the YMCA, site of the Salsa-Thon, she calls, "You girls have fun! I'll pick you up at four."

We walk slowly, Rosemary waving her mom off. When she finally pulls away, Rosemary giggles. "This is so excellent. Is your brother here yet?"

I scan the parking lot at the side of the building. "No. Wait, yes. Here he is." I smile at Rosemary. "Thanks again for covering for me."

"No problem whatsoever." She gives me a huge, tight hug. Apparently she is pro-hug. At least she's unambiguous about it: she spreads her arms so wide you can see from miles away that she's coming in for a landing.

"Good luck," she says. "Are you nervous? First day at a new job? Which you still haven't told me about."

"I will, I swear. I just want to get a few days under my belt." *And hell yes, I'm so nervous I could barf.* "Yeah. Kind of nervous."

She smiles, her eyes wide. "Text me, tell me how it's going? And later we'll go out to celebrate."

"Sounds good. If I survive. And if my parents don't find out and shoot me." Oh man. Bad choice of words.

Jeremy is as thrilled as ever to be my chauffeur. I wonder what excuse he gave Mom and Dad about going out so early. Doesn't matter; he has assumed the position of Jones Family Golden Child.

"Turn here!" He has the music so loud I have to scream directions. "Go up the hill!"

He shouts, "What? This is the way to the Pig Farm Party Shack!"

"I know! It's on the same road!"

When we get to Mr. Showalter's, the sun is just reaching the tops of the shorter pines. The place looks smaller in daylight. Jeremy swerves to a stop next to the beat-up truck, which is next to the white van.

Mr. Showalter materializes in the garage door, reaching overhead to pull it down behind him. The way he's dressed, rugged and sturdy, he looks like a hunter hyphen construction worker. No possum.

When Jeremy sees Mr. Showalter, he frowns and turns down the music. "You sure about this?"

Wha? I gape at my brother. Was that actual concern in his voice? I guess dropping me off in the woods with a stranger is the hidden trigger to some latent sibling protection instinct.

"Yeah," I say. "It's fine."

He shudders, shaking off his momentary lapse of hostility. "Whatever."

"Pick me up at 3:30, okay? And remember, as far as Mom and Dad and everyone else is concerned, I'm at the Y doing a dance fundraiser."

"I'll remember. Just so long as you don't renege on our deal."

I grab my lunch and backpack and open the door. "Just pick me up on time today. And tomorrow. And—"

"Our deal. Unlimited use of the computer and any entertainment devices. And you're doing my chores."

Sigh. Goodbye, internet. Goodbye, movies. Hello, mowing the lawn and doing the dishes. "Yes. That's the deal."

"Then it's all good. Go. Posthaste."

And then he's gone, and I'm alone with the mysterious Mr. Showalter.

It's freezing. I open my backpack and start piling on the extra layers I packed.

Mr. Showalter smiles a friendly, wide smile. "Morning, Sarah. Right on time." He sounds pleasantly surprised.

I poke my head through one of Stenn's old hoodies, then put my coat back on over it. "Hi." I pull on a hat and my red mittens—my Exhibit A, Telltale Heart mittens—which is some crappy planning, for sure.

Mr. Showalter says, "Ready."

I nod. *Ready as I'll ever be.*

"Let's get to work."

For the first hour, *let's get to work* means following Mr. Showalter around, tying thin yellow plastic strips to the trees that will be getting the axe.

The axe. Ha. Gradually, my nervousness wears off. It's pretty easy. I just walk and tie while Mr. Showalter identifies different types of trees and how to tell if they're ready for harvest. I try to pay attention, but it's way early and way cold. My fingers are extra-freezing because I have to take my mittens off every time I tie a plastic thingy to a tree.

Around 9:30, Mr. Showalter stops, rubs his chin, and turns around slowly. He nods. "This'll do, for starters." He strides back to the homestead; I have to trot to keep up. At the garage, he opens the side door and holds it for me. "Come on, then."

Oh. I hadn't realized I'd stopped short. Am I a moron? (Scratch that question.) What I mean is, why had it not occurred to me that I'd have to go back into the garage? And why does it bother me so much? It's not the gym, after all. But my forearm starts to throb as if Ruby had just sunk her teeth into it. Wonderful. Another place to be post-traumatic-stressed about.

All right, buck up, little camper.

I put my mittened palm on the doorframe and step in. The place is spotless. No bloodstains, no deer carcass. It's just like the gym: unless you'd witnessed it, you would never know anything bad had happened here.

How many places in the world are like that? How many places are the sites of murders or deadly car crashes and you just don't realize it?

185

Here in the garage, all that remains of the deer and that night is the deerskin, riddled with holes from the broken window, stretching on a rack on one of the workbenches. The antlers, cut from gray skull at the base of the horns, lie on the other workbench.

The swift animal was believed to speed the spirits of the dead on their way...

A frog-sized lump crawls into my throat.

"Sarah." Mr. Showalter is standing next to me. "It bothers you," he says.

I swallow hard. "Mr. Showalter...I'm sorry about what happened."

All he says is, "Prefer you call me Roy."

Allowing, wanting even, a lowly kid to use his first name? Not in this town.

He says, "Come along, Buddy." An unfamiliar *scritch scritch* from the floor. Mr. Showalter's—Roy's—possum scampers across the floor and climbs his pant leg. Buddy the possum winds its tail around his belt and releases its claw-hold to hang upside down. Buddy's pink snout glistens like he's had a runny nose, or maybe a sloppy drink of water. Or maybe that's normal for possums? It's been a while since my last shift at the zoo's rodent (marsupial?) house.

Roy—surely I will be labeled insubordinate for using his first name—walks over to the stretched deerskin, reaches around it, and returns with a pair of work gloves. "Here. Be big on you, but I don't think you can cut trees in those." Meaning my Telltale Heart mittens.

I take off my mittens and pull the work gloves on, shifting my gaze from the deerskin on the workbench to the wall behind it. There are random things pinned on a pegboard, some of them partially obscured by the deerskin: A bent plastic comb. A bubbling, faded Polaroid photo. A broken watch. A taped-together postcard. The glint of a thin gold chain. The top of a peacock feather. A leprechaun keychain. Clearly they aren't tools or anything meant to be useful. And now, in daylight, I see that there's a piece of gossamer thread around each thing, connecting one to another like a spiderweb.

"What do you make of it." Roy's voice startles me.

What do I make of it? There must be something important about this stuff, otherwise why would he ask? "Are they souvenirs? From trips?"

He looks at me like I've said something important. He nods once. "Something like that."

I wait for him to say more, to clarify. But (surprise, surprise) he doesn't. Instead of talking, he turns around, hefts a chainsaw down from a shelf, and hands it to me.

I repeat: the man hands me a chainsaw.

I must look completely shocked and bewildered, and also like I might tip over from the weight of the thing, because Roy laughs. "What, you thought the trees'd just fall down on their own?"

I blink at the chainsaw in my hands. There is a chainsaw in my hands.

Smiling, he shakes his head like I just told a good joke. "Would be easier if they did," he says. He grabs two sets of safety glasses and earplugs, and leaves the garage. I lug the chainsaw and follow, watching Buddy bump against Roy's leg as he walks.

Armed with the chainsaw, I follow Roy to the farthest tagged tree. He rips the yellow tag off the tree, then puts on his safety glasses and gloves. "Here. Set that down and I'll show you how it works."

Show me how it works? Show *me* how it works? I'm not just being a pack mule? I look around. Surely there are eighty workplace safety laws prohibiting minors from wielding chainsaws. The man is batshit crazy.

Well, hot diggity! This is the kind of crazy I can get behind. It's not like using a chainsaw is number one on my List of Things to Do Before I Die, but now that the gauntlet has been thrown down, I'm determined. It's time for something new.

Roy hands me the other pair of safety glasses, along with earplugs. After we put them in, he hollers instructions. Pointing to the scary end of the saw, he says, "The chain goes around and cuts according to how much throttle you give it."

I nod. "Okay."

He points to a small bar on top of the handle. "That's the chain brake. Stops the chain if there's kickback. Chain guard here. That's the throttle safety latch, that's the throttle interlock. If you let go of it, it kills the motor." He looks at me. "Safety feature."

"Throttle interlock. Got it."

He steps on the handle. "To start it, you stand on it here, and here's the choke, and then pull here." He takes his foot off the chainsaw. "Before we do that, two things. First: this thing can kill you or take a leg off right quick, and it doesn't care a lick about you."

"What's the second thing?"

"'Timber.' Always look where the tree's going, and always yell 'timber,' even if you think no one's around for miles. Aren't big trees, but they don't tickle."

Dude. You had me at *timber*. "I think I got it," I say, pointing to the parts. "Throttle, throttle lock thing that stops if you let go. Chain, motor, chain guard."

He nods. "Always use two hands and never cut above shoulder height. Short blade, but it's got some kick." He rubs his chin. "Ready to try."

"Can I watch you do one first?" See Sarah. See Sarah stall.

"Yep." He steps back on the handle and pulls the start chain. It roars, evil loud. Roy motions with his elbow for me to step back. Hefting the saw, he squats at the base of the tree. When he puts the saw to the trunk, it gets louder, louder, louder. Eventually, the motor cuts out, and Roy yells, "Timber!" There's a loud *snap* and the tree falls away from us, bouncing a little when it hits the ground.

He sets the chainsaw down. "Your turn."

I take a deep breath to calm my nerves. "All right. I think I'm ready." I step on the handle. "Here?"

He nods. "Give it a short, quick pull."

I do. Exactly nothing happens.

"Try again."

I pull harder and the thing kicks to life. I pick it up, holding the throttle lock like Roy said. It's super heavy and it's vibrating my arms into pudding. Carefully, trying not to behead or otherwise maim either of us, I crouch under the tree. When the blade touches the trunk, the whole chainsaw jumps hard. I guess that's what kickback means. My stomach drops to my toes. This is so dangerous and scary. I try again, pressing the blade to the trunk. And the chain starts cutting wood. Ripping, more like.

Terror aside, it is frigging awesome.

By the third tree, it's frigging hard.

An hour later, it's by far the hardest thing I've ever done, ever. I manage to cut down eight trees in the time it probably would take Roy to do twenty. Or twenty-hundred, but who's counting?

A while later, Roy suggests switching jobs. "I'll cut. You move and net."

Fine by me. Even after I put down the chainsaw, my arms are still shaking. My knees are jelly. But I still have two legs, two arms, and an attached head, so, victory!

Roy demonstrates my new task: dragging trees over near the garage, hoisting them onto sawhorses, then cutting off any straggly branches—done the old-fashioned way, with a big pair of loppers. After this manscaping, each tree has to be hauled over to a large metal ring with plastic netting scrunched around it. Roy shows me how to push a tree into the ring to catch the netting, then pull it from the other side, twisting as I go. And then you have it, the final product: a skinny cocoon tree. These get propped against the garage, their trunks parked in tubs of warm water.

Roy gives me a box cutter to cut the netting. Then he scratches his chin. "Do you need a break before we keep going," he asks.

"No. I'm good." Something about Roy is bringing out Scrapper Sarah. A person I've never really met before, but who I always hoped was in here. Somehow the work is transforming my snarkiness and sarcasm into stubborn pride. I will not complain. I will not wimp out. I will do what Roy throws at me, and then some. Maybe because

A) Roy seems so old-school and rugged.
B) Look at the hell he's been through with his wife and son. Who am I to whine about some work?
C) He's treating me like a capable human being instead of a broken teenager.
D) Most surprising: I seem to actually *like* this ass-busting work. Go figure.

After two hours of dragging, sawing, netting, and plunking tree after tree after into washtub after washtub, all my layers are off, down to my long-sleeve Salsa-Thon T-shirt (thanks, Rosemary) and yoga stretchy pants. My hair keeps sticking to my sweaty forehead. I twist it into a messy clump, secure it with the old elastic I keep twirled around the lip balm in my bag. I trek back into the rows to fetch another tree from Roy. Like me, he is shedding layers. He's now in patched overalls and a thermal under-shirt: Dukes of Hazzard Uncle Jesse Couture. I dig it. Buddy is snoozling on Roy's coat. That possum has it good. Makes me miss Rubes.

Roy nods over at Buddy. "Looks like a good idea, doesn't it. Taking a nap."

"How do you know he isn't just playing possum?"

Roy frowns. Then he smiles. "Well, goodness. She tells a joke."

I drag another tree to the sawhorses for trimming. It's the biggest so far, with long upper branches flying everywhere. The blasted thing will not behave. I try to shake it into submission, but only succeed in scraping up my arms, especially right near my bite. Awesome.

I'm still trying to prod it into the Net-o-nator when Roy comes over. "Lunchtime."

"I'll be right there."

"Can I give you a hand with that," Roy asks.

"No!" I say, a smidge forcefully. I'm making

involuntary sounds, like pooping grunts, as I fight the tree. "I got this."

Roy cocks his eyebrow like he isn't so sure. "Come on in when you're done. Kitchen's to the right."

"Okay." I wait for Roy to leave and then I jog around to the other side of the metal ring. I grab the trunk and pull. The freaking thing will not budge. I set one foot on the Net-o-nator and yank. The tree moves a little. Yes! More leverage. I lift my other foot off the ground and brace it on the other side of the Net-o-nator. I lean way back, nearly horizontal, and pull like crazy. Yank. *Eef.* Pull. *Arrh.* Tug. *Gah!*

The tree swishes through.

I flop onto my back like a dead fish.

The tree falls on top of me, squashing my boobs and knocking the wind out of me.

When I manage to breathe oxygen back into my lungs, I push the tree off and jump to my feet. I kick it, spin around and kick it again. "Ha. Take that. That's what you get for messing with me, tree." Karate chop. Slow motion Kung Fu destroyer goddess moves like the wind, devastates like a tornado.

I look up in time to see Roy on his front steps, watching me

    1. talking to myself

    2. pretending to jujitsu

    3. a tree.

Mother of God. The humiliation.

THE inside of Roy's house is straight out of the pages of *Better Homes & Gardens,* if it were actually called *Depressing Houses on Pretty Cool Tree Farms.* It's nearly empty. Extremely spare. Bleakly so. There is definitely no HGTV vibe. I wonder what his family's house in Brisben used to be like? The article had said his wife was a painter. Were there canvases on the walls? Did she have an artist's flair for decorating? Whatever it was like, it had to be nicer than this.

The front door opens into a living room in which—aside from a beat-up old recliner, a huge boxy TV, and a cardboard box of tattered blankets that must be for Buddy—there's nothing. No pictures, no other furniture, no decorations, no rugs, no curtains. Let alone throw pillows, Ikea accessories, or cut-flower arrangements.

Out of necessity, I use Roy's bathroom. It's not disgusting, but it is definitely no frills. One bath towel for the lone wolf. Over the sink, his medicine cabinet—hell yes, I snoop—holds precisely one tube of toothpaste, one toothbrush, one can of store-brand shaving cream, one yellow plastic razor, and one stick of Old Spice deodorant. Dang. Someone stage an intervention for this product-hog.

The kitchen is also straight-up utilitarian: a small electric stove, super old-fashioned refrigerator, dented sink, drooping shelf full of cans of soup, beans, tuna, and sardines. There's a small table, a folding chair, a plastic patio chair, and another box of blankets. Buddy is curled up in this one, his thick tail whorled into a curlicue over the edge. The coffee-maker and microwave are the only evidence that we have not, in fact, time-warped into a 1935 West Virginia mining town.

Roy clears junk mail off the table and gestures for me to sit. I plop down while he pulls the latch on his refrigerator. Man, he could sell that thing on eBay for big money. "Authentic Vintage 1950s Refrigerator ~ ~ ~ Still Works!"

"Coke or Pepsi," Roy asks.

Coke or Pepsi? Who buys both? Where is the man's brand loyalty?

"Coke, please." I open my lunch bag. PB&J never looked so good.

Roy hands me a can of Coke and sets another one on the table. From the fridge, he grabs a bag of bread, a jar of peanut butter, and a plastic squeeze-bear of honey.

"Thanks." I pop open my soda and sip while Roy dips a knife into the peanut butter, hardened from the cold, and mashes it onto a slice of bread. He dribbles honey over the peanut buttered slices. PB&H: the combination had heretofore not occurred to me. Most interesting. Looks yummy. Then again a baby harp seal straight from the endangered species menu would look good to me right now. I'm slightly ravenous.

We eat, quiet except for the smacking of sandwiches and the slurping of Coke.

"Want some cookie?" I take one out of my bag. "I make them really huge."

Roy looks hesitant. I bend the cookie until it breaks and set half on the table next to his Coke. "They're pretty good, if I do say so myself. I bake them mostly so I can eat the dough. Usually I can't get rid of all the cookies in time for the next batch."

Roy holds his part of the cookie up, turning it over to inspect it. "In that case, I'd be helping you out."

"You really would."

He takes a bite. And another. I have a convert on my hands. We wash down more cookie with another Coke.

"I can drink Pepsi next time. I'm not picky." Actually, I am all kinds of picky, but I'm trying to grow here, people. "And I can bring more cookies."

"It's a deal."

I start to help Roy clean up, but he motions at me to sit back down. "Nothing much to do," he says. "You just set."

He rinses our empty Coke cans and puts them in a paper bag. I watch him until I finally work up the nerve to ask the question that has been floating around my brain. I clear my throat. Why am I so nervous? "Um, Roy? Can I ask you a question?"

He wipes his hands on a grimy dishtowel and leans back against the sink. "You can ask. Won't guarantee an answer."

Harsh. Way to put a lady at ease there, cowboy. "I don't mean to be nosey," I say, "but...how did you end up with Buddy for a pet? I mean, not to be rude, he seems sweet and all. But I haven't seen a lot of..." I kind of taper off, not wanting to insult the man's possum. (That sounds bad.)

"Found him when he was little. Hurt on the side of the road. His mom and the other pups were already dead. I brought him home, fed him milk, fixed him up. Tried to set him loose but the little feller just kept scuttling back up my leg."

Sounds like Ruby, minus the trying to set loose part. "He seems pretty content," I say, looking at him dozing in the box.

"Sure does. Plus he keeps the riffraff away."

Is he kidding? Buddy's a guard possum? What does he do, sleep you to death? "How? Does he bite?"

Roy shakes his head. "More that it takes a certain kind of person to come up and chitchat with a man who's got a possum on his belt."

So he's weird Captain Possum on purpose. Interesting.

Roy's looking at me. "That all you wanted to ask."

Busted. "I did have another question." *Actually, Roy, there's so much I want to ask you that I could launch into a full-scale interrogation: How can you deal with the violent deaths of people you love? How do you keep going? Do you blame yourself? Do you ever expect to love anyone ever again? What's the point of going on?* And a bunch of other questions I'm way too chickenshit to ask.

"Go on then." His tone is matter-of-fact, but not irritated. It's more like *let's get your questions out of the way so we can get on with things.*

"Well, your garage? You asked me what I thought of the stuff on the pegboards. But then you didn't say anything about it."

Roy swishes the dishtowel onto his shoulder. "Uh- huh."

I give a smile that quickly devolves into rubbing my chapped lips together. My Burt's Bees lip balm isn't quite cutting it in today's outdoorsman/lumberjack scenario.

Roy sighs and pats his thigh. Buddy stirs in his box, scuttles over, and climbs his leg.

Roy shifts so Buddy can dangle. "Not something I talk about too much..."

Then why did you ask me what I made of it? "Oh, okay. I understand."

"Wasn't finished." He taps Buddy's tail, which seems to be some sort of I'm Pondering What To Say habit. "This isn't...what I mean to say...I get the feeling you can be trusted. Despite the circumstances of your employ." He blows out a breath. "I keep those things as reminders. From my work."

Okay. That clarifies everything.

I wait for him to elaborate.

Guess what? He doesn't.

Buddy scuttles down Roy's leg. He makes it halfway back to the box of blankets, then stops, cocks his head, and makes this bizarre *urrp* noise, like a squeak/burp/hiccup/cough combo. Roy chuckles. "Guess he's telling us it's time to get back to work. What say we muster trees."

"Sounds good." Because I was *born* to muster trees. Pretty sure. If muster means what it sounds like it means.

🌳 🌳 🌳

At 3:37, when Jeremy finally comes up the driveway, I stagger to the car. I almost don't make it, I swear. In my whole life, I've never been so tired. But not once—not once—did I complain, bitch, whine, or moan. Go me.

"Worked hard today," Roy says, surveying the trees propped against the garage. "Say a couple more days like this, we'll be square and then some."

Fantastic news. Fan. Ta. Stic. News.

"What say tomorrow. Same time." Roy hands me a piece of paper with his phone number. "Should have given you this yesterday. In case plans change."

"Okay. Thanks." I hand him my safety glasses and earplugs and peel off the work gloves he lent me. For some reason I feel shy again. "Um, see you tomorrow."

"Yep." He goes back to work.

Really, he should scale back on such long, sappy goodbyes. The sentimental bastard.

I climb into the car and sink deep into the seat as Jeremy maneuvers down the driveway. The music blares.

"Can we turn it down?" I ask/yell. "Just this once?"

Jeremy turns it down. I close my eyes. I am so so so so so so tired. But for the first time in a long time, I'm content. Tonight I'll sleep. Not just sleep, but Sleep The Sleep Of The Righteous, as Dad would say.

"The deal's off."

"What?" I open my eyes.

"I'm not driving you up here any more."

"Are you freaking kidding me? We had a deal."

"No longer."

"Fine. Be an ass. I'll make your life miserable. And I'll use the internet twenty-four seven. I'll tell Mom and Dad I have essays I need to type—"

"No you won't."

"I won't?"

He shakes his head and smiles like a smug turd. "Realizations came to me today, when Mom said something about you raising money at the dance thing."

"You didn't tell her!?"

"Not yet. That's my point. I've got leverage now. I'm not giving you any more rides *and* you'll do my chores *and* I get the computer whenever I want, however long I want it, or I'll tell Mom and Dad what you're up to."

My cheeks burn hot, then icy. This is a new low for my brother. Yes, he loves being a supreme irritation. But this—this is diabolical.

"You're such an…" I stop, take a breath. What about Stenn? Ruby? Driving? If Mom and Dad find out…I take another breath. "Please, Jeremy. I need your help. If I can't get a ride, I…"

"Not my problem." He starts to crank up the music.

"Why do you hate me so much? What did I ever do to you?"

He looks at me. "You mean besides ruining our family?"

My heart flops in my chest. "Ruining our…what do you mean?" It's nearly a whisper.

"Your friend died, but that's no excuse. You're a supreme bitch. All Mom and Dad ever talk about now is you. What a pain in the ass you are." He drums the steering wheel. "Remember when they didn't scream all the time? When everything wasn't always about you?"

Do I remember that? Oh, vaguely.

Tears are threatening to fall. What a shocker. "Please," is all I can say.

"Not my problem. Find another way up here. I have a splendid idea: Why don't you ask Mom and Dad for a ride?"

I'm so not the only one in the family with a snark problem.

CHAPTER 21

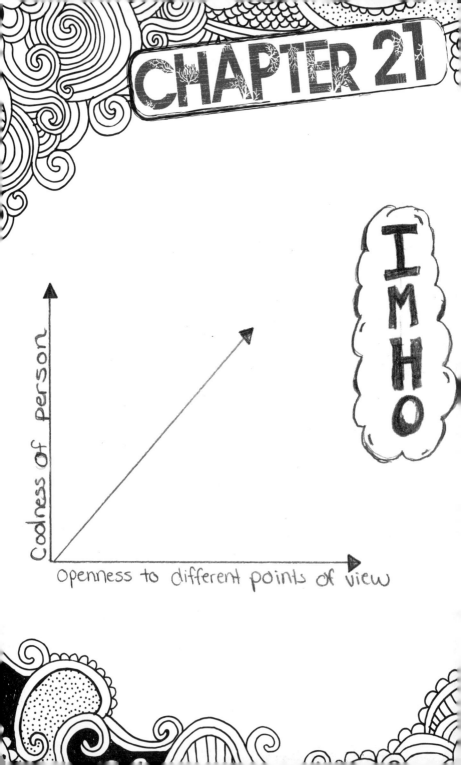

IMHO

Coolness of person (y-axis) vs. Openness to different points of view (x-axis)

AS a wronged sister and generally pissed-off teenager, it is my duty to execute a Class-A Car Door Slam when Jeremy drops me back at the Y, even though it hurts my aching bicep noodles to do so. I go inside and duck into the locker room. Thirty seconds later, Rosemary appears with some other sweaty girls. She hugs me, even though she's drenched. "My mom texted," she says. "She just got here, so we should go."

In the car, Rosemary and I discuss the Salsa-Thon. Because that's where we both were all day. When I get home, I drag myself up to my room and text Stenn to tell him I survived my first day of work. Then I curl up with Ruby and fall sleep. I pass it off as Salsa exhaustion.

Later, Rosemary calls to fill in some details of the Salsa-Thon and ask if I want to go out.

No, I do not want to go out. I want to potato on the couch with Rubes for the night, but

(1) There's the whole turning over a new leaf thing.
(2) I owe her for covering for me.
(3) I owe her. That counts twice.

Apparently my mom called the Y—not my cell phone, but the actual YMCA front desk—to check up on me. How awesome to be so trusted. Rosemary took the phone and handled it like a pro. Mom bought it completely, probably due to her manic elation that someone wants to be friends with me.

So. I'm going out. Without Stenn and without Ruby. I shower and put on my favorite jeans and sweater—cute but not overtly boob-centric, so dudes might make eye contact, at least every once in a while. Also so I don't look like I'm trying to look hot while Stenn's gone. The cat's away but the mice won't play, and all that.

Dad drives me to Rosemary's, asking the requisite questions about the Salsa-Thon. I tell him it was pretty good. Don't want to sound suspicious with too many details.

"Hm. Was it cold at the Y?" he asks.

"Why?"

He shrugs, too innocently. "Just wondering. You seemed quite chilled when you got home."

I try to sound blasé. "Oh, probably just from being out in the cold, you know, on the way home after all the sweating and dancing and everything." *Oh sweet cheezus, please do not check with Ms. Gliss directly.*

He eyes me. "Uh-huh. Probably."

Dad tips the Jeep's blinker, and turns into a driveway, and almost smashes into a gigantor orange dump truck and a hunormous yellow snowplow.

I look at the address in my phone. "Is this right?"

"Sure," Dad says, shifting into park. "Ed—your friend's dad—is head of the Chenango County DOT."

"You know him?" Duh. My parents know everyone.

Dad nods. "I talk to him every time it snows. He helps me decide whether to cancel school."

Holy guano, Batman! My jaw drops. This is shocking information. Shocking! My entire life I've tried to figure out Dad's algorithm for canceling school. Even Jeremy and his friends are devoted to the cause. The rumor is that it has something to do with backing his Jeep out of our driveway. A skid of greater than five inches = no school. And while it's true that sometimes he hops in the Jeep before he declares a snow day, that can't be all of it. No way. His OCD fascination with The Weather Channel, along with mysterious phone calls at the butt crack of dawn, hints at a more complicated decision-making system. But whatever it is, it's in the vault. This is the most he's ever said about it, ever.

Dad is chuckling. "Remember last December when we got a foot and a half of snow overnight?"

Dumbstruck. I am dumbstruck.

"Poor Ed got stuck in a snowbank somewhere. I had to talk to Rosemary instead. Seems like a real sweet girl." Dad makes a face. "I mean, a cool girl. No, I mean rad?"

"Please. Stop the madness. You are a dad. Whatever coolness you once possessed is gone forever."

"Not so. You better believe, back in the day, I used to be hot stuff."

"Let it go, Dad."

"I was! Ask your mother."

"I'm sure you were cool. No, I mean rad."

"Why are you so skeptical? Is it so hard to believe?"

"The math doesn't pan out."

"What math doesn't pan out?"

"It does not compute. I'll walk you through it, but only this once, so pay attention. Let's say 15 percent—even 20 percent, and that's being generous—of any given high school population is actually cool. Right? Yet 100 percent of parents claim to have held that status. Even if you factor in the adults who aren't parents, it doesn't hold water. Statistically."

Dad gives a goofy smile. "You should put that mind to work on your trigonometry, you know. And chemistry. And all your other studies."

"Wow, I've never heard that before." Knee jerk response. But I add, "I kicked butt on my test this week."

"I heard." He starts to fidget with the heat controls. "Okay, kiddo. Give us a call when you need a ride home."

"Okay." I open the door.

When he looks up from the dashboard, his eyes are heavy with emotion. It's a classic Meaningful Parental Moment look. And it doesn't take a rocket scientist to know it's because this is the first time I've been over to someone's house, beside Stenn's, SJD.

I wonder if Dad feels guilty about Jamie dying. Because it happened at school and, as he always says, everything that happens in the Norwich School District is ultimately his responsibility.

Why haven't I thought about it until now? He must. Dad must feel some guilt, even though it wasn't his fault at all. Those folding walls were there long before he became superintendent.

There's even some lingering legal talk about the walls. Every now and then, I overhear him talking to Mom about a class action lawsuit. At first, I thought it meant that the Clearys were going to sue the school—or sue Dad!—but then I looked up what it means. It means they're trying to make it the wall company's fault. Which it kind of *is*, but what's done is done at this point. No court can bring my Jamie back.

I feel bad for him, so I say, "Thanks for the ride. And thanks again for letting me do the Salsa-Thon." Damn it. Why did I have to bring that up?

He tilts his head, all wry. "About that. Good thinking, asking me first. Your mom told me about your big fight over working at Roy's tree farm."

Outwardly I shrug, but inside, an electric jolt shoots through me. The way he said Roy's name makes it sound like they're buddies. Great. He's buds with Rosemary's dad *and* Roy.

Dad cuts into my thoughts. "She's not the boss of everything, you know. Your mother's not the sole arbiter in the family."

"Um, have you met her?"

He laughs. "Well. She's not the *sole* arbiter."

Where is the man going with this? It's weird.

"I'm just putting that out there," he says. "Some of the decisions she makes...I might not necessarily agree with."

"Then why don't you veto?"

"One rule of power: the less you use it, the more you have. Keeps people off-balance."

"So basically you like to be completely random about stepping in. Sweet."

He laughs a little too hard. "Sometimes, with your mother, it pays to bide your time." There's hint of something in his voice. Mischief? Wistfulness? The man is an enigma. "Other things, like your grades and school—we're on the same page on those. And you should be too, young lady."

I roll my eyes.

"But there are times when she might need to see who wears the cowboy boots in the family."

"Gross."

"These boots are made for walkin'..."

I can't quite feed him the line, but I do eke out a smile.

It's like he *wants* me to triangulate them. He wants me to drive a wedge between him and Mom on decision-making matters? More often than I already do? Is he saying that if I'd gone to him first, he would have let me work for Roy? Because that seems to be what he's saying. Or is he manipulating me, trying to play Good Cop, with Mom as Bad Cop? Either way, his behavior is unprecedented. And bizarre.

Dad narrows his eyes and says, "Is there anything you'd like to ask me? Because I might be able to help you. Unless you're sneaking around and lying to us, in which case…"

It's a trap! Take evasive action!

"Nope. I'm good," I'm out of the Jeep and up to Rosemary's front door faster than you can say Forest Moon of Endor.

Rosemary ushers me in and leads the way upstairs. "It's totally humiliating," she says about the dump truck and snowplow. "Like we need the whole Department of Transportation fleet at our house? Ugh. We're already podunk enough without those things parked in our driveway."

Upstairs, Rosemary leads me down a carpeted hallway. She opens a door on the right. "Ta da! Home, sweet home."

Holy fuchsia! The pink, it burns my eyes. And the room has a theme: I Am a Dancer. With Lots of Friends. Worn-out ballet shoes by the mirror, lots of photos in "Friends Forever!" frames. Her bedspread, carpet, wallpaper: peony, fuchsia, pale rose. Ballerina tutu-ed teddy bears on her bed. Good gravy.

After scooping a pile of clothes from the middle of the floor to a basket, Rosemary unzips, steps out of her jeans, and puts on a different pair, then turns around to look in the mirror. "Do these make my butt look big?"

"No," I say without looking up from the stack of gossip magazines on her dresser. It's a library of glossy, gossipy *Not What's Truly Important In Life,* but it's sucking me in.

Rosemary sighs, then pulls off the jeans. "Nothing looks right. Let me try yours?"

I go rigid.

Her question sucks the warmth out of my body. I try to cover by turning the page of a magazine. No one has ever asked for the pants on my body. And nobody has tried on any of my jeans SJD.

Rosemary senses something's wrong. "I'm sorry! I'm shameless, a total clothes whore. My friends are always yelling at me for it."

"Where are they tonight?" I ask, trying to sound non-freaked-out.

She shrugs, "Away game. Michelle, Andrea, and Anna are all on Cheer Squad this year. They want me to join, but I have—"

"Dance."

"Yeah. I think that's why Ms. Gliss hates me so much, because I choose dance instead of cheering. Anyhoo. Your jeans are probably too small, anyway. You're tiny. I'll be right back. I'm going to check the dryer for other pairs." She swishes out of the room.

I rub my temples and sit down on her bed. Crap. I hadn't meant to dork out, but the whole jeans-sharing thing—the last time I did it was with James. The night before the accident.

She was wearing my jeans when she died.

She was all, "Let me try yours." Trying to get noticed by her crush, Rajas, a Ninja senior, which necessitated a good outfit. I handed her my biggest pair and she shot me that look of hers, equal parts annoyed and grateful. She tugged them on and groaned like an elephant in labor. "I got some junk in my trunk."

"You are not fat." My mantra to her. "You are bootylicious."

"Whatever, Miss I'm-Barbie-I-Would-Look-Hot-In-A-Potato-Sack."

"You're deluded. Unless it's my cellulite that makes me look like I have cellulite."

"Cry me a river. Size two cellulite." She inspected her butt from another angle, sighing miserably.

"I mean it!" I turned her around to face the mirror. "You are gorgeous, and you have a great can. And even if Rajas was available—which he's not, I am obligated to remind you—he isn't worthy of my Jamie."

We stood there, looking at our intertwined reflections.

Jamie finally relented. "Maybe."

It was a major victory.

"No maybe about it. Your pooper is super." I hugged her.

Because I used to be a hugger.

Damn. When will thinking about Jamie not make my heart hurt and my throat ache? When will it not cause actual physical pain? And when will it not freeze me out of social situations like a total head case?

No wonder I'm a social dropout.

I lie back and stare at Rosemary's ceiling.

Rosemary appears in the doorway with a laundry basket of jeans. She sets it on her bed. "Are you okay? You seemed a little freaked out."

I hold my breath, waiting. She's going to tell me I'll feel better if I go home. And she's probably right. I do miss Ruby. "I'm sorry," I say. "It's..." Ugh. How can I explain without weirding her out?

"Jamie, right? You got sad again?"

I nod.

She sighs. "We went to St. Bart's preschool together. I never knew her or Emmett that well, but I always thought they both seemed cool." It sounds genuine.

"Jamie thought you were cool, too." It's true.

"Is it hard for you to be here? I mean, with me?"

"It's different. But good?" Not sure who I'm trying to convince. "It's just that...I miss Jamie." It sounds simple, but it feels profound. To actually say it.

"Well, der! You're supposed to *not* miss her? She was your best friend. If you weren't sad all the time, it would only mean that you're some sort of ice cold bee-yotch."

I look at her. "You really don't mince words, do you? I mean, tell me what you really think."

She laughs. "I'll try not to be so subtle next time."

I pick up a pair of her jeans and look at the tag. We wear the same size.

"Wait! Not those!" Rosemary says. "I have the perfect pair for you." She dives into the clothes basket, flinging jeans all over the room.

I pull off my jeans, thanking the Lords of Kobol that I am not wearing granny panties. When Stenn's away at school, I don't think about what undies I'm wearing.

I pull Rosemary's jeans on. They are still warm from the dryer and so low-rise that if I bend too much, I'll flash some coin slot, but they fit. They fit.

And now I'm crying.

"Oh my God! What's wrong?"

I am a freak. I sit down on the bed and hide my face. "Nothing."

Rosemary makes some kind of tooth-sucking sound. "That is the crappiest answer, ever. Obviously, it's not nothing."

"You don't want to hear it. I've been enough of a pain in the ass already."

She makes an exasperated noise. "You know how I don't mince words? Well listen up. You have to give people a chance. Don't shut down like that. It's kind of insulting. You think I won't understand? Or can't handle it?"

Yes, and yes. "No, it's nothing like that."

"Then lay it on me already." The bed jiggles as she sits.

I sigh. Fine. She asked for it. "Jeremy won't give me a ride to Roy's anymore, and—"

"For work? Why not?"

"Because he's evil, and I can't ask my parents because—"

"Your mom already said no."

I nod. "And I have to work for Roy or he'll tell my parents I was trespassing up there and if they find out I was sneaking out they'll take Ruby away and stop me from seeing Stenn..." I explain the whole thing.

"That gorgeous creature!" she says about Ruby. Or maybe Stenn. She pauses, thinking. "Stenn can drive you when he gets home for Thanksgiving break, right?"

"If I'm still working by then. But that's not until—"

"I wasn't finished. I was going to say—"

"Before I rudely interrupted—"

"Yeah, which I would never do."

"Clearly."

"Clearly," she smiles. "I was going to say: Have you asked Roy if he could give you a ride? Pick you up from the Y in the morning?"

I give my head a little shake, trying to process her question. "I can't."

"Why not?"

ose. "You don't ask
ob."

, right? Have I mentioned
a chance?"

e says no?"

im, what if he says yes? Explain the situation and tell him it's temporary. You know his phone number, right?"

"Yeah."

"So get out your phone and call him."

I obey. Roy answers on the third ring. Damn it. Why is it that every time you want voice mail, the person answers, and every time you want the person, it goes to voice mail? His gruff voice says, "Roy Showalter."

"Er, Roy? It's me. Sarah."

"Yep."

I explain the situation while Rosemary stares at me, hopping around like she is literally on pins and needles. It's not a long conversation; soon enough I'm pressing the End Call button.

"Well?" Rosemary asks.

"He said he'll pick me up at the Y. He was pretty nice about it."

"Then why don't you look happy?"

"He said it'll only be for the morning and we'll have to 'work something out' for the rest of the time."

"What does that mean?"

"I have no idea."

Nano's is bustling when Rosemary and I walk in. Hot air blasts from the pizza ovens and we immediately peel off our coats, mittens, and scarves. The soccer team has claimed the booths in back; other tables are bursting with young families, more Youth of Today, and a few bewildered senior citizens who seem to be regretting their decision to go out.

I don't know why I'm here. I mean, I know why I'm here—new leaf and owing Rosemary and all—but we are here to meet up with her boyfriend. Can you say *third wheel*?

The whole team is stoked for their upcoming tournament. Rich From The Party is overfilling his teammates' cups from a pitcher of Coke. Exactly what these guys need right now: more sugar and caffeination. There's no room to sit, but Rosemary manages a one-cheek sneak next to Ron. I, on the other hand, continue to stand in the aisle like a dweeb. There isn't anyone I know well enough to cheek-sneak or lap-sit.

Where's Emmett? Any level of unspoken tension with him is better than standing here in the aisle flying my freak flag. Rosemary notices me scanning the restaurant. She doesn't miss much, I have to give her that. She says something into Ron's ear. He eyes her suspiciously, then seems to figure out why she's asking. "Emmett went out back a little while ago," Ron shouts to me over the din.

"I'm going to say hi," I tell Rosemary.

"Want me to come with?"

"No, it's fine."

"Okay," she smiles. There's way too much grin in her smile. "We'll save you some slices." Which is a nice idea, but doesn't seem likely with this crowd.

I go past the restrooms, out the back door into the cold, and spot Emmett right away. He's sitting on a concrete bumper in the parking lot. I walk over but he doesn't look up until I clear my throat. "Hi."

He fumbles with something, sticks it under his coat.

"Shooting heroin? Or checking your blood sugar? I'm hoping it's the first one."

He looks up and smiles, like he's relieved it's me. Just little ol' me.

I sit down—I'm so sore from working, even my butt hurts—and he pulls out his little computery thing to finish the test.

"How's everything going with that?" I ask. It's a stupid, vague way to say it, but I do want to know.

Emmett shrugs. His little contraption beeps. He frowns at it and tucks it into his jacket. "Okay. Kind of up and down."

I let it go. If he wants to tell me more, he will. After a while I say, "Want to go for a walk?"

Emmett scrunches up his face like it's a horrendously tough decision.

"Come on," I say. "I was in there for fifteen seconds and that was sixteen seconds too long."

He stands. To my surprise, he holds out his hand to help me up.

We walk through the parking lots that are strung together behind Nano's and the other shops on Broad Street. We cross West Main and meander through the park in front of the courthouse. Eventually we sit down on a bench to watch the dribble of traffic on Broad.

It's a somewhat amiable silence—not as uncomfortable as I would have predicted. I'm starting to appreciate the company of these strong, silent types: Roy, Emmett. They don't demand a lot.

"Ready for your games tomorrow?" I ask.

Emmett nods. Really, you can't shut him up.

"That game was great the other day. You were great." Great, great, everything's great.

Emmett glances over at me, then back toward the street. He smiles a little. "Thanks."

"Well you were. Kicking ass and taking names." I bob and weave to reenact his performance.

"I meant, thank you for coming."

"Oh. Sure. I'm glad I did. I saw your folks there."

Emmett reaches down and picks a blade of grass. He twirls it between his thumb and forefinger. "They fight."

Sweet. I'm so glad I brought it up: the not-sitting-together parents. Maybe I should kick him in the nuts while I'm at it. "Since Jamie died?" My stomach flip-flops, saying this.

Emmett nods and peels the blade of grass into two thin strands. "They're talking about a trial separation."

"No. Really?" That is terrible news. But it makes sense, in a twisted, depressing way. Some pieces fall into place. Like Emmett being at the Pig Farm Party Shack. Are his folks so self-absorbed and unhappy that they've slacked off in the parenting department? Wouldn't it make more sense for them to get super overprotective—even more than before?

Whatever. I'm pissed. They're slacking on parenting, and they're going to be separating? They're basically abandoning him. As opposed to my parents, who won't get off my back. Which, to be real about it, is better than abandonment.

Emmett is staring at the gazebo across the street.

We sit a long time, not really knowing what to say. Me, at least—I don't know what to say. Then we both kind of look at each other and, without speaking, make our way back to Nano's.

As I open the restaurant's back door, Emmett seems to hesitate, like he doesn't want to go back in.

"Hey?" I say. "Do me a favor and walk me home?"

Seeming to brighten, Emmett nods.

"Wait here a sec. Let me tell Rosemary, so she

doesn't worry that I've completely disappeared."

Rosemary makes an incredulous face when I tell her I'm leaving with Emmett. "Should Stenn be worried?"

"That's crazy. It's Emmett," I say.

"Yeah! *Hot* Emmett. *Cool* Emmett."

"How about he's-like-a-brother-to-me Emmett." From the look on her face, she's not buying it.

She stands to give me a good-night hug. What can I do? I can't leave the girl hanging. I hug her back. "I'll wash your jeans and bring them in the morning," I say into her hair.

"No hurry," she says, de-hugging but still staying close. "They look great on you. Besides, I have your Sevens. *Mwahaha.*"

"Your evil laugh."

"Very good!" she smiles. "See you in the morning."

I call my parents when I'm back outside, to tell them I'm walking home. And not to worry, because Emmett is walking with me. Parents like to drill that into your head: if you're a girl, don't walk alone at night, ever. As if there's ever been a mugging in my town.

Emmett and I are halfway to my house before he speaks. He doesn't look at me and doesn't slow his pace.

"Jamie's birthday's coming up," he says. His words freeze into the cold air in front of us; we walk right through them.

"It's your birthday, too. The big sixteen." I've been wondering if he's been thinking about it. But duh. Of course he has. "You doing the traditional day?" The traditional Cleary Get Signed Out Of School At Noon And Go Get A U-Cut Christmas Tree And A Sugar-Free Ice Cream Cake. (It changed to sugar-free five years ago, when Emmett was diagnosed. Morbidly, we all kept waiting for Jamie to become diabetic, too. But it never happened.)

Emmett's pace slows but he's still walking pretty fast. He shrugs. "Don't know."

"Haven't your folks said anything? About making plans?"

He shakes his head.

Now I truly want to kick their asses. "You should remind them. It's your birthday, for God's sake. You didn't die." Somebody needs to smack me.

"They'd fight the whole time, anyway."

We stop to wait for a car before crossing Hayes Street. The driver slows and waves us across.

"Well, you and I could go," I suggest. "We could get someone to drive us to Dale's U-Cut." If it's still there. I haven't been there in years. Roy should totally open his place up to DIYers. Save himself—and me—a ton of work, and still make money.

Emmett shakes his head again. "It's a school day."

"So we'll skip school. Stenn can drive us. He'll be home for winter break by then."

"Thanks. Seriously, thanks. But no. One more detention and I'll get suspended."

This is more news. "What, you're a big trouble-maker now?"

Emmett shrugs like it isn't a big deal. "Whatever. Some things don't seem as important—"

"As they did before."

"Yeah."

"I know what you mean. The things people get all worked up over, who cares? They're not the real things in life. The important things." I can't believe the things I used to care about: being a Ninja, expensive jeans, perfect hair, perfect makeup. *Pfffft.* It was all image and superficiality. But what's actually important is how you feel about people. And being here for each other. It's not about appearances anymore, it's about what's real. It's about relationships with people (and dogs) you love. And who love you back. I know this now, SJD. I know it in the rational parts of my brain but it hasn't passed through all the filters into the Core Knowledge Center Of My Being. Yet.

But that's also what's terrifying. Because you can lose those people at the drop of a hat. Or the smush of a wall.

We're in front of my house when Emmett says, "Sarah, can I ask you something?"

My stomach slips out of my body and slaps onto the sidewalk. Of course I knew this was coming.

And there's still no chance I can answer. Eight months after it happened, I'm just now starting to be able to think about it without going into a total panic attack. There is no way I can speak the words. Zero chance.

I lick my lips, chapping them more. "You can ask, but I can't guarantee I'll answer."

Emmett looks confused.

"Sorry. It's something a friend of mine says. Um, yeah. Ask away." I try to sound breezy. Breezy, for crying out loud!

I wait. It's evil of me, but I don't help him by prompting. I make him get the words out himself.

"Do you…," he manages to say, "do you still have the locket?"

The what? I slump onto my porch stairs in a puddle of relief. I loosen my scarf and pull my locket out from under my sweater. It glints in the porch light.

Emmett sits next to me, asking with his eyes if he can touch my necklace. I nod.

Mesmerized. It's a strong word. But it's the only way to describe the way Emmett looks as he holds my locket. From his expression, I can tell that he hasn't seen either part of our lockets since Jamie died. Poor kid. I don't know what I'd do without it. As steeped in grief and guilt and loss as it is, my necklace is still a piece of Jamie that's with me all the time. Does Emmett have something like that? He must.

But from the look in his eyes, maybe he doesn't.

Emmett is so close that I can feel the warm puffs of his breath. I wonder: Did he see Jamie after the accident? Did he have a chance to say goodbye? In the hospital, maybe? Did they take her there, even though they pronounced her dead at school? Or did she go to the morgue? Or straight to the funeral home? I don't know how those things work.

I didn't have a chance to say goodbye, and I was *there*. The last sight I had of Jamie, she was stooped over, trying to yank her necklace free of the wall hinge. And then she disappeared.

Jamie's calling hours and funeral were closed-casket. I guess because her body was mangled from the accident. Not that it's something you can ask. *Hey, Mr. and Mrs. Cleary? Can I open the coffin so I can see James one more time? Maybe climb in there and give her a hug? Pretty please?*

I was screaming on the inside. I wanted so badly to throw the coffin open, just for a moment, so I could give Jamie one last hug. I honestly didn't care what she looked like, how damaged her body might have been. It was still Jamie. Her essence, or spirit, or soul—I don't know what to call it—had probably left her body that moment in the gym. But what if it hadn't? I got the feeling, in the funeral home, and then at the church, and then in the cemetery, that Jamie was nearby. Hopefully floating around—not trapped in the casket; that thought is unbearable.

Emmett's voice tumbles out into the night, interrupting my thoughts. "This is your part," he says. The locket lies in his palm, its long chain hanging slack from my neck.

"Right."

He closes his fist around the locket. "If this is yours, where's Jamie's?"

"Your parents buried it with her. Didn't they?"

Emmett shakes his head, slowly.

"Maybe they kept it for themselves?" I ask.

His bottom lip comes unstuck from the top. It looks as chapped as mine. "No."

This is every kind of messed up. It makes no sense. Jamie's mom and dad knew how important her locket was to her. They had to. She died getting that necklace! "Are you sure?" I ask.

He nods, moving his head up and down but holding his gaze steady in mine. "They didn't even realize she still wore it."

"You asked?"

"Yeah. They had to pick out clothes for her. You know, for the funeral home. To be buried in."

"But you asked about the locket, specifically?"

"Yes! I was like, 'Are you going to bury her with the locket?'"

"What did they say?"

"They didn't know what I was talking about."

I shake my head. They must have known she was looking for a necklace when she died; I told the cops that much. How could they not realize it was her locket? It's crazy how parents can *not* know so much. I take a deep breath to try to make sense of all this. The locket is the whole reason Jamie ceased to exist, and now it's like it doesn't exist either—never existed in the first place.

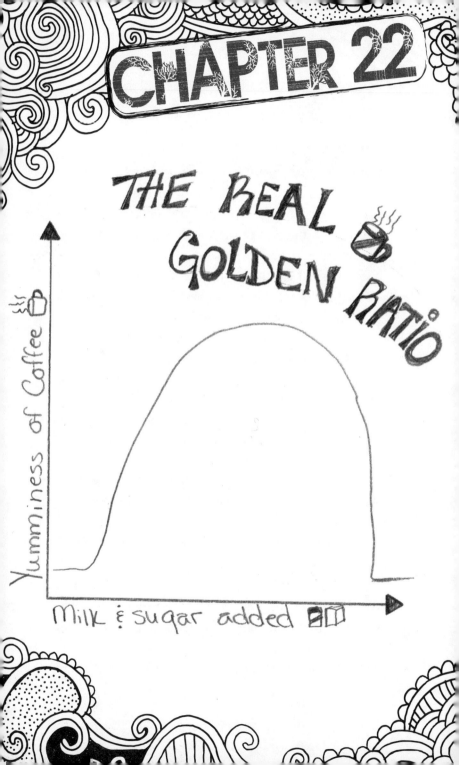

SATURDAY morning, Rosemary's mom drops us off at the YMCA again. After she leaves, I go back out. For her part, Rosemary's tired and pretty much over the whole extra-credit thing. An entire weekend of salsa dancing does seem like a lot of effort to appease one grumpy gym teacher.

Roy picks me up in the parking lot and doesn't stop talking the whole way to his place. Ha. Kidding. We ride without a lot of conversation. And by a lot, I mean any. He's as much of a morning talker as I am.

Even after busting ass yesterday, there's still a ton to do. Every muscle and tendon and ligament and joint and even the freaking marrow in my bones is so sore that I involuntarily groan every time I move. But I refuse to complain. In spoken words, at least.

Roy's quietness suits me fine. We've traveled from Awkwardville into Companionable Silence Territory. We get to his place, and get to work. While I net and drag and bikini wax the trees, I think about Emmett, and Jamie's locket. (When I use the chainsaw, I don't think about anything but not cutting myself in half.) And I wonder how much trouble Emmett is really getting into. It can't be that bad if he's still allowed on the soccer team; he can't be flunking out. But are his parents really headed for divorce? And also the tiny detail of him wanting to know how Jamie died. I don't know much, but I know this: just because he hasn't asked again doesn't mean it's not on his mind.

And then there's Stenn. He's coming home for Thanksgiving and a long break in a few days. Which I'm happy about. Really, really happy about. But that brings up the whole sex thing, as in, when are we going to have it? Plus, Stenn's being stingier than usual about his texts and phone calls. Which is probably all in my head, but it's not lost on me that he's around other girls, some of whom are evidently quite cool and down-to-earth. And I can be a bit of a handful. Sometimes.

Then there are the minor additional worries about Jeremy breaking our deal, Dad being cryptic, and Mom still holding her grudge. Not to mention that I'm physically exhausted, which I'm pretty sure I've already mentioned.

So after two hours of steady, sweaty work, I drag my tired schnookus over to Roy to suggest a coffee break. I've come prepared this time, with a big thermos of coffee and lots of cookies. Plus multiple sandwiches for lunch.

"Want to take five?" I ask Roy.

He looks stymied. Like I've asked him to sketch the schematics of a nuclear reactor.

"You know, a coffee break? With treats?" I wave the bag of cookies.

"Oh. Sure." He goes to the garage and comes

back with two tall white plastic buckets, which he sets upside down for us to sit on. Buddy curls into a ball on the ground between us. I pour some coffee into the thermos cap for Roy, and sip mine straight from the bottle. He takes a bite of cookie, a swig of coffee—and chokes.

"Are you okay! What's wrong?"

"The coffee. My goodness, that is sweet."

"Yes. I like it to taste like coffee ice cream. Except hot."

"Mission accomplished," he says, standing up. "Got my own inside."

I pick up the thermos cap after he goes into the house. Should I toss the coffee onto the ground? It's too tasty. And I'm willing to bet Roy doesn't have mono or herpes, so I pour every drop of the precious fluid back into my thermos. Roy comes back with a chipped mug of black coffee. He settles onto the bucket and bites his cookie. We don't talk. We eat. And I marvel at the unmitigated genius of whoever first combined caffeine and refined sugar and chocolate and carbohydrates. That person deserves a recurring Nobel Prize.

I eat another cookie. And one more after that. I'm fairly confident that lumberjacking burns one trillion calories per hour.

Way too soon, Roy stands. "Well, got more that needs doing. Let's see. Need to refill the washtubs— have to empty them nightly or they freeze solid— and finish felling and readying. Also got to tally up the inventory." He rubs his chin and looks around as if he's trying to prioritize tasks.

I finish my third cookie, pull my—Roy's—work gloves on. "How about I keep doing what I'm doing so you don't have to spend your time teaching me new things. And I can fill the washtubs."

"Makes sense. Hose is in the garage. Tap's over there," he points to a faucet near the front steps. He asks, "You aren't getting too tired out."

Holy hell YES I am too tired out. "I'm all right. Let's git 'er done."

He tilts his head, nods once. It looks like approval. It's a small gesture, but it has a huge effect on me. I am filled with an insane amount of pride.

Roy pats his leg and Buddy scampers up and assumes the old belt-hang. He flashes his nippy teeth and beady eyes. What with his gray patchy fur and huge, skinless rattail, he's as cute as a button. But he keeps Roy good company, and I'm glad for that. Han Solo has Chewbacca, I have Ruby, and Roy has Buddy.

"We'll probably be finished up an hour or two after lunchtime," Roy says. "If we keep working steady."

"Okey doke." Did I just say *okey doke*?

So I keep Working Steady.

And along with learning

1. How ridiculously sore a body can get, and
2. How loud a chainsaw is, and
3. How to wrestle a Net-o-nator

I'm learning something else about physical work:

4. It gives the mind room to mosey. Meander in a less tweaked-out way. It's very different than lying in bed or spacing out during class. Somehow the work here helps make things transparent and more comprehensible. Ergo:

Hard work + physical exhaustion + being actually useful = a smidgeon of clarity.

Time passes, and we work, and it's really hard. And we go inside to warm up and eat lunch, and we talk about nothing much. I tell him about school and we talk a little bit about the weather—he tells me he trusts the predictions from *Farmer's Almanac* over The Weather Channel any day of the week— and then we go outside and get back to work.

At two, Roy comes over to me at the Net-o-nator and says we can stop. He looks at all the bundled trees and turns back to me. "I'd say we're square. Debt cleared."

"Really?" That is Great News. But why does it also make me sad?

He nods. "And then some." He puts his coat back on, and I do, too. Stop moving and your sweat chills quickly. I gather my things. And I realize why I'm sad: I really like it here. I really like this work. I like being useful, and it makes me feel strong, because I am strong when I'm doing this.

Roy clears his throat and says, "Sarah. You probably don't want to, but I'm wondering. Would you like to keep working here."

My cheeks flush with pleasure. Yes yes yes, I want to keep working here! That is, *if* I can move my body at all, ever again. And *if* I can get my parents to let me, because I don't want to risk losing Ruby and Stenn and driving. Which are pretty big *if*s.

"There are some things I need to work out, but yes. I'd like to."

He smiles. I smile. I say, "I'll be out of school for Thanksgiving vacation, and then of course there's after school and weekends. So I could help a lot, if you want." I hand Roy his work gloves, pull my red mittens on.

"You can help me set up the stand downtown."

My eyes go big. "You're setting up a stand?"

"Yep."

"I thought you were a...what's it called. A wholesaler."

"Cutting out the middle man this year."

"So you're going into retail. Selling them yourself?"

"Yep."

Sounds good to me. Selling trees will be a lot easier than cutting them down. Oh. Wait. No! My cover will be blown. How can I remain incognito in town? Wear a ski mask? Sunglasses and a fake mustache? My parental units will find me out for sure.

Crudmuffins. I try to think of solutions while Roy takes Buddy into the garage. He comes back *sans* possum.

"Well," Roy says. "What say we do some trail-blazing."

"Say what now?"

"Can't give you a ride everyday. Here," he sets a compass in the paw of my mitten.

"Are you serious?"

"From here, I believe your land is east-northeast."

"How do you know where I live?"

"Little thing called the phone book."

The phone book. How quaint. Anyway, he can't be serious. I need to get back to the Y, not My Land!

"Well, go on. Lead the way," he says.

He's serious.

We walk.

$$ \text{♀♀♀} $$

When Roy oh-so-politely suggests yet another course change after the zillionth tree branch whacks me across the face, I get the distinct impression that the compass is for my benefit alone. Roy seems like the kind of person who could find his way across the Himalayas with his eyes closed. And fashion a snare out of a shoelace while he's at it. And then rub some sticks together to start a fire. And make tea in a pot he whittled out of a pinecone.

Me, on the other hand… Well, between trying to

read the compass (a skill my one year of Brownies left me woefully unprepared for) and working out how to hide from my parents, bypass my house, and proceed to the Y, it's—*gah.* I look at the compass again and keep walking.

Roy ties those yellow plastic strips onto branches to mark the trail.

When the descent levels out, I pray to the compass gods that it means we are near my house.

Crick. Crack. Branches and twigs crash in front of us. Ruby! What a sight for sore eyes. My sweet ferocious girl.

She's tearing through the trees with a mole dangling in her teeth. She drops it at my feet, her almost completely healed tail whirling in circles. Another poor critter to bury.

"This must be your dog."

I nod, and swallow my fear of Roy's reaction, remembering what she did to his deer. "This is Ruby." I tell her to sit so she can make a good impression, and so I can properly introduce her to Roy.

"Do you know how to *shake*," he says to Rubes.

Ruby holds up her paw. Roy takes it in greeting.

You could knock me over with a feather. My dog never listens to anyone except me.

"Nice to meet you, Ruby. You're quite a hunter, aren't you."

"That was my fault! What happened the other night with the deer. I am so sorry. And Rubes didn't mean to…"

"Dog's only as good as its owner."

Wow. That is harsh.

He scratches his chin. "Looks like you've got a good dog here."

Again my cheeks flush. A compliment for Ruby, and me. I don't know him that well, but I think it would be out of character for Roy to veil an insult. The man might not spill his guts at the drop of a hat, but he's earnest. Which is remarkable, when you think about it. I mean, how many people can you name who aren't facetious, or snide, or smart-alecky, or sarcastic, or snarky, or at the very least *ironic*, some of the time? None, that's how many.

And Roy doesn't layer on the compliments, either. So if he says something, you know he means it. If he trusts me with a chainsaw, it's because he thinks I'm strong and clearheaded and capable enough to use it. Unlike how Jeremy, and Mom and Dad, and overprotective Stenn, and the rest of the universe see me.

"Now that you've got your own way to get to work, I'll see you tomorrow," Roy says. "Same time as usual."

I'm pretty sure it's a question, and it would probably be okay if I say no to tomorrow, but yes to later. But what what comes out is, "I have to have lunch with my family. But I can come in the afternoon."

"Sounds good."

"See you tomorrow."

"Reckon you can bring your dog, if you want."

"Really?" My heart lifts. "But what about Buddy?"

"We'll leave him safe inside."

"Wow, that'd be great. Thanks."

Roy nods. I'm about to go when he holds out his hand.

I take off my mitten to put my hand in his. He wraps his other hand around mine and says, "Sarah, it's been another real good day."

He squeezes my hand, then turns and hikes back up the hill.

I look at the sky through the tree branches. There was respect conveyed through those cracked, leathery hands. That strange feeling of contentment comes through me again. And hope.

Until it's time to sneak past home, convince Ruby to stay there, and get my ass over to the Y. Details, details.

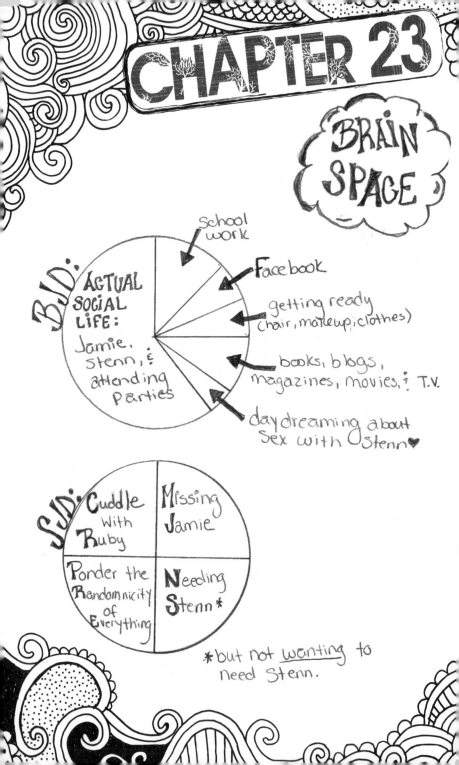

CHAPTER 23

BRAIN SPACE

BJD:

ACTUAL SOCIAL LIFE: Jamie, Stenn, & attending Parties

school work

Facebook

getting ready (hair, makeup, clothes)

books, blogs, magazines, movies, & T.V.

daydreaming about Sex with Stenn♥

SJD: Cuddle with Ruby

Missing Jamie

Ponder the Randomnicity of Everything

Needing Stenn*

*but not <u>wanting</u> to need Stenn.

moves along. I manage to not get caught going to work Sunday afternoon. My dad keeps giving me these You're Up To Something, Aren't You? looks, but Mom seems pretty normal: crabby and texty and Bluebird Dinery and breakfasty.

Stenn shows up at Emmett's soccer game two days before Thanksgiving. He texted me when he left Mercer, but once again he shows up earlier than expected. Kid has a lead foot; no wonder he and my mom get along.

Ruby and I run down the bleachers to greet him. He hugs me but he's scowling and his eyes are bleary. He looks wiped out. He gives me a prude, Parents Are Around cheek peck. He says quick hellos to people and we return to my roost at the top of the bleachers. Rosemary chats with Stenn a moment (*How is boarding school? What's it like?* kinds of questions), but then she smiles and goes to sit with another group of friends, because it seems pretty clear Stenn wants to be alone with me.

"I'm so happy to see you," I nudge him with my shoulder. "How was your exam?" Stenn hates math. I help him sometimes over texts and e-mails, since we're both taking trig.

He shrugs.

"How was the drive?"

"Fine."

This is weird. Bad weird. Being this terse goes against the entire Wagner ethos.

"What's wrong?" I ask him.

He glances at me and flicks his eyes back to the game. No answer. He starts to chew a fingernail, looks at it, and switches to the cuticle.

"Stenn. What's going on?"

"You mean you actually want to know?"

"Um, yes?" This comes out snarky. Oops.

He rubs his hands together like he's suddenly remembered he's not supposed to bite his nails. He sighs. "Why are you here, Sare?"

"What do you mean?"

"What do you think I mean?" Pure acid, his tone. He stares at the game but no way is he paying attention to it. "What am I supposed to think about you coming to Emmett's games?"

"What?" I almost laugh. Almost. Thank Christ I have the sense to stifle it. "Stenn. This is only the second game I've been to this year. I used to go all the time."

"That was to watch me. Or so I thought."

"Of course. But I like soccer. And I thought you'd be glad. That I'm reaching out to friends."

"Friends," he snorts.

"Friends," I repeat. "Rosemary. And Emmett. We are friends."

"Right. Friends." His hand shoots back up to his

mouth and he gnaws at his pinky nail. "Famous last words."

He seriously cannot be jealous. No way. First of all, Ninjas like Stenn do not get jealous, as there is no need. Second: "Emmett is my best friend's twin brother. There is no way anything is going on with—"

"Sure. Nothing other than, oh, let's see…hanging with him at the soccer party, coming to his games, leaving Nano's with him Friday night…"

"He's like my brother."

"You already have a brother."

"He's like a *nice* brother. Think of me and Emmett as Luke and Leia. You're my Han." I nudge him again.

He doesn't respond.

"If you want to talk about jealousy, I'll give you an Emmett and raise you a Midge and an Apple."

He almost gives a hint of a smile.

"Look, I'm not hiding anything here. I always tell you what I'm up to."

"So do the guys. You know how many texts I got when you left Nano's with Emmett? How do you think it looks, Sare?"

"What, you're turning into your mom now? Worried about how things look?"

He puffs out an angry breath and looks at me like he hates me. It *was* a low blow. But there's always been a touch of his mom in him, and I don't think

Mercer is helping. How Things Look is to be considered at all times. It never really bothered me before; it never really came up because I cared about it, too—BJD.

"How it looks isn't what's important," I say gently. "I told you everything."

"Sure." It's practically a snarl. "Everything. Like you always do."

In record time, his jealousy has gone from surprising to mildly annoying to truly irritating.

"Meaning?" I press.

"Oh, just that..." He stops midsentence. Shakes his head. He's super angry but he keeps his voice low, for appearances. "You don't tell me anything. Sure, you tell me when you hang out with Emmett, but you never tell me what you talk about. And there's the whole deer thing that you didn't tell me until later. Why wouldn't you want to tell me right when that happened? I'm supposed to be your boyfriend. And—oh, I don't know—how about *every single thing* you feel about Jamie that you never, ever talk about. To me, at least."

Eesh. It's not just that Stenn is jealous. It's that he feels frozen out.

"You're like a robot, Sarah."

I manage not to try to make a crack—*C3PO or R2D2?*—because I'm honestly a little too scared of getting dumped right now.

Wordlessly, we sit. I stroke Ruby (robotically)

until Emmett scores a goal and the crowd smashes our brittle quiet.

"Can we go somewhere?" I finally ask.

He doesn't look at me. "You sure you want to miss the game?"

"Stenn. Please."

He sighs and relents.

We walk past the soccer field to the elementary school playground, Ruby trotting in front of us. Our feet sink into the thick mulch as we go to the swings. Site of our first kiss, over a year ago. We each sit on a swing. Ruby sniffs around and sits at my feet. The playground is deserted. We each sit on a swing. I have a huge urge to sit on Stenn's lap and kiss him hard— distract the hell out of him. And me. But not only does it not seem like a good idea at the moment, it doesn't even seem possible. Right now he's undistractable.

Strangely, I keep thinking about Rosemary and how she said I need to give people a chance. And Roy, how he's been so kind and fair to me. I owe Stenn that much: kindness, fairness, a chance. It's not like he hasn't put up with a lot from me: depressive girl-friend who stops wearing makeup and stifles all meaningful communication. And that's on my good days.

So. I take a deep breath. "I'm sorry people gave you a hard time about Emmett and me. I should have thought about how it would look. I guess I figured you'd trust me…"

"Damn it, Sare!"

"Wait. Please. Let me say this."

Stenn's jaw clenches.

"You have to believe me. Nothing is going on with Emmett. We…I…" *How do I put it?* "It's nice to have someone who understands."

"That's as bad as hooking up with him. If you ever talked to *me* about that stuff, then fine." His gaze rests on something distant. "But you don't. Like, ever. Which means Emmett's getting a part of you that you won't even let me touch."

"I don't hear you complaining about touching all the *other* parts of me that Emmett doesn't get to have," I shoot back.

Stenn stands up. "Don't. Don't say that. What are you even talking about? I am not some guy who wants to bang you and doesn't care how you feel. And by the way, you were the one who was so wanting to do it. And now you're the one who wants to wait."

"Oh, so I'm your mercy non-screw? Thanks." I don't even know what my argument is. I'm just mad.

"I cannot *deal* with this!" The look on his face— he's more furious than I knew he could get. "I never. Ever. Pressure. You. We have never done *anything* you didn't want to do as much as I did. Half the time I can't get you off me. It's like you use it to avoid talking. And you know it."

"This is bullshit." I get up. Ruby gets up. My whole body wants to dump his ass and run. Get rid of him before he gets rid of me.

Instead, I sit back down. Breathe. Dang, this giving-people-a-chance thing is hard as hell. I whisper, "You know what? You are absolutely right. I'm sorry."

He scoffs. "You're sorry. Sure."

"No, I am." Another deep breath. "I was totally out of line." I chew my lip. This honesty thing, it's like pulling my own teeth. "It's hard to talk about...everything. It makes me so...whatever. And I never realized, until...until Jamie died, how different we are."

He sits on the swing. "What do you mean?"

"I don't know. In terms of what we believe, I guess." This is self-dentistry using a wrench. "I mean, I respect that you have this faith in God but I...I'm not so sure about it all. And when I did try to talk about it, pretty soon after it happened, you got this look on your face. Like you were super worried. Or scared. So I don't talk about it. I can't stand thinking that you'd be worried about me."

Stenn sighs. "Sare. I worry about you anyway."

"Really?"

"You're an idiot. Yes, I worry about you. All the time."

"Then I owe you another apology. I didn't know you worry about me."

He gives me a look.

"Well, I sort of knew, judging from your finger-nails."

He kind of laughs. "Yeah. My mom's on my ass about them. Again."

"Then I definitely owe you a really huge apology. Giving your mom something else to criticize."

"True."

I think some more. "If I tell you something about Emmett, will you take it as me trying to open up to you? And me having this friend who happens to be a guy? And not be jealous?"

"I don't know."

"Well, you want me to talk about things with you, right? Things on my mind? Even if that's Emmett?"

"Artful manipulation. Well played."

"Thanks."

"All right. Let's hear it."

"Okay. First, to repeat: Emmett's like a brother to me. Fully Luke and Leia. So us hooking up is not something you ever need to worry about, ever."

"On Hoth, Leia practically sucked Luke's face off."

"Oh no! I totally forgot! Incest." But it's a relief to laugh. "Okay, bad example. Bad. Example. Still, I'm worried about him. So I sort of get how you must feel about me—"

"I doubt it. Unless you've been going out longer than a year, and you love him."

My stomach somersaults. He loves me.

I love him, too. Even though we're a lot different than we were a year ago. I still really love him. I say, "It's like this. I feel that I owe it to Jamie to look after Emmett. He's been getting in trouble, and of course there's his diabetes to worry about, and now their parents are maybe getting a divorce."

Stenn tilts his head to the side like he's sorry to hear this. Because Stenn is a good, decent, kind human being. Solid that way.

"You know our lockets?" I ask.

"Of course."

"Well Emmett asked me where Jamie's part of the locket is." My breath hitches with a strangled sob. I touch my necklace and pull my locket out from under my shirt, looking at it a long time. "And he doesn't know what happened to Jamie. How she died. I mean, everyone knows she died in the gym wall, but he wants the whole story, all the details. Why we were there, what really happened, how. He wants me to tell him."

"Damn. Are you going to?"

I tuck the locket back. "Honestly, I don't think I can. I've never had to say it out loud, not since that day, when the cops came. I mean, I've never even told you."

"You could practice. With me."

"I don't think I can go through it again, saying those words." *Because then you might agree it's my fault.*

"It could help," he says.

"Look. If you want me to talk to you more, I'll try. But not about the accident. I just... I can't."

He bites a fingernail, thinking. "What if you write it down? And then show it to Emmett? That way you can tell him what happened, but you won't have to say it out loud."

I stare at Stenn. Oh my Genius. Why didn't I think of that? And also, how sweet is he, trying to help. "I think maybe I can do that."

"Yeah?"

"Yeah."

"Do you think you would ever let me read it?"

Stumble. Because that question rubs me the wrong way—like this is suddenly about Stenn, not Emmett. I make my voice neutral and say, "Maybe. I think so. I don't know. Let me think about it."

He looks disappointed. "Well, at least I know what's up with you, more than I have in a long time. Will you keep trying?"

"To open up a little more?"

He nods.

I lean over and kiss him—a hungry, after-fight kiss. "I'll try, but when we're together, I'd rather...you know."

Stenn pulls me closer. Oh my, the boy is just so beautiful. "That is okay with me. More than okay. Most of the time"—he's talking through our kiss—"but not all the time."

"What are you, the girl in this relationship now?"

He bites my lip, gently. "I'm most definitely the guy in this relationship. But we can play around however you want."

I melt. When he makes me feel this way, I know it's going to happen. We're going to have sex—not here at the playground in broad daylight, obviously, but it's going to happen. Soon. Even though it makes no sense to complicate things more—we have enough drama already.

But right now, it's what I want: sex and complications.

CHAPTER 24

SEX ?

	STENN SAYS	PARENTS SAY	TRUE*
Wait until you're ready	✓	✓	✓
It's an expression of love	✓	✓	✓
It complicates things		✓	?
You're not ready yet		✓	
Always use birth control	✓	✓	✓

* conjecture. Not evidence-based. (yet

THE day before Thanksgiving, Roy and I set up the sales lot. He is renting the parking area of Mr. Big's, the older of Norwich's two highly esteemed soft-serve establishments, both of which are officially closed for the season.

As far as Mom and Dad are concerned, Rubes and I are spending the morning at Rosemary's and the afternoon at Stenn's. Both of which I'm allowed to do, yet I am still not allowed to work. A state of affairs that must change, but I can't figure out how. In the meantime, I really need to not be seen skulking about—aka working—with Roy.

Roy picks me up at the corner of Locust Street and West Main in his rusty pickup. Ruby jumps in the truck with me after I wrestle the door open. (Buddy is safely snoozing in a box at Roy's place. Must keep animals separated.)

At Mr. Big's, we sit, sipping coffee and surveying the place from the warmth of the truck. While Roy checks his handwritten list, I ponder the meaning of the universe and stuff.

"Rented a moving van," Roy says after he's made some checkmarks on the list. "To bring the trees down. Shouldn't take but two trips. Three at the most."

"It's still a lot of trees. How about we enlist some help?" I ask.

I figure Roy will say something about the two of us managing fine, but he surprises me: "Help would be nice."

We make some calls. I round up Stenn and his older brother Stiv, who's home from Brown. Things feel slightly awkward on the phone with Stenn, but the Wagner boys never refuse a request for assistance. Their mother would kill them if they did. She enjoys feeling superior too much. As for Rosemary, she has to help her mom with Thanksgiving prep, but she offers her dad's DOT dump truck.

"Really? Your dad would let us borrow it? Isn't it government property or something?"

She says, "Whatevs. He's weirdly cool about lending it out. Something about Robin Hood and the haves and have-nots. Who the hell knows with that man? The only thing is you can't tell anyone. Keep it on the down low."

"He won't let it get back to my dad that I'm involved in hijinks, will he?" I ask.

"Not a chance. Anyway, that'd mean getting himself in trouble."

I decide to take her word for it. Never look a gift truck in the mouth.

With Stenn and Stiv's help, the four of us get all the trees moved in one trip. Roy takes the pickup; Stiv drives the dump truck—he seems to secretly enjoy it—and Ruby and I ride down to Mr. Big's in the moving van with Stenn. I can't believe the van can make it over Loblolly Road.

In town, I hunker low in the seat, keeping eyes peeled for family members or spies. And try to figure out how Stenn's feeling about our fight yesterday. And the making up. I swallow my pride and ask Stenn, "Are we okay, do you think?"

Stenn glances over at me, then back to the road. "I don't know, Sare. I hope so." He lifts his thumb to chew his nail but changes course halfway and scratches his shoulder instead. "Do you think we are?"

"I think we will be." Is it a lie? Is it wishful thinking? Is there a difference? "We've been through a lot together, you know? I mean, you're my best friend. I really do, you know: I love you."

"I know."

"Okay, Han," I say.

"You know, though, I like the *Battlestar Galactica* line better. When the president finally says, 'I love you,' and Adama says—"

"About time," I say in a deep, gruff voice.

Stenn is familiar with my Edward James Olmos. "Yeah." He smiles.

"I like it better too." *Because it's about time I tell you what you mean to me. And because I've been a teensy bit of a high maintenance lady by keeping my distance. But I'm going to try, really hard. So don't you dump me!*

And I think he gets it—I hope he does, because I can't say all those words. Can I? I can't.

We're back at Mr. Big's. Stenn starts to open the

door, but I touch his arm to stop him. He looks at me. "What?"

"I just want to say…the whole 'about time' thing? I get it."

He gives me this look, and I can't tell if means What Are You Talking About? or if it means Go On, I Want to Hear You Say This. Either way, I need to keep going. I triple-dog-dare myself. "I get scared because of what happened to Jamie, that you're going to—"

"I'm not going to die, Sare."

"You can't say that! You don't know. But let me finish. I was going to say…" Shit. It was so clear in my mind, what I need to tell him, what he needs to hear. And now it's all jumbled up again.

"You were going to say?"

"That I'm trying harder. I get scared because things are finite, and I don't want them to be finite with you."

"Are you sure? You seem like you're changing. And I can't tell if you want to take me along on the changes."

"I am changing, sort of. But it's more like I'm *not* changing. Like my changes are shedding away the outside stuff, stuff that doesn't matter, but the inside stuff? That's all the same. And you're inside stuff, Stenn. You're not outside stuff." Eureka! Holy crap! I figured it out! "That's what it is. I've been worried that you are…that we are…that we're only outside stuff. Because you always act so perfect, and you go to Mercer—"

"Sare, I'm not—"

"Let me talk! And everyone's always saying we're the perfect couple, and you're a smoking hot Ninja—"

"Please, not the Ninja Continuum—"

"Hush! My point is, you're *not* outside stuff! You are part of the important things to me, the 'core values' or whatever it's called. And"—holy cats, more things are falling into place for me—"And I'm worried that you want me to be outside stuff. Like how I'm not dressing up as much, and makeup and parties, I guess I've been worried that bothers you and you'll dump me because that *has* changed. I mean, I see how your mom looks at me these days. I know she's all 'Run a brush through your hair, young lady.'" I take a deep breath. Yowza. That was a lot.

Stenn is looking at me. Not the lack-of-makeup, old-jeans-and-sweatshirt aspect of me, but my eyes, my heart. He kind of chuckles. "Sarah. Are you done?"

Why is he laughing? I spill my guts out and he thinks it's funny? "Is this amusing to you?"

"No no no," he says. "No, I don't think it's funny at all. I think it's awesome. I think I love you more than I did five minutes ago."

My heart doesn't know whether to settle down yet. It's gone from beating with excitement to pounding with anxiety to fluttering with happiness. "Really?"

"So much." He puts his fingers on my cheek and kisses me. We kiss, the melty kind of kissing, except we are in the parking lot of Mr. Big's and Roy and Stiv are waiting.

But it's all mixed up, this emotion and realization and kissing, and I feel more open to Stenn than I ever have, like soul-split-open open. And out of me spills the following tidbit of information: "Stenn, I got the patch."

He looks bewildered. "The patch?"

"The birth control patch."

"Oh." His eyes go wide. Then a big, goofy smile. "Oh," he says again, much happier. "Yeah?"

"Yeah."

"Wow. Really? Where?"

"Planned Parenthood."

"No, I mean, where on your body? I haven't noticed—"

"I haven't put it on yet. But I'm going to. I think I'll put in down here," I pat my butt. "So nobody will notice." Especially my parentals.

"When?"

"All the time. You have to wear it all—"

"No, I mean, when are you going to put it on? When can we...you know. How soon does it work?"

Oh. Deep breath. "I have to wait for my period. Then I put it on the first day."

"When's that?"

"Couple weeks."

"And then does it work right away?"

"The nurse said use a backup for the first week. But the website says if you put it on the first day of your period, it works pretty much right away." Another deep breath. This is so not the time and place to be talking about this! A rental van in Mr. Big's parking lot.

"You think you're ready?" he asks.

"Yeah. I'm nervous. But I think so. Are you?"

He looks at me like Are You Crazy? Of Course I'm Ready.

"Just asking. I don't want to assume that because you're a guy you want to have sex all the time."

"You can definitely assume. Yes. I'm ready. I've been ready for a long time."

"Okay then. Soon."

"Should I"—he looks like a kid all of sudden—"should I make reservations or something? We could have a romantic dinner? Or I could try to find a bed and breakfast?"

"A B&B for teenage sex? Sure, set that up." It's sarcasm, but happy, crazy-with-anticipation sarcasm.

"I want it to be special. For you." He looks down, then flicks his eyes back up to mine.

My heart is in my throat. "What about you? Don't you want it to be special, too?"

"It'll be special, as long as it's with you."

I groan. "Did you really just say that?"

He laughs, "I really said that." He looks so happy. I feel so happy. We kiss. He slips his hand under my coat.

And Stiv taps on the window. "Get a room, kids. Let's go."

Red faced, we kiss one more time and hop—or, at this point, it's more like I slide—down from the truck.

Right. Back to work. Try not to think about sex. Do not think about having sex with your boyfriend. Think about Christmas trees!

Impossible.

Okay, but at least I can work while I daydream.

The four of us unload everything fast. Ruby trots around, supervising. Roy and Stenn and Stiv are all really sweet to her. I stay deep in the trees, as far away from the street as possible. Oh my sweet crazy-cakes! Am I really going to have sex with my boyfriend? I am. Aren't I? Yes. I'm ready. Aren't I? Ugh. Am I really having this debate with myself while sneaking around a Christmas tree lot? Oh, the hell my parents will unleash if they find out where I am, what I'm doing right now—even though it's totally innocent. And what about the sex?

Keep working. Keep unloading trees.

When we have almost everything out of the trucks, Stenn comes up. "Jeremy drove by."

The news is a bucket of ice in my face. "Did he see you?"

"Yeah, he kind of nodded."

"He didn't see me, did he?"

Shaking his head, "I don't think so."

"What about Ruby? Did he see Rubes?"

"Maybe."

Wonderful. I send Ruby to the bed of Roy's pickup and tell her to stay while I work.

An hour later, Stenn and Stiv need to return the van and dump truck in time to get ready for some fancy-pants lunch for Sir Wagner's work. Ah, the life of the obscenely rich. How those two boys have turned out so down to earth, helpful, decent, and nice is a true mystery. Probably to spite their mother.

They both shake Roy's hand before leaving. Stenn jokes to Roy, "Don't work Sarah too hard."

Roy makes a puffing sound. "She works hard whether or not I say so."

Stenn looks surprised. They both look at me. Stenn says, "Well, I care about her a lot."

Overshare! Awkward! "Don't you have to go?" I remind Stenn, practically pushing him to the van. I wave goodbye to Stiv, who's already revving up the dump truck. "Thanks again for your help. This has been really good."

Stenn kisses me. "See you soon?"

Oh-bi Wan Kenobi, I'm melting again. "Yes. *Soon* soon. Like we talked about."

"Text me when you get home." Stenn looks drunk, he seems so happy. He starts up the moving van. "Good luck," he calls, and then he and Stiv are gone in clouds of exhaust fumes. Hello, global warming.

Roy and I set to work in earnest. With some two-by-fours, nails, and twine, Roy constructs racks; I help him. The wood bounces and jostles every time the hammer hits. Then it's my turn, and I try to drive the nails in fast and straight. We drag the unloaded trees over. I'm still sore as hellation, but my arms feel like they're changing from mush to muscles. If I keep up the lumberjacking, I'll have Madonna arms soon.

Soon…

Stenn and I are going to deflower each other. Will I feel different about myself after sex? Emotionally? Probably. Physically? Sore, maybe. But anything else? Will it change things in my vaginey? I wonder if it will sound different when I pee. Or if tampons will feel different. I need my best friend! She wouldn't know the answers—not firsthand—but at least we could look them up together.

"Over here, Sarah."

Busted out of sex-zoning. "Oh, okay. Should we arrange the trees by height?"

"Yep."

As I sort—ducking every time a car passes—I say, "I have another idea." Anything to get my mind off sex: planning sex; having sex; sex sex sex.

"What's that."

"What do you think about selling wreaths? People pay tons for ugly, fake plastic wreaths. Bet you they'd pay big bucks for a real one. Especially if we advertise that they're handmade." I lean a tree against one of the racks that Roy and I made, and I pause for a moment: I helped make that. Pretty cool. "Which they would be. Handmade."

"You know how to do that." It's a question.

Another car goes by. I step behind a tree until it passes. If Roy is wondering about my super-spy moves, he doesn't show it. He's probably immune to my weirdness by now. I shrug, "Sure. We've got tons of extra branches and pinecones. All we need is some wire, dry-cleaning hangers, and creative flair."

"Wire I got. Hangers we can get. Creative flair I'll leave up to you."

Around lunchtime, we get into his pickup to round up wire and branches from his place, and hangers from the dry cleaner. Ruby hunkers down in back. I stay low to avoid being seen, and cup my freezing hands over the pickup's heat vents.

"You been cold today," Roy asks.

"A little," I admit.

"We can fix that."

When we get back to Mr. Big's, Roy goes straight to the detached shed where they store picnic tables off-season. He drags out an empty oil drum, adds some pine branches, lights a fire. "That should do it."

I smile my gratitude. It's a fully hobo solution, and it works like a charm.

Roy has set up the fire in the back of the lot, behind all the trees, away from passing cars and spying eyes. It's almost as though he knows I don't want to be seen. Maybe I haven't been as sneaky as I thought. Or maybe he does it for himself as much as for me. He likes his privacy.

As for Rubes, she rewards Roy's thoughtfulness by licking his hand before plonking down next to the fire. I sit on an old blanket and start making wreaths while Roy cuts the netting off the trees.

Memo: we have to de-net and re-net. De-net so people can size up the trees in all their branchy glory; re-net for the trees' trips to their new homes.

After a while, Roy joins me by the fire. "Open early Friday. Imagine plenty of folks want trees then."

Right. And I'm going to hide from the public exactly how? Invisibility cloak? Facial transplant?

Roy says, "Remember, we're square. If you don't want to—"

"If you could use the help, I'll keep working." Somehow.

"I could."

We smile at each other. In Roy language, it's like we're running across a sun-dappled Austrian wildflower meadow to embrace. He's swinging me around in circles.

Roy says, "We haven't talked numbers. How's fifteen dollars an hour, or 10 percent of profits, whichever is bigger."

I frown. "That seems like way too much."

"It's settled, then."

Should I argue? Remind him that, despite my profound level of maturity and extraordinary capabilities—especially with a chainsaw—I am, in actual fact, a member of the Youth of Today, constantly mooching off of my parents? Roy clearly needs the money more than I do. I look at him again. He seems resolute, so we shake on it. And he returns to the trees.

Making wreaths isn't as physical as moving trees, but it's honest work. Productive.

Get me a possum; I sound like Roy.

I'm wiring bent pine branches into a circle when a wire flips out and pricks me. A small droplet of blood pops through my thumb pad. I wrap it in my sweatshirt. It gets me thinking about that glass sliver in my forehead—how the deer crashed into the gym, of all places. And Roy had cleaned up the deer, and put it in his garage, and Ruby ran there. And Ruby's bite. And how escaping from Roy's led me back to Emmett. How I've gotten to know Rosemary because of Emmett's soccer game. And how I've started opening up to Stenn partly because he was jealous of Emmett.

And then there's Roy. He seems to trust me—seems to value me as a capable human being. And he, too, has survived something awful.

Each one of us has our own story, my connection to each of them unexpected and undeniable. The deer tilting the kaleidoscope, setting so much into motion.

The swift animal was thought to speed the spirits of the dead on their way...

The deer has certainly sped spirits. Jamie's? Don't know about that. But it has brought the spirits of this one small group of people closer to me. Or brought me closer to them.

My fingers are tingling, like there's something else. Something else to figure out. I look at the wreath beside me and float my fingers over the tips of the pine needles. I finger the wire spool, pick up a pinecone.

The rest of the Wikipedia entry: *which perhaps explains the curious antlered headdresses found on horses buried at Pazyryk.*

Bam. That's it! I have it.

Yes, James is gone. Even her part of the locket is gone. I will ache for her forever. And whether or not what happened is my fault, whether I should be blamed, whether I can ever be forgiven for leaving her, the truth is I played a role in her death. I did.

If I could, I would do anything, *anything* to bring her back.

But tough shit, because I can't.

But there is something I can do for someone she loved, someone who is aching, too. I can do something for Emmett.

I hold my breath and let the idea get brighter, glow, until it illuminates a plan. A totally brilliant genius plan. Not to toot my own horn. But *toot toot.*

Stenn probably won't like it, but he'll get over it. He's got more of me now than he did this morning. And he's about to get all of me.

I jump to my feet and jog to Roy, who is stacking wreaths and extra branches in the storage shed. "Roy? Can I ask you something?"

"You can ask, but I—"

"Can't guarantee that you'll answer. I know. I'm just wondering if you'd do me a favor? For a friend of mine."

"Ask on the way," Roy says. "Time I got you home."

"Drop me off on the corner again?"

His eyebrows rise. He regards me with eyes that say Don't Think I Haven't Noticed You're Sneaking Around. But he doesn't ask. Because he's Roy.

In silence, we finish packing up and get into the truck, Ruby on my lap.

As I give Roy the general outline of my idea, he chuckles. "Sure. We can manage that."

"Really?" I'm so excited, if I had a tail I'd be wagging it.

He nods. "Count on it."

I take a swig from my water bottle and offer it to Roy, who shakes his head. I say, "Speaking of plans…I don't want to be nosey, but I didn't know if you have plans for Thanksgiving?" The thought of him spending the holiday alone in his depressing house is sad. I can't invite him to my house for our Thanksgiving Late Lunch—way too fishy—and I can't offer him a place at the Wagner's feast, which I attend in the eventide. "Maybe I could come up for a while in the morning?"

"That's real nice of you to ask. But no. Tends to be a busy time for…work."

The man's not talking about the trees. "So this is janitorially speaking, I presume?"

"Yep."

"Really? Do a lot of deer crash through windows on Thanksgiving?"

"Something like that." He's quiet a while, and it's a heavier quiet than usual. But then he seems to shift thoughts. "Tell me more about this plan of yours."

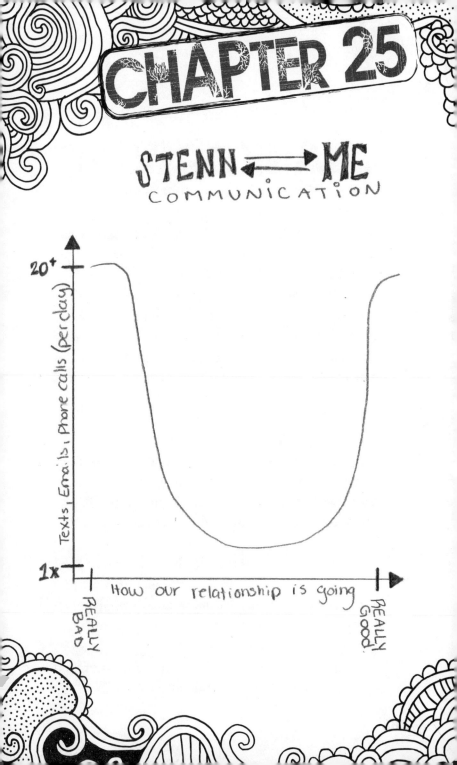

THANKSGIVING

Late Lunch with my family isn't that bad. It isn't that fun, either, but all things considered, it's better than a sharp stick in the eye. Maybe my family can tell I'm trying for less snark, more…what? Chitchat? Let's just leave it at less snark.

I help Mom cook—and do all the dishes since Jeremy is still holding the Salsa-Thon over my head. For dessert we have a big batch of freshly baked chocolate chip cookies. Jeremy is somewhat civil, for a dickhead. Dad is Dad: dorky but sweet. Mom is still holding one of her hundred grudges. The woman is impossible.

But eventually it's five o'clock and time to go to Stenn's (Ruby's not invited) and get through their Thanksgiving feast so we can go downstairs and get it on. Yes, Stenn and I talked about the patch, and I'm still planning to use it, but now I can't wait that long.

I change into the satin lace bra and undies I got that day with Jamie. I pick out a demure skirt and cardigan that will meet Mrs. Wagner's approval. It feels very Innocent Outfit Hiding Sexy Vixen.

Cue the Barry White.

Dad drops me off at the Wagner McMansion and Stenn's mom greets me at the door.

Scratch the Barry White.

There's a crystal goblet of wine in Mrs. Wagner's hand. With her, alcohol can go three ways:

1. Blood Alcohol Content (BAC) .05–0.10 = normal judgmental self, watching with hawk eyes, but prone to random smiling and demure hiccups.
2. BAC > 0.10 = 50 percent of the time, she gets friendly, even downright silly. *But—*
3. BAC > 0.10 = 50 percent of the time, she becomes mean as a rattlesnake, striking with no warning, and nasty venomous fangs.

Mrs. Wagner must be hovering around 0.08, because she's smiling a little more than usual, but she still has me under constant surveillance. Her scrutiny is exhausting. No girl on this blue planet will ever be good enough for either of her two princes.

Stenn's dad is generally pleasant but distant—as in, never-around, always-working distant. The few times when he is home, he doesn't feel the need to relate to the under-forty crowd. At all.

Thank God, Stiv is always cool and nice, and their favorite aunt is fairly normal (and tipsy), because I'm seated between them, with Stenn far away across the table, between his mom and her bitchier sister. Place cards. Believe it.

Acceptable conversation topics: the success of Mr. Wagner's businesses; recently published biographies of Great Thinkers; the quality of education at Mercer and/or Brown; the future of the internet, specifically monetizing social media and content marketing; tennis; the weather as it relates to flower gardening. Prohibited topics: partisan politics; weather as it relates to climate change; public schools.

Dealing with Stenn's mom and family is as tiring, in a different way, as working at the tree farm—and I'd prefer lumberjacking. By the time Stenn and I start clearing plates, I feel like I've been mud wrestling grizzly bears. Probably look like it, too.

After dinner, the other members of the Wagner dynasty scatter around the many upstairses, drinking more wine or watching one of their huge screens or passed out in tryptophan comas.

Stenn and I retreat to the basement rec room, alone at last.

So, here we are. I don't have the patch on yet, but we both know something's changed in the air between us. It's go time.

Stenn bought condoms with spermicidal lube. They are about to meet their prophylactic destiny.

Wow. This is it. We're going to do it. This is huge. I'll never be a virgin again.

I want it. I want to. But I'm shivering with nerves. So, like a complete and utter wuss, I start *The Empire Strikes Back* on their big screen. I sit on the marshmallow leather couch, poised to watch with utmost attention. Like it's the first time I've seen anything like this crazy moving picture! It takes place in space! *Space!* What will they think of next!

Without complaint—but with a hint of disappointment in his face—Stenn sits next to me and we watch. After a while, about the time Han mounts a Tauntaun to look for Luke, Stenn pulls me over to snuggle on his chest. His lack of pressure is excellent reverse psychology. It's totally making me love him even more. Well played, sir.

We snuggle, tension rising, while Luke snags the legs of an Imperial Walker.

This is it. Everything's perfect. I kiss him, watch his eyes liquefy as I undo the buttons of my cardigan.

Stenn kisses me hard, sliding his fingers over the top of my bra. "This is really pretty."

He scoots me down and lies on top of me. Starts kissing my neck, my chest, pushes my bra down.

"Are you sure you want to?" he asks.

I nod. "I think so."

He starts lifting my skirt. "I want you to be sure. I don't want you to regret anything."

Am I sure? I'm not sure. How will I ever know if I'm sure? The more you think about whether you're sure, the less sure you feel. "I think I'm sure."

He puts more of his weight on me, kisses me again. He whispers, "We can wait if you want."

"I want to."

He lifts up a bit. "Want to what? Wait? Or do it?"

Do it. Wait. Do it. "I—" *Air! I need some air!* I push him back.

Stenn sits up. What's his expression? Frustration. Annoyance. Some softness there, too.

We sit, kind of blankly looking at the TV. He is quiet.

Way to ruin the moment, Sarah. I mean *ruin* the moment.

Onscreen, Leia kisses Luke. Brother-sister tongue kissing. And suddenly I can read Stenn's mind. I know he's thinking—we're both thinking—about Emmett, about our conversation on the playground during Emmett's soccer game. And by conversation, I mean fight.

The freaking movie. It keeps going. Leia storms out in a huff. Chewie roars something to Han. Luke makes a face like an idiot.

And Stenn finally speaks. "You know what?" He's still looking at the TV. "I can't do this, Sare."

My scalp goes numb. "You can't do what?"

"This. You and me."

My ears start buzzing. "What do you mean?"

"Here we are, and I'm thinking, finally we're going to be together, you know—"

"Have sex," I say.

"Yeah. And it's like you're not even into it. I mean, do you want to be with me, or don't you?"

"I got a little freaked out back there. That's all. I'm fine. It's all good. Everything's fine here now. Thank you. How are you?"

He heaves a huge sigh. "That's great, Sare. Make everything a *Star Wars* quote. Is this all a joke to you?"

"It's not a joke. You make with the quotes a lot too, you know. Let's not make a big deal about this." I tug his shirt. "Why don't we pick up where we left off?"

He moves. It's not a push, not really, but he makes it so I have to sit up and slide away. He says, "I'm not into it anymore."

What? This is not happening. I'm offering up my virginity on a platter, and he's turning it down? How much of a loser do I feel like right now? Slowly, I smooth my skirt, fix my bra, start doing up the buttons of my sweater.

So quiet.

"I just...," Stenn says, "I need some space."

I look at him. And because I'm terrified, the snark box kicks into gear. "Isn't that supposed to be the girl's line?"

He tilts his head. He's not taking the bait. "You know, Sare, everyone keeps telling me I should break up with you."

"Everyone! Everyone who?"

"Guys on the team—"

"Soccer guys?"

"Yeah. And also Midge and—"

"Awesome. You're talking to Midge about me."

"Yes, I am. Because she's my friend. And I keep telling Midge, and everyone else, they're wrong. I keep saying no, you're not yourself, you're depressed and still, like, grieving. I keep thinking you'll get better. And the other day at the playground, and then Mr. Big's? That was so...hopeful. But you know what? Maybe this is it. Maybe this is who you are now."

"And your point is?"

His eyes look sad. "It's tiring. You are tiring. I need a break."

"Well, you got it." I finish buttoning my sweater and put my shoes on. My coat's upstairs; I'll get it on my way out.

"Sare, you don't have to storm off."

"Oh, but I do."

"Let me give you a ride home, at least."

"No."

"Sare, come on."

"No. Don't follow me. Don't call me. Don't try to give me a ride home. You want space, you got it."

Alone, freezing, dark. Walking.

Damn it. Where is he? Why don't guys realize they're supposed to chase you when you storm off? Even if you say, "Don't follow me."

Especially if you say, "Don't follow me."

Irritating.

More irritating: Why do I expect Stenn to know this is the one time I want him to do the exact opposite of what I said?

I blame my misery on every romantic comedy ever made.

And it is misery. A long, miserable, lonely walk home.

CHAPTER 26

HOW I'M BECOMING A BRICK SH*THOUSE

Physical Pain of Lumberjacking (building muscle) →→

Time

BLACK Friday. The day after Thanksgiving. Black not so much for sales and shopping but for how my heart feels. Black and blue.

Is it over? Did we break up? Stenn's been mad before, sure, we've had arguments. But he's never asked for space. What does that even mean? Does "I need space" mean *we're breaking up*? Or does it mean *I'll call you later tomorrow when I feel better*? Why can't it mean the stars/cosmos/galaxies kind of space? That's the kind of space I can get behind. Stenn's space sucks.

His FB status still says *in a relationship*. Click, refresh. Click, refresh. Still *in a relationship*. So that's something. Maybe this is just a bad fight.

For breakfast, I force down a plate of leftover mashed potatoes and gravy while Mom hovers. She hands me my Zoloft and unloads dishes from the dishwasher as I put my phone, industrial strength lip balm, and a water bottle in my bag, next to the bag lunch I packed last night.

Mom looks at her watch. The woman wears a watch. Un-ironic retro. "Tell me again why you're going so early?" she says.

"Rosemary's mom wants to get to the mall, stat.

It opened at 5:00 AM or something. Can I have some money?" Soon I will have tons of my own cash, thanks to Roy. But for now I'm still relegated to sponging.

Mom sighs, because I'm such a hardship. "Use your debit card. I'll transfer money into your account."

"So you can forget and I can be publicly humiliated when my card gets declined? Again?"

"Text me a reminder."

"Fine."

"And text me so I know when to expect you home and whether you will have eaten."

"I'll probably be back in time for dinner." Not that I feel like eating anything. My insides are staging a revolt. Massive. Full-on Rebel Alliance in there.

I bundle up while Ruby wags. How can I possibly take her? *Oh, by the way Mom, I'm going to take Ruby and pretend like she's staying in the car all day but really I'll be at Mr. Big's selling trees and she likes it there.* Besides, Roy and I have agreed to take turns bringing our pets. Today is Buddy Day.

"I'm sorry, girl," I say to Rubes. "I'll walk you when I get home, okay?" She wags her tail and my heart breaks a little more.

I meet Roy at the corner. We're at Mr. Big's by 7:30. We set out the wreaths and a sales desk, then dump out the icy water in the washtubs, flipping them and smashing out ice so we can fill them again. I manage to get my feet soaked with the most freezing cold water ever known to man. Roy sees me do it.

He doesn't laugh or make me feel like an idiot. He just reaches into his pocket and hands me a book of matches. "Why don't you start the fire."

I stuff branches in the oil drum and light it up. Thank you, caveman who discovered fire. Thank you, hobo who first used an empty oil drum for a firepit. Thank you, pine needles for exploding into flame.

By noon, half the town has bought trees. Crazy. I don't get the early buying of Christmas trees. It's still November, people. But I'm clearly a minority voice. The tree lot is rocking.

I have to admit it pulls me out of my funk. A little.

It's hard to pout when you're maniacally busy.

Roy and I spin around like Tasmanian Devils— selling, netting, carrying, tying trees to the roofs of cars. I try to lay low, do the backlot work, but it's kind of fun to see who's coming, and when. Families with little kids are the first wave: haggard, tired parents dragged around by little snow-suited munchkins. Mellow older couples drift in around midmorning. Families with teenagers come later—edgy and argue-y. And the wreaths are selling like crazy. Big hit.

Ms. Franklin and Dr. Folger buy their tree/wreath combos within an hour of each other. I hide in the shed the minute I see Dr. Folger's car. Rat fink. There is not a chance he won't remark upon my presence here to the paternal parental. I watch through the crack in the shed door as he pumps

Roy's hand to congratulate him on the booming business.

When Ms. Franklin comes, though, I decide to risk saying hi. Ratting isn't her style.

At the cash table, she asks me how my Thanksgiving break is going.

"Busy." *And I think I got dumped. But I'm not really sure.* I smooth out bills to make change. We are a cash-only establishment. Kicking it old school. "And yours?" I ask.

She tucks the money into her warehouse of a purse. "Hon, this time of year gets busier the older I get. So much to do at home, I hardly have time for work at school!" Conspiratorially, she leans close. "A snow day or two would sure be helpful."

I put my hands to my mouth. "Ms. Franklin! You're not suggesting I ask my dad to cancel school. That would be positively scandalous!"

Ms. Franklin swats the air. "Oh, you! I'm kidding. I'm sure your father is impervious to your requests. Although I bet sometimes it's tempting to try."

"You don't know the half of it," I say. Because she doesn't.

After three o'clock, the stream of customers dwindles. Roy and I haven't eaten lunch; we haven't had time. And now I'm starving. Boyfriend drama or not, work works up an appetite.

"Wow. I can't believe how busy it's been," I say, crunching into an apple and warming myself by the oil drum. Thank Zeus my shoes have dried. Note to self: pack extra socks next time.

"Yep." Roy has his usual peanut butter and honey sandwich.

"So enough small talk. Let's get down to business." Roy cocks an eyebrow.

"My plan? The favor?" I say. Stenn can ruin my life if he wants, but it won't stop me from trying to un-ruin Emmett's. "I figure we'll get to your—"

Beep. Beep. Beep. I look around. It's not my phone. I frown at my apple.

"It ain't your lunch." Roy pulls something out from a pocket. A pager.

A pager? Do they even make those anymore?

Roy has a pager. Well this is some new information. So he's not just a tree farmer and a part-time janitor, he's also a drug dealer. I mean, who else uses a pager nowadays?

Roy presses a button, tilting the pager to read the display. "Goodness. Bad timing."

"What's up?" Translation: *Do you need to get to your meth lab or what? Is your cook going to explode?*

"Looks like I have to go."

"Really? Now? Where to?"

"Yep. These things don't wait." He stands and surveys the lot. "Guess we'll have to close down."

"But you might lose money."

"It's too much work for one person. It was tricky when you hid in the shed." He winks at me. Okay. So he noticed that.

Moving right along. "What if someone can fill in until you get back? How long do you think you'll be gone?" I ask.

"Not sure," Roy says. "But keeping the lot open would be a big help. I'd pay whoever helps, of course."

I nod, thinking, but not about the money or the trees. What kind of janitorial business requires a beeper and won't wait?

"Suppose you're wondering," Roy says as he packs up his lunch, "what it is I do... What else it is I do."

"I mean, if you want to tell me…"

"It isn't that I don't." Roy makes a face, shakes his head like he's changing his mind. "It's…complicated. Prefer not talking about it."

"Your cleaning business?" *What do you mean, it's complicated? How can it be complicated? Someone has a mess, they beep you. End of story. Are you a meth dealer or what?*

"Specialty cleaning. People call me when they have…emergencies."

"I know. Like the deer," I say.

He nods slowly but doesn't say anything.

I say, "Or if a toilet bursts? Or someone's house gets flooded?" I can see how that wouldn't be able to wait.

Roy is still nodding. "That. And other things."

"Sounds disgusting." Nice. Tell the man his job is

disgusting. Quickly, I add, "But important. I bet people are really grateful. I know I would be, if you came to help me with a job like that."

Roy raises an eyebrow. "Appreciate you saying so." He looks like he's deciding whether to say more.

Jedi Mind Trick: *You want to tell me everything. Keep going.*

"Well. It's not only when a pipe bursts. Sometimes it's...other kinds of accidents."

"What do you mean?" The air starts getting heavier. Starts *whooshing* a little.

Roy is just standing there. "Sometimes it's—"

"Got it. Stop. Got it." Oh my God. Like his son and wife? Or worse. Suddenly I have too much information. I cannot—do not want to—hear another word. Not one more word.

His pager beeps again. He thumbs it off, looks at the display. "Really should attend to this."

"Sure. Yeah." I stuff my lunch back into my bag. "Let me see if I can find someone to fill in until you get back." And a bucket to puke into. Because now I'm even more nauseous than I was this morning.

There is a car horn—a familiar car horn—and I look over, and the need to hurl gets worse.

It's my dad's Jeep.

CHAPTER 27

PRO vs CON
Being the Superintendent's offspring

	PRO	CON
Everyone knows our family	?	✓
Staff & teachers kiss my butt a bit	✓	✓
Dad's never home b/c of meetings	✓	✓
Get in less trouble from teachers	✓	
Kids always want us to tell him to do stuff.		✓
Held to a higher standard		✓

OH. My. God. It's too late to make a break for the shed. He's already seen me. He honked his horn on the way in.

Did he come here for a tree? Or did he know I'm here somehow? Did Jeremy narc?

This is so, so bad. Beyond bad. A shudder travels through me, like fingernails are raking chalkboards all over the tree lot.

Dad steps out of his Jeep looking strangely calm. Zombie calm. He's wearing his cowboy boots.

He ignores me and goes to Roy. They shake hands. "Good to see you, Roy."

"You too, Earl."

They're on a first name basis. How nice.

"I see you've got Sarah working for you."

"Yep." If Roy's surprised by Dad's need to state the obvious, he doesn't show it.

They stand there.

Roy hooks his thumbs in his pockets. "She's a fine worker, Earl. Real hard worker."

Dad's eyebrows shoot up like Really? Are You Sure This Is My Daughter You're Talking About?

Way to believe in me, Dad. But he looks kind of proud.

Roy says, "Don't know what I'd do without her."

And even through my mortal dread, I swell with pride. To hear that from Roy is like winning an Emmy-Grammy-Oscar-Tony.

Dad turns his back to me, but I can still hear him. "Why didn't you let me know she was working for you?"

Roy looks past Dad to me. "Reckoned that's between you and Sarah. I'll give you two a minute." He goes to the shed.

Dad doesn't come any closer. He crosses his arms. "Well, young lady. Lying to your mother and me. Going against her express wishes."

"I'm sorry, Dad. You're right. *Mea culpa.*"

He looks surprised. My lack of sarcasm probably threw him off. "What?"

"I'm sorry I lied about where I've been. But I'm not sorry I've been working for Roy. I tried to get permission—"

"And your mother said no." He has regained his footing.

"But she was wrong to say no! I'm good at this. And Roy needs me, and I...I like it. *This* is what I need. *This* is what's going to help me. Way more than stupid counselors."

"So you know, better than your mother, what's best for you?"

"Yes! In this case, yes." My heart is pounding. I have to make him understand.

"But you can't sneak around, lying to us. Your mother said no."

"And that was so not fair. And before you tell me that life isn't fair, don't. I already know it isn't. Believe me."

Something in him softens. Is that—is it compassion on his face? Rosemary's words pop into my head again: *You have to give people a chance.* So I take a deep breath. "Maybe I should have talked to you about it."

"Yes. You should have. And I gave you lots of chances to." He sighs. "Say goodbye to Roy."

I howl, "Forever?"

Dad laughs. He actually laughs. "No, kiddo. Not forever."

In a million years I will never figure the man out. "You mean...I can come back? I'm not in trouble? But I lied to you guys. And when I ditched school you said if I did one more thing wrong..." Oh for the love of all things good and holy, why am I still talking?

"Sarah, you may not believe this, but I love you. Your mom loves you. And we are pretty smart human beings." Dad presses his lips together. "Salsa-Thon? Really?"

"You knew this whole time?"

"I'm not happy about you lying to us. There will be consequences for that. But there's a world of difference between lying in order to cut school versus lying in order to hold a responsible job."

"That's very moral relativist of you." Seriously, what is wrong with me? Why won't I shut up?

Dad cracks his knuckles. "You have a lot, and I mean a *lot*, of making up to do with your mother.

Groveling would probably be a better word."

"But?" I say hopefully.

"But..." His mouth twists into a wry smile. "Let's just say I'm the one who wears the cowboy boots. Sometimes, at least."

"Are you forbidding me from Stenn? Driving? Is Ruby safe?"

The compassion in Dad's eyes is unmistakable. "Sarah, we couldn't stand to take your dog away from you."

"You were lying? All this time I've been scared shitless! You lied to me?"

"Language, kiddo," he says reflexively, then, "It's no fun being lied to, is it?"

Deep breath. Relief. Anger. Relief. "No. It isn't."

"Tit for tat."

"So we can call it even?"

"Nice try." He reaches over and rumples my hair. It's awkward and goofy but it's sweet. "Now. About these boots," he says, total non sequitur. "You want to know something about these boots?"

"They're made for walking?"

He gives a Happiest Dad In The World smile. "And that's just what they'll do." And then he practically snaps me in half with his hug.

Thank God for a man who can't hold a grudge.

Mom, on the other hand...

She's just tickled pink when I walk through the back door with Dad. Her eyes are like daggers. "You are grounded. Forever. Until you learn not to lie to us."

I don't even have my coat off yet. I'm still petting Rubes hello. "But Dad said I can work for Roy!"

She looks mad enough to spit. Spitting Cobra, Hawk A Venom Loogie Into My Eyes spit. "You will go to school, you will go to work, you will come home. You will do all your homework. No computer except for schoolwork. No phone. No internet. No TV. No Stenn. No Rosemary. No anything."

Fine. Banning Rosemary is harsh, but I can see her at school. Obviously Mom doesn't know that Stenn may have dumped me, may even now be changing his FB status to *it's complicated*—or worse, *single*. No reason to tell her now. But she didn't say no driving. And she didn't say no Ruby. So Dad was probably telling the truth. Ruby is safe. Safe!

"Scratch that. You will have your phone. For limited use. You will text when you arrive at work. You will text when you leave. You will text me when you get home. You will be available to take my calls or texts at any time. You will call or text no one but your father and me. You will leave your phone on the kitchen counter at all times when you are home. We will have free access to your call history. No other texts, no internet. Are we clear?"

I nod. I have the sense to keep quiet for a change.

"If you make one false move—I mean *one* false move," she lifts a finger in warning, "if you skip one class, tell one little lie, make one unauthorized call, you can kiss your working days goodbye. I don't care what your father says."

And it hits me. I get it: sure, she's mad that I've been lying. And she's fuming at Dad for standing up to her. But deep down? Under all her anger, she's happy. No, she's fracking *ecstatic* that I have something to do that I really care about. Because now she has real leverage. And also because, maybe, she's happy for me. Maybe.

But the woman's on a roll. "And by the way. Your grades will come up. You will show us all your graded work, and we will be checking in with your teachers every single Friday. If they're not up, forget working. I'm talking mostly A's again or forget it."

"What if I'm honestly trying really hard but I get a B? Chemistry's a bitch, Mom."

"Language, Monkey." She narrows her eyes suspiciously. "We'll see. I'll take it under advisement."

I nod and act like the oppressed Youth of Today that I am—and hide the breakdance of joy I'm about to do.

Until I realize that now I'll have to sneak out to do The Big Plan for Emmett.

Turd burgers.

CHAPTER 28

PUSHING LIMITS

	Physical	Mental	Emotional	Parental
working for Roy (ACTUAL WORK)	✓			✓
making sense of the world SJD		✓	✓	✓
fooling around w/ Stan	✓		✓	✓
trig, chemistry & computer programming		✓		
that 5k "fun run" with Jamie	✓			
GOOD TO TEST — should do more often	✓	✓		

IT'S back to work the next day. I get to bring Ruby, and I don't have to lie to my parents. What a strange notion. I don't have to sprint to the shed every time I see someone I know. How will I get my cardio now?

Roy's pager summons him a couple more times, and I force myself not to think about why. Fingers in ears, eyes closed—I will not think about it, I will not think about it. We manage to keep the tree lot open, thanks to Rosemary, who tags in when needed. And no thanks to Stenn, who I still haven't heard from. I miss him like crazy, and I'm freaking out, but I refuse to cave; I will not contact him first. He's the one who overreacted, so he should be the one to call. I was trying to be honest and open. He's the One Who Done Me Wrong in this scenario.

During a lull on Sunday afternoon, I brief Rosemary on her role in The Big Plan. She's picking at a glob of pine sap stuck to her mitten.

"Do you think you can manage it?" I ask.

"Totally," Rosemary says. "As long as it's cold, it's infinitely do-able."

"Great. I'll call you when the plan's in motion. *Mwahaha.*"

"Nice evil laugh!" She thinks for a moment, petting Ruby. "So I'll need to unplug the other phones in the house... This is going to be so cool." And then, because she's so mellow and chill, she pops up and starts leaping around, scream-singing, "It makes me feel like dancing! Dancing! Dancing!"

Sweet lords of disco.

She keeps going. "Footloose! Footloose! Everybody cut, everybody cut!"

And then I start crying. Because I watched that movie with Stenn. And because Rosemary somehow always hits the jackpot when she pulls the handle of the tear-dispensing slot machine that is me.

"Oh no! What's wrong? I don't suck that much, do I?" She sits down. "Is it Jamie again? Oh. Was she a Kevin Bacon fan? Or was she more of a Kenny Wormald *Footloose remake* girl?"

And now I cry harder—because I wasn't thinking about Jamie! Which just loads guilt onto my shoulders and into my heart, because *forever* is the whole freaking point of BFF.

Rosemary pets me like a dog. Ruby tries to lick the tears off my cheeks. I wipe my face and say, "No, that's not it. Well I mean, who doesn't love the Baconator?" I try to laugh but it mixes with runny snot and I make an awesome choking-on-my-own-phlegm sound. "No. It's Stenn. I think... I think Stenn might have broken up with me."

"Oh my God! What happened?"

"I don't know! One minute everything's perfect, well not perfect, but fine. I mean we were going to have sex..."

"You were?"

I nod.

"You guys have done it before, though, right?"

"No. Why?"

She looks surprised. "I guess I figured…you've been going out so long…"

"Yeah. Well. We've been waiting."

"That's cool." She nods.

"It was supposed to be special, you know? And it was going okay, and then the next minute he's telling me I'm too high maintenance and he needs space."

"Ouch. Why?"

I sniff. "I don't know."

"Is he jealous of Emmett?"

I give her a What Are You Talking About look. "What? No."

"I bet he is. Guys are like that. Possessive."

"Not Stenn."

"Yes, Stenn. He has a wiener, doesn't he? Then he's a guy. And guys are like that."

"I disagree with your gross overgeneralization."

She crosses her arms. "Listen, Brain. You're doing this big plan—which could get you in huge trouble, by the way—to surprise Emmett on his birthday. So Stenn's jealous."

"Stenn doesn't know about the plan."

"Aha! Keeping secrets from him. That's even more reason for him to be jealous."

"That doesn't even make sense. I don't like Emmett like that. He's a brother to me."

She narrows her eyes until she's almost squinting. "I don't buy it. Maybe when you and Jamie were besties."

"*Besties*? You're going with *besties*?"

"Yes, and I'm sticking to it. Now stop interrupting." She thinks for a second. "When Jamie was around, Emmett was like a brother to you, I'll give you that. But Jamie's gone now—sorry. Everything's changed."

"You can say that again."

"Everything's changed."

"You're funny."

"I know." She shrugs. "You know, I think Jamie would be okay with it."

Which makes me hiccup a tiny leftover sob, which makes Ruby shift closer. "You're crazy."

"You knew her better than anyone, but if it were me? And I died? I think I'd be cool with my bestie— yes, *bestie*, shut up—wanting to get it on with my bro."

"That's gross."

"Whatever. Emmett's hot. And he needs you, I bet. More than Stenn does. And you need—"

"Don't say it—"

"Maybe you need Emmett as much as he needs you."

Riiiight. As if I don't have enough on my mind, let's pop that little nugget into a bong and smoke it.

"Anyway, Roy's back," she says, looking over my shoulder, "and I have to get home before my mom stacks the dishes in my room."

"Your mom puts the dishes in your room?" I thought *I* had it bad.

"Don't ask. Are you going to be all right?"

I nod. "Always am."

"Call if you want to talk later, promise?"

"Sure."

"I mean it. Don't make me kick your ass."

I hold up two fingers. "Scout's honor. I'll call if I need to."

"Hi, Mr. Showalter," she says to the boss man, then turns back. "Bye, Ruby. See you later, Sarah."

Roy winces at being called by his last name. He nods at Rosemary.

"See you," I wave. "I'll call you in the morning." To set The Big Plan in motion.

Team members are briefed. Everything is ready. The Big Plan is set. There's only one thing left for me to do: call Emmett. Which would have made me nervous even before Rosemary's disturbing hypothesis. Add to that the fact that I'm forbidden from using the phone and you get a jittery mess—I'm a complete disaster. I can't hold still, so I throw Artoo for Ruby to fetch over and over while I hide in the back hall with the home phone. Waiting, waiting for Emmett to pick up.

He answers his cell on the third ring. "Hello?"

"It's Sarah."

"Oh. Hi," he sounds surprised.

"Hi. How's it going?"

"All right." He sounds like, *Why exactly are you calling me?*

"I wanted to wish you Happy Birthday."

Pause. "It's tomorrow."

"I know! I'm just saying it in advance."

"Oh. Thanks?"

I throw Artoo for Rubes again. "So, do you have any plans? For tomorrow, I mean?"

"My parents said we'd go out for dinner. They said we'd get a tree. From Mr. Big's."

"They're not taking you out for your half-day off? They're making you go to school all day?" Way to rub salt in a wound! But my fingers are crossed that the answer is yes.

He's quiet for a while before he says, "I guess."

"That's too bad," I lie. "Maybe we could do something after school? I have a present for you. Nothing big, but—"

A beep. Call waiting. Dang. I'm not supposed to be on the phone. But if it's my parents, they'd want me to answer the home phone, right? If I'm here alone and it rings? We did not cover this scenario.

It beeps again. I should answer it. If it is my parents, then obviously I'm supposed to answer. And if I'm not supposed to answer, at least we'll clear up the confusion.

"Sorry, Emmett, but can you hang on a sec? There's another call."

"No problem," Emmett says.

I click to the other line. "Hello?"

"Sare." It's Stenn. My stomach drops. Crashes through the floor, through the basement, through the ground to the hot molten core of the earth.

"Hi."

"Hi. Your cell's off."

"Yeah. I'm not supposed to use it. Long story." Ruby sets Artoo down. And then I remember, "Wait, can you hang on one second? I'm on the other line."

"With whom?"

Crap crap crap. If I tell him it's Emmett, he might freak out. Why is he asking, anyway? Why does his question sound like an accusation?

"I'm on the phone with a friend. Is that all right with you?" It comes out distinctly pissed-off. But *he* called *me,* so maybe I should try to meet him halfway: "Sorry. I'll call you back, okay?"

"Whatever." *Click.*

Damn it!

The line clicks back to Emmett. Tears are threatening. "Sorry."

"No worries."

"Anyway." Where were we? Besides in a galaxy far, far away from my boyfriend, and getting light years farther every minute. "Um, tomorrow. Right. I have something for you. Meet me at Nano's after school?"

"Sure. Okay."

We say goodbye. I take a deep breath. I dial Stenn. He does not pick up.

His voice mail comes on. I need to say something. But what? Where am I supposed to start? On a freaking message. I open my mouth and all that squeaks out is, "Hi, it's me. I—I hope we can talk soon? Good night." Which is the stupidest thing ever.

Ruby nuzzles my leg. We go into my room, but I come back and dial a local number—one of Mom's secondary office lines—and hang up on the first ring. Thus if any suspicious parentals hit redial to check up on me, it won't be Stenn's number they reach.

Ruby and I pad into my room. My heart is in two: half happy for tomorrow, half broken by Stenn.

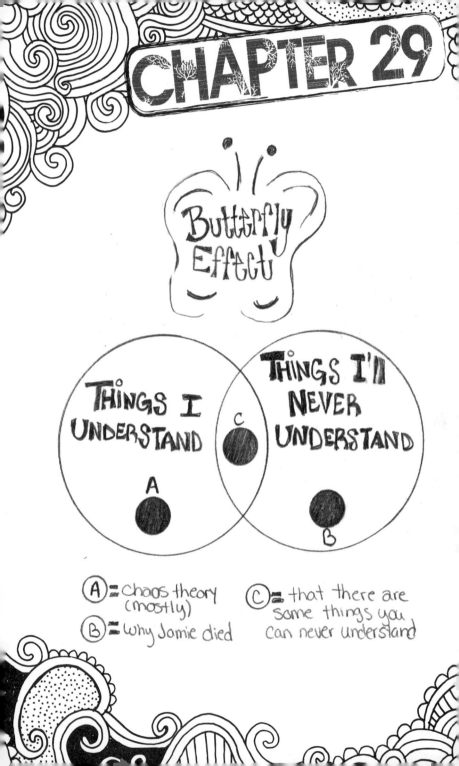

MAYBE a butterfly flapped its wings in China, or maybe it's completely random. Whatever the reason—if there even *is* a reason—I look out the window at 4:00 AM on Emmett's birthday, and the weather is perfect. Perfect! Plump puffs of snow float down from the sky to decorate the ground. Trees, houses, lawns, cars: everything looks like it's frosted with frozen buttercream.

When we go outside, Ruby snaps at whirling snow. Fat flakes stick to her black fur. It's one of those moments when the beauty of the world can elbow out even the most depressing fights with a boyfriend, can push thoughts of overbearing parents into the hinterlands.

As I twirl in slow circles, the snow glows and twinkles in the light of my headlamp. Jamie would love this. Love it.

4:15 AM. It's not only Emmett's birthday. It's Jamie's, too.

I start with the driveway. Bucket after bucket after bucket after bucket after bucket after bucket. Thank crikey I'm a physically righteous lumberjack.

When the driveway's done, it's time for the wheels. Both my parents' cars. Eight wheels, four tubs of greasy Crisco.

When all the wheels glisten like glazed donuts—mmm yummy, hydrogenated vegetable oil—I stagger through the back door, wet and nearly hypothermic. Crystallized ice on my jeans makes a smushing sound as I move. I clench my jaw against convulsive shivers. I whisper to Rubes, "I think I'm frozen."

She whips her tail in crazy circles.

I can't help but giggle. Seriously, this plan? Genius. Genius, I say! *Mwahaha!*

"Let's finish and get back to bed," I tell Rubes. "Dad will be waking up soon."

I open the door to the basement. And I freeze—more than I'm already freezing.

A voice, and someone's eyes on the back of my neck.

"And what, pray tell, do you think you're doing?"

Jeremy.

Busted.

Slowly, trying to think of an escape maneuver, I close the basement door and turn around to face my arch nemesis. "Go back to bed," I whisper. "This is none of your business."

Jeremy inclines his head to look down his nose at me. "Seems like it might interest Mom and Dad."

Never in my life have I wanted to bitch slap someone more than I do right now. "Please, Jeremy. Just leave me alone."

"What are you doing?"

I sigh. There isn't time for this! I have to turn off the electricity and call Rosemary, stat, or my plan will turn into a pile of steaming dog poop. "Look, I'm busy here."

"Doing what?"

"If I tell you, will you leave me alone?"

"I don't know," he shrugs. "Perhaps."

"Fine!" I tell him the plan, whispering fast, staring at the kitchen clock, willing the seconds not to tick.

Jeremy is quiet, like he's contemplating how to best use this information to make my life a living hell.

"It's for Emmett," I say. "It's his birthday, all right? And it was Jamie's, obviously, and he's lonely. I'm surprising him."

Jeremy's mouth goes slack. "You're doing this for Emmett? Not your own selfish reasons? That's hard to believe."

"Believe what you want. But please don't tell Mom and Dad. I want Emmett to be happy for once."

Jeremy stands there. The clock is literally ticking. Any second Dad could wake up. Everything will be ruined.

Finally, Jeremy kind of sniffs. Translation: *Wow, you are genuinely awesome, little sister! A true friend and patriot. Good on you.* Or something like that. "Fine."

I'm so relieved I actually smile at him. He's letting me go!

When I'm halfway down the basement stairs, I hear him right behind me.

"Wait! How are you going to make a phone call? Your cell is confiscated and cordless phones need electricity."

"I got an old one down from the attic. It doesn't need power, just the phone line."

"Oh."

I must be delirious from cold, because I swear he sounds impressed.

"Please go back to bed, okay?" I beg.

"Whatever, Dork."

Jeremy slowly closes the door.

I almost whisper up the stairs, into the darkness, "Hey, Jeremy? Thanks." But I keep it in. Death before surrender!

♟ ♟ ♟

Upstairs in my bed, warming up under tons of blankets, I hear Dad's cell phone ring down the hall.

Perfect timing. I snuggle close to Ruby.

In my parents' bedroom, something tumbles to the floor. Probably books from Dad's bedside table, knocked over as he fumbles for his phone. He mutters something I can't make out.

What's this? Can it be? Is that Jeremy I hear? Through the wall? Giggling like mad? My brother, giggling. I should record it. Talk about leverage.

My parents' bedroom door opens and Dad's voice gets clearer. "Wasn't expecting it to be so bad" —quiet grunts as he pulls his cowboy boots on—

"thanks for the call. Give your dad my best." His phone chirps when he ends the call.

Dad clomps up the hall. He flips the light switch. *Click. Click, click.* "What in the Sam Hill?" His boots go quiet as he steps onto the carpet of my parents' bedroom. Voices again. A drawer slides open and shut. Heavy footsteps in the hall again. A circle of light slides past the crack under my door, disappearing with Dad as he stomps down the stairs. I wait for Mom's slippers to shuffle after him, then I tiptoe out of my bedroom, resting a hand on Ruby to keep her quiet. Jeremy is already perched on the top step, listening.

He scoots over so Ruby and I can sit next to him. Which is a pretty nice, non-douchey move.

Downstairs, Dad says, "Power's out in the whole house."

"Did they call for this bad a storm?" Mom asks.

"No." Dad's voice fades like he's in another room. "Doesn't look that bad out."

Mom's voice gets more distant, too. "Street lights are on. There's power outside."

"Guess I'll have to use the old reliable."

"You haven't done that in ages." Their voices get louder as they make their way back to the kitchen.

Keys jingle. The back door opens.

Jeremy and I look at each other with wide eyes.

And wider smiles.

My brother and I are sharing a moment. Next we will hold hands and sing "Peace Train."

"Be careful, dear," Mom calls.

Dad's response is difficult to hear; he must be on the back porch.

Mom says, "Oh, give it a rest, will you? It was only that one time."

"What did Dad say?" I whisper.

"Shhh! I think he's threatening to use her car."

I stifle a chortle. Ruby thumps her tail between Jeremy and me.

Everything is going perfectly.

Oh.

Shit.

I forgot to pick up the Crisco tubs. They're still out there! Four empty tubs, between the cars and the driveway.

I'm dead. My life is over. It was nice knowing you, Roy. I love you, Ruby. Stenn, I'll miss you, even though you're being a big jackass right now. Goodbye, cruel world!

Outside, Mom's car starts.

Which means—how has Dad not seen the Crisco containers? And come right back inside?

Is the jig not up?

On tiptoe, I race to the hall window. I press my forehead against the cold pane to get a good angle of the driveway. *Wham!* The wall shakes.

"What was that?!" I ask.

Jeremy's doubled over, laughing.

"What just happened?" I ask again.

Between snorts of laughter he says, "Dad crashed into the house!"

"No way."

Jeremy grabs his stomach. His whole body is shaking. "I guess it worked," he says, trying to catch his breath. He looks at me. "Why aren't you happier?"

"You're looking at a dead woman. I forgot to pick up the—"

"Evidence?" Jeremy waves his hand, beckoning me to follow him down the hall. He opens the door to his room. There is his disgusting bed, stinky socks, messy closet.

And also. Four empty Crisco containers.

I slap my hands over my mouth. "How did you... *Why* did you..."

"I get half the bragging rights. More than half."

I beam. "You got it. You know this is going down in the annals of history."

"You'd know about all about the anals of history."

Dad slams back through the door. We run to the top of the stairs to listen.

"The driveway is a solid sheet of ice! I slid through the bushes into the house! It's a f—"

"Language, dear," Mom says. The back door opens, then slams a few seconds later.

"Son of a bitch!" Mom yells. "You crashed my car!"

"Language, dear," Dad says, shuffling around the kitchen, opening and closing drawers and cabinets.

"Lydia! Where did I put the list of cancellation phone numbers?"

"I think it's—" Mom starts to say. But we don't hear the rest. We're too busy breaking into *Hammer Time. Stop. Hammer Time.*

The Big Plan, Phase One: complete.

CHAPTER 30

DIAGNOSES THAT SHOULD BE IN THE

DSM-IV

(DIAGNOSTIC & STATISTICAL MANUAL)

CODE	DISORDER	CATEGORY
296.08	Morning Person	Mood Disorders
308.72	Kaleidoscopic Shift	Adjustment Disorders
348.00	Batsh*t Crazy (the good kind)	Awesomeness Disorders

WHY do parents always *wake you up* to tell you that you can sleep in because it's a snow day? Sadism? Schadenfreude? Revenge? Passive-aggression?

Jeremy and I both feign sleepy surprise. After Mom and Dad shut themselves in the bathroom for their sordid mutual grooming rituals, Jeremy sort-of-almost helps me by keeping watch while I sneak back down to the basement to flip all the circuit breakers back on. I don't want to give the parentals too much time to contemplate our lack of electricity. If they notice that not only are the streetlights working, but the neighbors' lights are on, Dad will call the power company to complain. And the customer service rep will be all, "Are you sure your daughter isn't trying to bamboozle you into declaring a snow day?"

Mom whoops from the bathroom. "Power's back!"

Smug at the magnitude of my awesomeness, I sneak to the home phone and dial Emmett.

"Sarah." He sounds sleepy.

"Happy birthday!"

"Thanks."

"Guess you get your birthday off from school after all."

"Yeah. It doesn't even look that bad out. Random."

I beam. "Maybe random, maybe not. I have big plans for today. Can you meet me?"

"Sure. What's up?"

"You'll have to wait and see."

♀♀♀

Mom and Dad have to work, so after they leave—on foot! Because the driveway is so icy! *Mwahaha!*—I offer Jeremy twenty bucks of my new wages to cover for me while I go out to meet Emmett.

Jeremy squints. "This 'covering for you'"—he makes air quotes—"what would it entail?"

"Being here to answer the phone if Mom or Dad calls. Tell them I'm in the shower. Then call me right away. Please? For Emmett's sake?"

"Fifty bucks."

"Thirty."

"Thirty-five."

"Deal."

Something has changed between us. He's being human...almost. But he's still not doing favors for free. Which seems about right. It's a capitalist, free-market relationship—we're not comrades—but at least it's a relationship. Progress.

I hotfoot it out the door before Jeremy changes his mind. Ruby and I set out for the courthouse park.

When we get there, the fluffy tufts of snow have melted; wet pavement glistens in the sun and the ground squishes under my boots. Ruby curls up with Artoo on the bench next to me. The dog lives for snow days—even more than the students of Norwich School District. Middle of the week and she gets to hang with me all day? Hot doggity dog.

Emmett lifts his hand when he sees me. He comes over and Ruby gives him a hello sniff.

"Happy birthday."

"Weird that school was cancelled."

"Well…" I've been smiling so hard my cheeks are sore. I probably look stoned out of my gourd. "In point of fact, it isn't that weird. It's part of your birthday present."

Emmett's eyes go wide and then narrow. It's

Surprise + pleasure / curiosity + suspicion

I stand. "Come on. I'll explain while we walk."

The marshy ground sucks at our soles until we get to the sidewalk. We head toward my house. Because my parentals both had to walk to work, they'll spend all day at their offices. No meeting somewhere for lunch together. No running errands. So I don't worry too much about being spotted.

Emmett's wearing his heavy soccer hoodie; he shoves his hands in its front pocket as we walk. Ahead of us, Ruby trots with Artoo.

"So. Here's the thing. I thought it was awful—criminal!—that your birthday would go by without…" I frown. How do I put it? "And Jamie's. Birthday." Our footsteps punctuate my words. "Anyway, I hope it's all right with you. I thought it was a good opportunity for us to do something to…I don't know…acknowledge Jamie. Say goodbye."

Emmett pulls up his hood. "That's what the funeral was for."

My stomach twists. Oh wow. I am totally, completely wrong. About everything. The funeral was enough for Emmett—enough to say goodbye, put things to rest.

Which would mean my entire Big Plan is completely pointless. And worse: presumptuous.

I open my mouth to apologize for my stupidity, but Emmett says, "I asked them if I could say something. At the funeral. Know what they said? They said it wasn't a good idea. They said it would make me more upset.

"Can you believe that shit? That got me so mad I could hardly talk. Literally." He looks at the sky, back down. "So I didn't. Talk. In that receiving line, I didn't want to. And there was this guy. He shook my hand and said, 'It's fine to keep quiet. Fine to wait until you have something to say.' And that's how I felt, you know? Like I did have something to say, but they took it away from me. So I'd wait."

"That's why you hardly talked for a while there." Makes sense.

"You noticed."

"Yeah." *Even though I was avoiding you like the plague. My bad, about that.* "Who was the guy?"

"Not sure." Emmett droops, like all this talking has depleted him.

We walk. Ruby looks back at us to be sure we're following.

A block later, I say, "I just thought that we should do something special. Our own way of saying good-bye."

Emmett nods.

I take another breath. "And it's time for me to tell you what happened. The details. Whatever you want to know."

Emmett stops walking but doesn't look up.

"Is that okay?" I ask in a cracked whisper.

Emmett meets my eyes. "Yeah. It is."

We stand here. I study my boots and the cracks in the sidewalk. Ruby sets Artoo down and waits until Emmett starts walking again.

He says, "But first, tell me how you managed to get school cancelled."

Ruby runs ahead of us, into my backyard, as I recount icing the driveway and the rest of The Big Plan.

Emmett smiles and shakes his head appreciatively. "I can't believe you did that."

"I know! Don't I rule? And aren't I humble?"

"Very."

I say, "The buckets were super heavy. All that

water. I thought I would freeze my toes off."

"Huh. Why didn't you use a hose instead?"

Oh. My. God. I smack my forehead. "That is an excellent question. Which I'm going to try to forget you ever asked."

He laughs. "Rosemary seems cool. Will she get in trouble? For calling your Dad and lying to him?"

"She doesn't think so. Her dad is a big practical joker, so if he finds out, he'll probably be impressed. She said he'll be proud of her for 'sticking it to The Man,' whatever that means."

Emmett nods to my parents' cars in the driveway. "Crisco. Genius."

"I have to wash it off before they get back. I hear Dawn dish soap cuts through grease."

Emmett is quiet for a while, staring at my driveway, the ice melting at the edges. "You did this for me."

"For you. And Jamie."

He smiles. "But also, you're going to be a legend."

"Jeremy will steal the credit."

Inside my house, I add some extra socks, bottles of water, and sugar-free wafer cookies to the bag I packed earlier. Like a good Cub Scout, I'm all about being prepared these days. I throw my backpack over my shoulder, and Emmett, Ruby, and I cross my backyard and start up West Hill, following the trail I marked with Roy.

"So, where are we going?" Emmett asks.

"You'll see. It's a surprise."

We walk in silence, the wet ground *thwuck, thwucking* under our feet. Ruby's paws and belly are splotched with mud. I'll have to wrangle her into the bathtub later.

About halfway up the hill, I push a tree branch aside to reveal a tiny clearing I noticed on my previous hikes. It's a secret little Narnia, perfectly ringed by hemlocks. The tree canopy gives way enough for the sun to stream in; golden shafts of light illuminate the space. I drop my backpack. "We're here."

Emmett gives me a We're Here? Where's Here? look.

"Don't look so disappointed. This is merely our first stop." I unzip my bag and pull out an old blanket, which I snap open and lay over a fallen log. My heart is pounding. Sweat prickles my armpits. My mouth is cottony dry. And it's not because of the hike.

I pat the blanket for him to sit, and I take a deep breath. I pull a small velvet jewelry box out of my backpack. "For you."

Slowly, Emmett takes the box and turns it over in his hands.

"I want you to have it, and I want you to be able to hold it while you…while you find out," I say.

Emmett opens the jewelry box. Inside is half of my half of the locket. Rosemary took it to the jeweler for me, her grounded friend—I gave her money from my wages. She asked him to split my locket piece and loop half of it onto a thick, boyish chain.

Emmett looks from the box, to me, and back down, but doesn't say anything. He slides his thumb over the necklace.

My heart is punching the inside of my ribs. "I wrote it down for you. I'm sorry, but I just can't say all of it out loud. But if you want to know anything, anything at all, you can ask."

I hand Emmett the pages. At some point the words had morphed from something written for Emmett into a story I needed to write for myself. An account. An accounting. Accountable.

Before he unfolds the pages, Emmett tips the jewelry box so the necklace slips into his palm. He curls his hand around it. As he reads, his knuckles go white, gripping the locket tighter and tighter while he finally learns the whole story about how his sister, my best friend, died…and why.

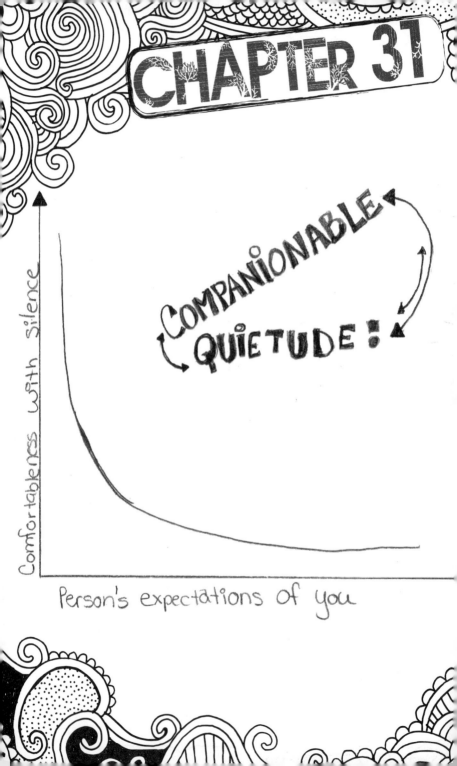

CHAPTER 31

COMPANIONABLE QUIETUDE!

Comfortableness with silence

Person's expectations of you

**EMMETT** stares at the pages for such a long time that I can't tell when he's finished reading. I look, finally, at his face. Tears are running in rivers down his cheeks; snot drips from his nose onto his sweatshirt.

"I'm so sorry," I say. There is a cascade of feelings in those three words. "The police said the wall…it malfunctioned. It should have stopped. I tried to stop it. I'm so, so sorry." I take a deep breath.

Emmett doesn't say anything.

"I never—we never should have cared that much about a stupid necklace."

"It obviously wasn't a stupid necklace to Jamie."

"But it wasn't worth dying over."

"Obviously," he says again. He doesn't say more.

"Do you hate me?"

He gives kind of a gasp. He wipes his face on his sweatshirt.

"You do." Confirmed. Worst fears, confirmed. Millions of invisible spiders crawl up my neck, scattering over my scalp. "It's my fault. I pressed the button."

Emmett shakes his head. "It was an accident."

"But I left her."

"Jesus, Sarah. Stop. This isn't about you. I don't hate you."

"Really?"

He nods.

I say, "It's not about me, okay. But do you...do you think Jamie does? Hate me for leaving?"

"No." He shakes his head. "Definitely no. You were going to get help."

I cry, hard.

"What else could you do? Anyone would have done the same thing," he says. "I would have."

Oh my God. Oh my God! How long have I been waiting to hear someone say that? From someone who loves Jamie as much as I do. I start shaking, but not from cold. From relief. From forgiveness.

It's almost unbearable, the sudden feeling of release. You don't know how much you need to be forgiven until you are.

Emmett wipes his face again. "Sarah?"

I sniff my own dripping nose. "Emmett?"

"Thanks. It's better, knowing." He holds up the necklace and tugs down his hood. "Help me put it on."

My shivering makes it difficult to work the clasp. After I finally get the necklace on him, I lay my hand on the back of his neck. The feel of his skin, the fine hairs over the bumps of his vertebrae, it's tender and warm. We stare at the trees in front of us. I try to stop shaking. After a long time, I clear my throat. "Ready for the rest of your birthday surprise?"

He puts his hood back up. "I don't think I can take any more."

"The next part will be more fun. I promise."

���

Our moods brighten a little as we hike. The sun warms the earth, and winter songbirds chirp their appreciation. Ruby prances in circles and trots along. By the time we tramp out of the woods onto Roy's land, muck cakes our shoes and our cheeks are glowing rosy pink.

I sweep my hand toward the rows of stumps, and the remaining trees. "Ta da! Your own private birthday cut-it-yourself Christmas tree farm. Courtesy of my friend Roy."

"Wow." Emmett smiles from under his hood. "Cool. Roy's your boss?"

I nod. "You'll like him." I nudge Emmett with my shoulder. "Come on. I don't think he's at Mr. Big's yet. Let's go see if he's here. I want you to meet him."

Roy is sitting on the front steps of his house. "Hey there," he calls as he comes over to us. "Turning into a nice day for—" Roy goes silent. His eyes are on Emmett.

Beside me, Emmett breathes, "You?"

Roy nods. "You."

"Wait. You guys have met?"

Emmett says, "Once." He presses his arms tight to his sides, pushing his hands straight down in his sweatshirt pocket.

"Okay…" something's not adding up. "So, what's wrong?"

Silence.

Roy says, "Think you two best come with me."

"Is it safe for Ruby to come?"

"Yep. Buddy's inside."

We follow Roy to his garage in a single line, like a slow train. The light of the day, the sunlight, begins to feel stark. Begins to drain color from the world around us. The air starts to *whoosh*.

This is not quite the jovial finale to the birthday festivities I'd intended.

Roy stops in front of his garage. He grabs the door handle and pulls, sliding it overhead and securing it with a hook. Emmett and I step onto the concrete floor and watch Roy pull two big, empty buckets from a stack. He sets them upside down on the floor. "Sit."

We do. Ruby sniffs around but seems to know something's wrong. She lies at my feet. Roy stays standing, shifting his weight. He rubs his hands together and blows on them, but I don't get the feeling he's cold. Finally he says, "Sarah, you should know where Emmett and me met." He looks at Emmett and asks, "That okay by you."

Underneath his hood, Emmett nods.

Roy turns back to me. "Met at your friend's funeral."

"Jamie's funeral? Why were you—" I look from Roy to Emmett, back to Roy. "Why would you be there? You didn't—"

Emmett interrupts, "He's the one who told me it was okay not to talk."

Roy looks surprised. "You remember that."

"Yeah."

Roy dips his head once, like Emmett said something important. Then he pulls another bucket from the stack, flips it, sits down.

"You still haven't answered me," I say. I'm getting panicky and I don't want to think about why. "What were you doing at Jamie's funeral? What's going on? You guys are freaking me out."

Roy's gaze is steady on mine. "Sarah. Don't want to upset you. But it's time."

Time? Time for what? My ears get hot. The answer is already dripping through the filters of my brain. My stomach knots. I look at Emmett. *Help me!*

But he looks hollow, like no one's there. My eyes move desperately, flitting from object to object: the deer skin, the objects on the pegboards, connected with thread. Buckets and mops and cleaning supplies—

No no no no. No freaking way. "Roy. Why were you at Jamie's funeral?"

"Because I always attend services for the victims...for the accidents that I...that I clean up after."

Holy. Freaking. Crap. I stand up, sit back down. Maybe it's been obvious. He cleans emergency situations. The pieces of the puzzle have been right in front of me this whole time. Maybe I just...barricaded it. Kept it suspended above the filters. I didn't want to know.

Then again, why why *why* would I put that together?

"That's what you do?" Emmett is asking Roy. "You clean up after stuff like that?" He sounds respectful but disgusted.

Roy sighs. "Yep."

"How did you..." Emmett shakes his head. "Why was it..." He stops again. "How do you do it? I mean, I get how. But..."

"Why," Roy says.

Emmett swallows. "Yeah."

Um, yeah, thanks but no thanks. I don't want to know. I'd rather sear my cheeks with hot curling irons. Or stab toothpicks under my fingernails. But beside me, Emmett nods, waiting.

"I respect your wanting to know," Roy says. "I had something happen. Something awful. And messy. After the police were gone, after the under-taker…" He rubs his chin. "Thought sure someone would come along, knock on my door with mops and buckets, offer to clean up the blood."

I moan. So it started with his wife and son. The blood of his own family, splattered all over his house.

"Well, no one did," Roy continues. "Had to do it myself. Thought maybe—"

"You thought you could help other people," I say.

"Not to have to go through the same thing," Emmett finishes.

"Yep. It isn't much, but—"

"No," I say. "It isn't much. It's a lot."

Roy smiles sadly. "Sarah, I owe you an apology. At first I wasn't entirely sure it was your friend. Then when I was certain…I've been struggling. With when—how—to tell you."

I take in a shuddery breath. "I guess I should have put it together. But also—" I feel anger rising. Anger at people withholding information, thinking they know what's best for me, lying to me for my own pro-tection. Not Roy! I don't want to lose him to the dark side. "Just…tell me why you didn't say it. Before today."

"Sometimes things aren't clear. Sometimes you do your best, muddle through."

"But I don't see—"

"Sarah," Emmett cuts me off. "He needed time."

"Why are you taking his side?"

"He needed time like *you* needed time," Emmett says. "Like you needed time to tell me about Jamie."

I blink. Right. Good point.

Roy runs a finger under his eyes. Oh wow—he's crying. "Have something for you, Emmett, from Sarah. And Sarah, I got something for you, too." He shakes his head and whispers, "Goodness. I'm sorry," almost like he's talking to himself.

The mouth of his bucket scrapes the concrete as he stands. He walks to one of the workbenches and pulls a towel off the antlers.

He picks the antlers up, holds them in his open palms. He helped me mount them onto a small burl of pine.

The antler points seem to slice the air as Roy gives them to Emmett.

"Are these from the deer that…" Emmett trails off as he takes the gift from Roy. He rotates the antlers, studying their arcs, curves, points, velvety bases.

"They're from Jamie's deer—the one that died where she did," I say.

"My mom told me about it." He presses his fingertips to the antler points. He looks at me. "I know what we need to do with these." He sounds certain, decided.

Tools clatter along another workbench as Roy slides the rack with the skin aside, revealing the pegboard behind it. He reaches up and picks something off a hook, snaps the thread that's connecting it to the other things, brings it over. He opens my hands with his calloused fingers, and sets it into my palm. A thin, broken gold chain. And on the end of the chain, shining up from the nest of my palm, is Jamie's part of the locket.

CHAPTER 32

COMPARE & CONTRAST

	ROY	OBI-WAN
"CRAZY OLD MAN"	✓	✓
LIVES ALONE / HERMIT	✓	✓
SURVIVAL SKILLS	✓	✓
HAS SOMETHING THAT BELONGS WITH YOU	✓	✓
JEDI	?	✓

**JAMIE'S** locket. I never thought I'd see it again. I thought it was gone forever. I gape at it. Then at Roy. "How did…"

"Keep something from each accident I clean. Something small."

I breathe in sharply. "Isn't that illegal? To keep things?"

"I'm there after the police. After the families. Anything that's important, they take it away long before I get there."

"But…why?"

Roy looks from me to Emmett to the peg-board. "It's a tough job. Keeping something makes it more human. I tie the things together to remind me it's all connected. Somehow. We're all connected."

We're all connected.

I look down at the locket in my hand.

Roy says, "Noticed your gold necklace on occasion, Sarah. The chains are the same."

"Yeah," I manage to say before I start crying. "We each wear half. We each wore half."

Emmett holds his hand out, like asking if he can see it. I don't want to hand it over; I want to hold it forever. But he needs it as much as I do. I give it to him.

Emmett studies it. "It looks busted."

Through my tears I laugh.

Emmett gives the necklace back, spooling it into my palm. Roy returns to his bucket chair. We sit, the three of us—Roy looking at the garage floor; me staring at Jamie's locket; Emmett holding the antlers—and we let our tears go. Not all of our tears. But a lot. We cry until our sleeves are full of snot and tears. The three of us are beyond embarrassment; it's like we've created a place where we can let each other just…be.

Finally, Roy stands. He rubs his hands over his face, reaches down to pat Ruby, who thumps her tail for him. "Might could do with some coffee."

"Want me to make it?" I ask.

He smiles. "Goodness no."

"When do you have to leave for Mr. Big's?" I ask.

"It can wait a few more minutes."

I nod. "I brought hot cocoa for me and Emmett."

"I'll get the water started," Roy says. "You two come on in when you're ready."

"Thanks," Emmett says from under his hood.

"Welcome."

Emmett and I snuffle our noses and swipe at our tears. Emmett looks at me with red eyes and ruddy cheeks. "Do you think Roy would drive us to the cemetery?"

I nod. "We need to go there?"

"I don't know why, I feel like these belong on her grave."

"I read about some people who lived way back, before the Roman Empire, I think. Deer were symbolic to them. They thought deer helped send the spirits of the dead on their way."

"Really?"

"I feel it, too. Like maybe the antlers can help guard her spirit. Let it be free."

He looks at me, surprised. "Yeah. Exactly."

We sit quietly a while longer. Then I ask, "Want to go inside?"

"Sure. But I can't drink the cocoa."

"I brought the sugar-free kind."

"You think of everything, don't you?"

"Oh sure. I think of everything." I grab my bag.

Emmett helps me find some rope so we can tie Ruby to Roy's front steps. She looks pathetic, gives me big sad mournful eyes, but it's the safest thing. She's caused enough trouble here. But also—*thanks, Rubes. For setting good things in motion that night.*

Still, we don't need her sinking her teeth into Buddy. Wouldn't that be perfect?

In Roy's kitchen, the fluorescent lights jar my watery eyes. The coffeemaker is burbling on the table, spitting brown liquid. Roy's got a big, dented pot of water heating on the stove. There are three mugs and a couple of spoons on the table.

I sit on the stepladder that's been enlisted as a third seat. Emmett sits on the plastic chair. I pull the sugar-free cocoa mix and snacks out of my backpack.

Roy pours hot water into our mugs, returns the pot to the stove. Emmett and I tear open our packets and put in our cocoa, stirring, watching the brown powder darken, sink, dissolve. Roy sits and I fill his mug with coffee. We all look wrecked. But also relieved.

There's no talking. There's no need.

Emmett's spoon clinks against his mug. Roy takes a slurp of coffee.

I breathe. I feel the kaleidoscope shift.

It's a big one, this swerve my life took.

And I might catch hell from my parents when I get home, I might never patch things up with Stenn. I'll never have Jamie back. But for this moment at least, I'm okay.

I've got these friends, see. Who need me as much as I need them.

Go, Jamie. Let your spirit speed on its way.

We're good here.

FROM THE AUTHOR

The epitaph on Donna Showalter's grave is from Kahlil Gibran's *The Prophet*. It's a beautiful book, available at almost any public library. Super highly recommended.

Norwich, New York, is my real hometown, but I've fictionalized it. A lot. With the exception of Ruby, none of the main characters are real; also, I've moved things around and invented new places. Norwichians: enjoy the parts you recognize, but don't speculate too much about the people and places you don't. Because I made them up. Because that's what writers do. Which is why I love being a writer.

ACKNOWLEDGMENTS

This book wouldn't exist without the help of many, many friends. Noah and Sam Wichman bolstered me through four years of rejection. So did the members of Adverb Fight Club: Jennifer Harrod, John Claude Bemis, and Stephen Messer—true friends and great writers all. My agent, Ginger Knowlton, has believed in me for a long time, and I thank her for that. Kathy Landwehr is not just my editor but also my friend. (And dance-off archnemesis.) Nobody puts Kathy in a corner.

The whole Peachtree crew has been dreamy to work with. Maureen Withee came through again with phenomenal art, graphic design, and typesetting. Seriously, it's like things go from my brain straight through to Mo's pencil. Thanks also to Jessica Alexander, Vicky Holifield, and

Stephanie Fretwell-Hill for copy edits and proofreading. And there's Melissa Bloomfield, Samantha Grefe, Emily Rivet, Farah Gehy, Lesley Rowe, and the rest of the crew who do so much for me with courtesy and professionalism. Thank you for making this process so lovely. Also a big shoutout to Margaret Quinlin for fantastic food and conversation in NYC.

Earl and Juanita Johnson are not just my enduringly supportive parentals, they are also excellent proofreaders. Lisa Wichman, too. Thanks again to the Everetts for two contract celebrations down the pub in one week; and to Michelle, Andrea, Anna, Jen, Nishi, and Salma for early reads. Maddy Sweitzer-Lamme provided a helpful Youth of Today focus group. And to all my good good friends— you know who you are: you guys are the bestest. Thanks, cheers, and up your kilts.

THE THEORY OF EVERYTHING was written in loving memory of B. A. M., with continuing fondness for K.